The Bunker

L.T. Kodzo

ISBN: 978-1-943960-81-1

DEDICATION

To Langston's friend Michelle Leiser who
recognized Courtney's story didn't end in The Center.

PART I

The Present

CHAPTER 1

Nightmare sweat clings to the nape of my neck. A fake morning sun glows against my curtains and I pull the heavy comforter to my face. "It's only a dream," I whisper, folding my soft pillow against my wet cheek.

Seeking comfort and peace, I lean over the bed and pick up a fluffy slipper and press it to my heart. Shoes are safe. I'm safe.

Bunkerville is safe. Nightmares aren't real. Soft slippers, warm feet. Relax. Nightmares suck.

I collapse into my fluffy bedding as the battery-operated oil dispenser on the wall puffs the scent of lavender into the room. It can't compete against the bacon, but it tries.

A slight twist of my neck allows me to see the clock next to my bed. Glinda must have turned off my radio. Strange since I didn't know it could be turned off. It wasn't a standard radio with multiple choice channels like I remember from another time, but it was locked on one frequency. I tried to turn it off once when I first moved in, but I couldn't. My roommate told me the entire town listened to the same station. I rotated the radio dial, but the channel didn't change. The news came on every morning at the same time. Everyone in town heard the same message.

But not me. At least not this morning. I tighten the grip on my slipper. Routines don't ever change in Bunkerville. The slightest shift makes me pet the fur on top of my slipper.

A ton of things are going on. My surgery is in seven days, which means my mother arrives in Bunkerville today. My father soon after. Problem is, both of my parents are like strangers in my mind. I don't really remember them. Dr. Baum told me it was because of the tumor. She's my naturopath and hypnotist. She's the reason I'm not on drugs or in pain. And while I don't understand how a growth in my gut can erase memories of my family, I trust her completely.

The rumble of bike wheels over a cobblestone road reaches through my second-floor window. I stop rubbing my belly bump. To ease the rising anxiety about visiting parents and the impending procedure, I slip my feet off the bed and pull the slippers onto them.

A gentle sigh escapes my lungs. A combination of peace wells up in me. When my feet are protected, I'm protected. Even from the mass in my middle which continues to grow daily.

Sometimes it moves.

In seven days, surgery will eliminate it forever and my mother and father will be here while I recover.

That's what loving parents do.

Even if I can't remember them, it's nice to know they love me. Once I remove the tumor, I can stop the hypnosis and aroma therapy that keeps me dull. Dr. Baum assures me, I will remember them and the deep love I currently can't feel for them. The thought pulled me from my bedroom and into the small kitchen Glinda and I share.

"Good morning, Dorothy, did you sleep well?" Glinda says as she puts the wrapped cheese in a storage crate and the two remaining eggs in a liquid solution intended to keep them fresh without refrigeration.

In Bunkerville, electricity is reserved for maintaining the screens that make up the sky and horizon. Or for pumping water through pipes and temperature through vents. Remnants of my old life contain computers and television and phones. Those distractions don't exist in Bunkerville.

Here we play board games and read. We talk to people face to face. We ride bikes or walk. We don't have a movie theater, because the majority of our power is channeled to the high-definition screens which transform an underground cave into a comfortable oasis.

The sacrifice is worth it.

"What are you smiling at?" Glinda asks me with suspicion.

"Life."

My roommate leans against her curvaceous hip in a model pose. She's six-feet tall in her stocking feet, which are covered in ankle high sneakers. Red patent leather. Nice. I love a fancy pair of shoes.

"Me too," Glinda responds.

"Oh, did I say that out loud?"

"No problem, you're allowed a slip or two."

"Thanks, friend."

She rolls her eyes as if she doesn't believe we are friends. She's done that before, but I can't help but call her that since she's the only person I know in Bunkerville besides Dr. Baum.

I stuff the scrambled eggs on toast into my mouth as

Glinda shuts off the gas canister. The flame on the stove whisps away without the fuel to feed it. I remember my manners and say, "Aren't you eating?"

"I already did." She drops the sentence as if she's super annoyed at me.

"What's wrong?" I say between bites of bread.

"Actually," she wipes her hands on the kitchen towel. "I was wondering if you wanted to visit a place with me before we go to the market."

"Where?" I dab my mouth with a napkin.

"A special place I know."

"Really?" I'm surprised and honored.

"Yes, really."

I ignore her sarcastic tone. While it's obvious she's in a bad mood, it must not be at me or she wouldn't be inviting me to someplace special. "Yes, I'd love to." I stuff the rest of the breakfast into my mouth and hurry to the bathroom.

As quickly as possible, I complete my morning hygiene routine including securing a wig to my bald head. The wig is temporary. My hair is almost long enough to no longer need it, but the curls against my scalp make me look like a boy. I'll have to wear it until the length is more manageable.

In the walk-in closet, I pick a mid-length summer dress covered in white constellations. We don't see the real stars anymore. I could be sad, but life has choices. And Bunkerville is worth it.

I move to the tall shelf of shoes. A pair of white Keds sends additional joy through me. My worries are small. Today I not only get to go to the fish market with Glinda, but she's added a new and special place.

At the front door, Glinda's smile has finally found her face, showing off her high cheekbones. She's such a sweet lady. And beautiful. A fact she seems to try to hide. I pull on my jacket. Her pale features stand out against her dark mane. "You know what, Glinda, if you wore your hair down, you'd look less severe."

"Who cares?" She opens the apartment door. "I've more important things to worry about right now."

"Like what?"

She gently shoves me out the door. "Like where I'm taking you."

I skip backward down the open hallway. "Are we going shoe shopping?"

"No, better."

I laugh as I exit the building. "Nothing's better than shoe shopping." I inhale the soft smell of last night's rain. The sprinklers are timed to provide ambient moods. Rainstorms contribute to the show, as well as Bunkerville's attempt to grow plants underground. The chrysanthemum beds have their own growth bulbs with timers to meet their light versus dark needs. Although we had rain last night, the sidewalks are dry. The sun glistens off the lake. A flutter from my tumor tries to ruin my happy, but I'm not going to let it. Not when I have a surprise coming.

A few people roam the sidewalks, but not many activities happen this late in the morning. Glinda links her arm with mine. The blood in my veins tickles with anticipation.

We stop at the coffee shop. I half remember the world above where people make coffee in their own homes. But in Bunkerville, only one place offers the caffeine fix for those like Glinda who can't imagine a day without it.

The barista prepares my roommate's order.

At the table next to where I stand, a middle-aged woman sits with a twenty-something young man. "You should be glad your sister's willing to come," she says.

He gives a slight shrug.

"I'm serious, my parents disowned me for coming to this place."

"No way," the guy says. I lean closer to hear the reason for such hatred of Bunkerville, but searing drops of coffee splash against my bare legs.

"Ouch," slips from my mouth, although the pain doesn't hurt my skin as much as my heart at the sight of brown coffee seeping into my white shoes.

"I'm so sorry," Glinda says and mops up the mess on the floor. "Clumsy of me."

"It's okay," I say, although it's not. I doubt the stain will ever come out of my shoes.

"Maybe we can ask your father to bring you a pair."

At the mention of my family visit, I turn toward where the couple sat. Although I'm not sure I would have asked the woman more, now I couldn't if I wanted to, because they were gone. And for a split second, I wonder whether Glinda spilled her coffee on purpose. I press my hand to my stomach—and not for the first time—wondering why I know so little about where I live and why I live here.

I glance at Glinda who suddenly seems to be more like my keeper than my friend. And from the paranoid place where my dreams arise, I believe we were actually enemies in a former life.

CHAPTER 2

My roommate foregoes another cup of coffee. And we step into the artificial day. Glinda hasn't left my side since the moment Dr. Baum told me I needed surgery.

I avoid looking at my stained shoes as we pass the barber shop, and the grocery store, which contains canned vegetables, bottled pasta sauce and bagged rice or beans. I'd like to buy something fresh for mother, but unprocessed produce is impossibly expensive in Bunkerville. The greenhouse is still an unsuccessful experiment and shipments only arrive monthly. I can't afford fresh. All my fruits and veggies come in a can.

"What about spaghetti?" Glinda asks me.

"Sure," I say trying to sound normal.

"We could make it with fish."

The crazy idea does distract me a bit. Fish with spaghetti. That's nuts. And if Glinda is anything, she's not insane. Careful, yes. Intense, sometimes. But crazy. No. For now, I decide I don't want to doubt our friendship. If she were dangerous, I'd know it. Right? I mean we live together. "Who in the world eats fish with spaghetti?"

Her laugh makes me feel better. "People," she says, "I read about it."

"From where?"

"The internet."

"You get to use the internet?"

"I'm on the staff remember?" Glinda laughs again as we take a side street I've never been to. My nerves prickle. And like a flash, my doubt returns full force. We're not on a street as much as an alley. A dark building, backlit by the city skyline stands at the end of the sketchy passage.

I bite my lip. "This is my surprise?"

She takes my hand as we enter and I'm too frightened to let go. Exposed bulbs swing from a two-story storage facility. Our steps echo as if we were in a cave. "I don't like this place."

She squeezes my hand. Her smile takes on a determined expression I've never seen before as we head to a door in the rear. I hold my breath as Glinda opens it.

Inside, the room looks like it might be a living room. But that couldn't be. People in Bunkerville don't live in places like this. The designers have taken pride in creating comfortable sustainable apartments.

"But not for the staff."

"What?" I ask, realizing I've slipped again.

"Many people don't live in the nice apartments. Some live over shops they run or in warehouses like this." She waves her arm across the room. A painting hangs on the wall covered in random splashes of color.

"What is this place?"

"This is my home," she says casually. She releases my hand and opens the coffee table trunk.

"But you can't live here, you live with me."

"Only for now. This is my home."

"Why bring me here?"

"To test a theory." She lifts the trunk lid and retrieves a stuffed animal. An elephant. Gray like the painting in Dr. Baum's office. She hands me the plush toy.

My heart races and I can't breathe without panting. Everything about the place elevates my nervousness. "Who's this for?"

"It's for the baby."

I study my shoes.

Breathe.

"Baby, what baby?"

I wiggle my toes willing the leather in my Keds to calm my rising anxiety.

"You'll see."

I exhale. Glinda couldn't know I have frequent nightmares about babies. More specifically, I often dream I'm pregnant, and the child is in danger. When I wake up, I have to spend at least ten minutes in my closet touching my shoes until I'm calm enough to slip into a pair of fluffy slippers. The horrible dreams are impossible since I'm still a virgin.

"I want to go."

"Not yet," Glinda drops the elephant on the beat up sofa and opens the door to our left. "Follow me."

I stand in place. I don't mean to, but the terror holds me.

"It's okay, it's a spare room I made just for you."

"But I like my place."

"I don't mean now. I mean later. If you decide to move from the apartment, you're in."

"Why would I do that?" I squeeze the fingers of my right hand with my left and take a step back. None of this feels right. "I don't like this."

"You don't have to stay." Glinda put her hands on my shoulders commanding my attention. Her eyes aren't mean or menacing. They're kind. Her voice is soft as she says, "You don't have to make a decision today, I'm just asking you to look."

Taking a deep breath, I nod. "Just a look, and then we go."

"Yes, a look and then we go."

Okay. I force my feet forward. At the threshold I peek into the room. On the walls, a cartoon sun and two-dimensional grass provide nursey rhyme characters a place to dance. To the left of the mural, Glinda stands next to a sheet covering what looks like a tall box.

"I brought you here to confirm an idea." Glinda fingers the blue linen. "Something about your surgery feels off."

"My surgery?"

"Yes."

"Did Dr. Baum ask you to bring me here?"

A shadow passes over Glinda's face. It remains for less than a second and disappears. Odd because I know Glinda and Dr. Baum are friends. A team sent to help me and the others get healthy.

"I'm wondering," the tall woman tugs gently on the sheet and the fabric floats to the floor revealing a wooden crib. "Do you have a tumor? Or are you pregnant?"

I cringe. A baby lies on the small mattress. The smell of soap and baby powder makes me nauseous. I watch my shoes and try to calm down.

Nightmares aren't real.

Nightmares aren't real.

Nightmares aren't real.

"Tell me," Glinda insists.

"No. No. No." The familiar sensation of nausea rises from my stomach. Glinda lifts the limp newborn from the crib. A small blue ribbon attached to his bald baby head.

A boy, like in my dreams.

I turn and close my eyes.

"I want to go home. Please, take me home." I run from the room and straight into Dr. Baum.

Thank goodness.

I hide behind the doctor as if I'm a toddler and she's my mother. Not logical given she's too young to be my parent and I'm white and she's black. But Glinda triggered a childlike fear through me. As I peek around my protector and see my roommate defiantly place the baby into the crib. It didn't cry or move.

"What's going on in here?" Dr. Baum asks.

"Testing a theory." Glinda's voice is filled with what sounds like accusation.

I look back and forth between the doctor and Glinda. Anxiety rises within me, like when my parents fight. Only, I don't remember my parents enough to have seen them fight. Yet, somewhere in the recesses of my brain another couple fought when I was a child.

"Glinda, this was a bad idea."

"Was it? I've followed all your rules to the letter. And while I understand the change you are trying to make in these inmates' lives, I don't believe in abortion without the mother's consent."

I gasp and instinctively touch my belly.

"Who said anything about abortion," Dr. Baum scoffs.

"Is Courtney pregnant or not?"

"Who's Courtney?" I wonder if they are talking about me. But my name is Dorothy. And I'm not pregnant.

"We'll talk about this later." Dr. Baum grabs my elbow

and ushers me toward the door. But Glinda follows her.

"We can either talk about this here, or we can talk about it on the streets of Bunkerville. But either way. I want to find out if you are attempting to perform an unrequested abortion on this inmate."

Dr. Baum stops and turns to her accuser, "For crying out loud, will you stop being so melodramatic? Yes, this inmate is pregnant, but HIPPA says that's not your business."

"It is if you plan to operate on her without her consent."

"For your information, she approved of this."

"Oh really," Glinda faces me. "Did you know about this?"

I freeze as the taller women approaches me.

"Rowena, will you stop. You are confusing her."

The name trembled within me.

"Look, don't you see she's trembling?"

Dr. Baum put her arm over my shoulder, "Come to my office tomorrow and I'll show you the paperwork. For now, can you stop interrupting her progression?"

Progression? What progression? I glance toward the crib and my ears ring. My temples throb and I rub them trying to dislodge the confusion. Am I pregnant? Is that what the nightmares are all about?

Dr. Baum comforts me, "It's okay, we'll get this all sorted out."

The pressure of my dreams pushes hard against my skull. "What about the baby?"

"That is a doll, not a baby."

A shiver quivers through me. I let the doctor guide me away. How could this not be about a baby? The door closes on the room. What was Glinda—or Rowena—trying to do to me? I follow Dr. Baum down the hall.

My tumor rumbles inside of me.

The reality of my situation floods my senses.

It's not a tumor, it's a baby.

Dr. Baum's façade drips from my mind like the sheet over the crib in the other room. She isn't Dr. Baum. Her name is Dr. Maggie. Glinda, who isn't Glinda but my old nemesis Rowena, clomps behind me. And I'm not Dorothy. I'm Courtney Manchester. An inmate of The Bunker.

Shock has me keeping step with Dr. Maggie. Thoughts swirl through my mind. I don't have a tumor, I'm pregnant and big at that. Why would they do this? I hug my unborn child.

And Rowena, what was that all about? Since the day I entered The Center, the woman made it clear she only cared about keeping inmates under control. She never did anything to help me. Why would my enemy help me now? Why pull me from hypnosis? And worse and more important in this moment is the solid evidence Dr. Maggie wants to trick me into killing my baby.

CHAPTER 3

"Let me go." I pull away. "Let me go. It's not true. It's not. I don't want to kill my baby." I race toward Rowena as memories of being an incarcerated criminal push through the fog in my brain.

"Let's not do this out here," Dr. Maggie's voice rises barely above a whisper.

"No! We talk now!" My hand shields my baby as if it were made of steel.

"Fine," she looks between me and the other guard. "I don't know why you keep talking about an abortion. This isn't about an abortion, it's about a c-section. I'm not trying to kill your baby, I'm trying to give you an uncomplicated delivery."

Rowena's eyes tighten into a squint as she ponders this statement.

"Then why tell me it's a tumor?"

Dr. Maggie's brown eyes are gentle. "Because you signed up for Reconstruction. In your new life, you're not the angry mean girl they told you about in Truth, now you are a college student getting ready to start your first year of school."

"I'm what?" Panic pounds former-life memories through me. Uncle John, the illustrious senator from New York. I was six years old and we were eating pizza in a small San Diego restaurant. My patent leather tap shoes were smudged, and my face itched from performance makeup. Mom came. Dad was absent as always. Uncle John had flown across the country to watch me for seven minutes in a three-hour long dance recital.

History.

My history.

A history Dr. Maggie was trying to erase.

"Rowena, are you satisfied? Can I please get this patient back on track?"

"I'll be by your office in the morning."

"Sure, no problem."

The tall guard frowns as Dr. Maggie tells me to follow her. I don't know what else to do, so I go. She leads me off the back street onto the main road of Bunkerville. We pass from Rowena's fake factory home into a small town scene. The quiet streets around me misrepresent The Bunker's caverns. While the big screens and piped in smells make the place as creepy Disneyland-real as possible, Dr. Maggie's hypnosis provides me a storyline. A new life without a record or mistakes like an unplanned pregnancy.

The empty neighborhood feels creepy. The streets appear evacuated. The fake sun shines as if it's noon. I rub my growing stomach, terrified of how deep or long I've been under. As we walk, I want other people around. Maybe even my worst enemy, Rowena. Why did she show me the baby? She hates me. Her motives can't be good. At least not for my good.

This power struggle between the awful guard and the crazy doctor reminds me I can't trust either of them.

Dr. Maggie stops at the corner and turns into The Shoe Shop.

My favorite store.

As the door opens, a familiar bell rings. Worry drips off me as I inhale the scent of leather and polish. Shoes of every kind cover the wall displays. I approach a pair of blue Louboutin's with a red heel.

"Do you like them?"

"I love them."

"I know, you come here practically every day to hold them."

"I do." The previously forgotten memories begin to fade.

"Want to try them on?"

"Can I?"

"Sure, let's see if the shoe fits."

"Lets!" I sit in the chair and peel off my stained Keds. A slight hesitation makes me wonder where they got the ugly brown blemish. "Have I been outside?"

"Yes, Glinda took you for a walk."

"That's right. You're mad at her." I slip the pump over my right foot and grin. It fits perfectly. They are used, but I don't care. The second shoe slides on as if it were made just for me.

"I'm not mad at Glinda," the doctor says. "People have disagreements, that's all."

I make my way across the floor without a single stumble. The heels are high, but somehow, I naturally navigate the room.

"In fact, you don't remember what she and I talked about, do you?"

Stopping to look out the window, I honestly can't remember why I thought the two friends disagreed. In fact, I'm pretty sure they agree on everything. "No, I don't."

"I thought not."

"Can I buy these shoes?"

"Remember, these are for after your surgery."

"Oh yeah." A small mirror leans against the wall. Standing before it, I examine my feet at every angle. Amazing. Truly and wonderfully amazing. In seven days, I will own these shoes. They will be mine to wear whenever I want to.

"Maybe there's a way." Dr. Baum takes my hand and leads me to the chair where I have to take off the beautiful shoes. "We could call your father, see if he can't come early."

"Early for what?"

"To move up your surgery."

"Surgery?" I allow my eyes to shift from the blue leather.

"Yes." She points to my expanded stomach.

My head hurts as I try to sort out blank spaces in my brain. Tap shoes came to mind. Small child-sized tap shoes.

"The sooner we have the surgery, the sooner we can begin your recovery?"

The shoes were so comfortable. And pretty. "Okay. Let's call my Dad."

Dr. Baum smiled. She's such a stunning woman. "Yes. I believe that's doable. "How about I talk to the owner. I bet he'll let you take these home tonight, as long as you promise not to wear them until after the surgery."

"We are going to remove the tumor."

She nodded and headed into the back office. An inkling in my heart told me to be nervous, but I couldn't. Not around all these wonderful shoes.

An old man appears before me with an open shoe box. He smiles a familiar smile at me. "Your doctor said you are ready to move your surgery."

"Yes, if my Dad can make it."

The old man nods, "He'll come. I'm sure of it. Your doctor is on the computer in the back now."

I slip off the shoes and watch as the store owner gently places them into the box. At the front counter, I sign the slip of paper making the transaction complete. Money and credit cards aren't necessary in Bunkerville. Each person has a certain amount of points that get recorded in the system, and I'm sure I've used my entire month's clothing allowance on these shoes, but they are totally worth it.

Dr. Baum returns with the good news. "Your Mom will be here in a couple hours." She takes my hands in hers, "And your Dad will be here tomorrow in time for a picnic lunch. After that we'll all get you prepped for surgery in two days."

"Not seven." I say flatly.

"Not seven." She picks up the shoe box from the counter and extends it toward me. "Let's go to my office."

"For what?" I hug the shoebox.

"You have paperwork to sign."

PART II

The Past

CHAPTER 4

August 5th.

The date was scrawled on the wall in my Bunker cell. Not big and unruly, but neat and about two inches high. It's the day I entered The Bunker. The end of my first trimester and all the horrible vomiting. The day Jackson proclaimed his love to me. The day The Center burnt to the ground.

Below the date were three weeks of chicken scratches. Six vertical lines with a single horizontal line across the middle. Yes, I'd become a cliché, counting days on the wall with a bar of soap. A line at the completion of each lights-on-lights-off cycle.

Time dragged. I slept, ate, and paced thousands of steps. A female guard picked up my breakfast tray. She wouldn't answer my requests to see Dee Dee or Ángel. She only shoved a tray into my room and ran away. Maybe she was busy. Maybe she was afraid of me. I did some crazy things while in The Center. Enough to earn me an electronic taser.

I rubbed my wrist.

The taser had been taken off within a day of my arrival. So had the GPS bracelet that kept track of us in The Center. No need for high-tech electronics when you've got your prisoner locked behind thick cement walls.

I leaned against the door and watched for any activity outside of my cell door. The mesh on the small window limited my view. A prison documentary I'd seen in school replayed in my head over and over. Solitary confinement. One man had spent his entire life sentence in segregation, but he was a murderer of murderers. I hadn't killed anyone. I picked at a hole in my uniform left by an ember.

The same uniform I came in with.

The same uniform when I last saw Jackson.

The thought saddened me.

I didn't want to think of Jackson.

I didn't want to think of The Center.

I didn't want to think of anything.

To divert my energy, I moved away from the wall and slid under the bed to work on the mural I had started about a week ago. Hygiene items, dirt and leftover condiments became my paint. With the tip of my finger, I smudged strawberry jam into the outline of a pair of red high-heeled shoes. My fingers became brushes, and time passed.

Sometimes I fell asleep under my bunk only to find another day had passed and a new tray of food waited by the door.

Crumb dust from a Cheeto made a perfect pair of work boots, footwear I never would have thought of until I'd lived in The Center. Black business shoes had been made from the dirt off the bottom of my own shoes. Once I finished the high heels, I would have the clad feet of six different characters. I didn't stop there. Depending on the food I received, the shoes filled with legs up to the mattress level. Lighting and supplies were my biggest issues. I frequently had to slide from under the metal bed to check my work.

Maybe I'll be here long enough to finish.

The thought made me drop the jam container and slide to the middle of the room. Closing my eyes, I hugged my stomach. What in the world was I doing? I lay on the ground and rocked my child. The fear of going insane crept through me. Was I really creating a mural on a wall with toothpaste and jam? The fire had to have ended by now. The guards should have taken those of us who survived the fire above ground. Maybe they had. Maybe everyone else was gone. Maybe I was the only one left.

I rushed to the door and pounded. I wanted out. The fear of being buried alive made me envy those who'd been burnt alive. The walls felt closer. I pounded until the light at the end of the hall blinked out.

It had begun.

The waterfall of lights out.

I hurried to the bed as complete darkness descended. The thin mattress absorbed my frame. I pulled the coarse blanket over my face and waited. Hoped, actually. A deep desire overflowed me for The Bunker's night noise.

But it was silent.

The quiet tugged at my worry. I'd spent my life hating people, yet, here in the dark seclusion, the need for human contact crept through me. The faces of inmates I never took the time to meet wandered in and out of my mind. The smell of my own sweat permeated the bedding. The thought of weeks-old sheets didn't bother me as much as the idea of total isolation.

I didn't want to be alone.

Please let me not be alone.

Touching the concrete wall, I forced myself to imagine people on the other side. Anyone.

Then someone howled.

My heart soared.

I was not alone.

Before I could return the animal call, another inmate beat me to it. Connections. Yes. That's enough. I folded the flat pillow under my head.

As much as I didn't like people, being buried for so long made me miss them. I tried to remember what my family looked like. Uncle John on C-SPAN, the illustrious senator from New York. Nanny Bella, flour handprints on her floral apron. Father, international business consultant, in a suit on his way to the airport. Mother on her computer ready to ghost another story. And Kat.

I swallowed.

The little sister who stole my father's heart, smiled at me in the darkness. The memory stabbed against my brain. No matter how many awful things I did to her, Kat the Brat still loved me. Adored me. And hidden in this abyss, it hurt to accept this. My heart could be as cold and dark as The Bunker's night.

Loud weeping entered my cell.

I felt my eyes to make sure it wasn't coming from me.

The sorrow echoed down the hall, touching me from under the door.

I hugged my belly and comforted my baby.

The crying could be Dee Dee. Maybe it wasn't an inmate. The forest fire had forced guards and counselors underground. They may not have slept in cells, but they were as buried alive as the rest of us.

Jackson had warned us about the negative effects of The Bunker's solitude. Only Fisher wanted to see what the above ground pyramid led to. Fisher, the convicted rapist who had attacked me had been sent down here weeks before the fire.

A chill ran through me.

I turned and stared through the darkness toward the door. All desire for companionship evaporated.

I twirled the pearl at my neck.

Those thoughts didn't help. I needed to find a way to cope until the lights came up.

CHAPTER 5

Lights on. The illuminated bulb high above my head pulled me from sleep. I didn't move anything but my eyelids. What was the point? The sooner I got up, the sooner the tedium would start. Once my feet hit the floor, the boring, endless hours of nothingness would begin. Sleep burned time. Staring and listening became important early morning activities.

Water in pipes.

The whir of recirculated air.

The rattle of cart wheels.

My stomach gurgled like Pavlov's dog. Breakfast time. The lock on my door clicked open. A tray scratched across the floor. The door closed.

The guard no longer spoke to me when she came by each mealtime. She ignored my screaming and begging and whimpering. She ignored questions like, "What's going on? When will we go upstairs? Isn't the fire out?" There was no point in talking, to myself or anyone else. No point in getting out of bed.

We'd been forgotten by the world. I would probably have to give birth to my baby alone. A dreadful idea. I should have been more frightened, but I just felt numb. From my bed I stared at the caged bulb. Even light didn't modulate in The Bunker. Above ground, the sun and shadows shifted throughout the day. A cloud could darken a room and disappear while the room brightened again. But not down here. Light was either steady on, or steady off. No gray fade between hours.

The smell of buttered toast wafted over me, I rolled over. The tray had the customary breakfast. And something else.

Something new.

I got up.

Unbelievable.

The staff had given me more than food.

For the first time in over 21-days, something different lay next to my hard-boiled egg and toast. I hurried from my bed to find a letter-sized document on the tray. A push of air from under the door made pages flap like the wings of a wounded bird. A small bottle of juice and a regular bottle of water stood next to the unexpected written words.

I leaned over without picking it up. A stupid stack of papers shouldn't have thrilled me. It could've been nothing. But even Raman noodles tasted delicious when you were hungry. I crept to the window and peeked, trying to catch a glimpse of the person who'd delivered it, willing my heart to slow.

The hall was empty.

The room across from me never received food trays. It wasn't the only vacant cell.

Nervous energy had me pacing again. I didn't want to rush this one variable in my monotonous existence. At the sink, I kept an eye on the stack of papers and grabbed my underwear. Dry. Good. I slipped my pants off and the pile didn't move. I pulled on my clean undies and the pages remained on the tray. I brushed my teeth, keeping my eyes on the document while I spit and rinsed. This strange new addition to my day was bigger than Christmas.

I sunk onto the bed, staring at the printed gift waiting to see if it would disappear.

It didn't.

After three weeks of isolation, what would this crazy place give me to read? I closed my eyes imagining creative titles.

"The Spelunker's Guide to Life." I laughed.

The sound bounced around the room. Intentionally speaking my thoughts aloud, I pointed at the pages. "That could be a prisoner's guide to life underground." I argued with myself. "No, you're right, it couldn't be that. I'm an expert in that. No." I scratched my head. "Not that. I mean, they can't keep us down here forever. They have to let us out, they have to. Maybe this is evacuation instructions?"

I froze.

Could it be?

I turned toward the document with new hope.

It had to be.

"How to Prepare for Your Departure."

My heart beat harder.

"Life Under the Sun."

The days of sameness could be over.

"Please proceed to the upper levels." I clapped my hands. Three weeks was plenty of time to extinguish a forest fire. I hurried to the tray and quickly grabbed the mystery at the stapled corner. Raising the legal sized pages to eye level, I read, "The State of Virginia vs Courtney Anne

Manchester."

My court record.

A chuckle forced itself from my chest.

These jerks had jokes.

If I'd had a match, I'd have set the entire package on fire, tray and all.

I stood as if facing a jury. There weren't any cameras, so I spoke to the ceiling.

"You all think you know me."

I paced to the wall, conviction in hand.

"You think you've got me all figured out."

I tore the top page free of the staple and dropped it on the blanket.

"You remember my temper tantrum in The Center and think I'm going to repeat myself."

Rip.

Another page free.

I laughed manically. "You don't know me. You don't know anything about me." One more page floated from my hand. "Not one little thing." By the time I was done, a total of twelve pages laid released and unrestricted on the makeshift bed. I smiled. It was time to have some fun.

With my back against the bed, I folded the paper using my fingernail to make it tight. I reversed the fold a couple of times until it would tear easily. Clean straight lines for my creation, I wished for an audience. They wanted me to worry, to sweat at the meaning of these words. Dr. Maggie or Rowena would love to get into my head and scare me. But they couldn't.

I was stronger than both of them.

Fold.

They could not invade my mind.

Tear.

Once my baby was born, I'd have Ángel take him above ground.

Fold.

Bring it on ladies. I was ready to battle every head game the guard and psychologist wanted to throw at me. Those two had made my life a living hell since I'd met them. Neither of them had cared about rehabilitation or release. They'd enjoyed lording their power over inmates. What did I care? They might be able to crack every inmate in this place with guilt or drama. Not me. No way. I would out-game them. With every calculated fold, I grew surer of myself. By the time I'd created fourteen origami swans and seven airplanes, my lunch had arrived. The uneaten breakfast was removed by a female guard and my stomach growled. I left my project by the bed and slid to the wall to consume a sandwich of processed meat, a bag of chips and a squeeze container of applesauce.

For the first time in a long time, I enjoyed a Jackson memory. As I folded more creations, I reminisced about the sunny day hundreds of feet above me when the handsome guard had taught me how to make swans from shiny square pieces of paper. Back then, The Bunker was a mysterious structure. A metal Louvre-shaped pyramid, out of place in the Rocky Mountain forest. Life had been better then.

Holding my sandwich in my left hand, I retrieved one of the three remaining half pages. Between bites, I created a paper fortune teller. I didn't have a pen to write numbers or colors or names on the triangular flaps, so I creased the page with the words on the outside. I pinched the pyramid and began to play, I picked a word like "drugs" or "victim" and opened and closed the game based on the number of letters. From the chosen section, I selected a word inside to find the surprised sentence seeking to judge me. But all these fortunes were about my past. The conviction and sentence had already landed me in this place. Their judgment no longer frightened or weighed me down. I would survive for my baby and my baby would survive for me.

When the guard returned to claim my tray, I was ready for the real fun to begin. With the fortune teller in my back pocket, I'd lined up the paper swans on the mattress and sat across the floor from them. With as much precision as possible, I'd thrown a paper airplane at a stiff bird.

Miss.

Shoot.

Miss.

All seven airplanes had floated past every waiting bird. I tried again. And I'd reached a 50% hit rate when the key scraped in the metal lock on my door.

The door swung open slowly.

I smiled, fully expecting a disappointing look from the female guard who delivered my trays, for making such a mess, but the disappointment was mine.

In the rectangular frame stood Dr. Maggie.

CHAPTER 6

My counselor's presence was intrusive. I wasn't exactly afraid of the diminutive woman with her cat-eye glasses and perfectly spiraled afro, but she could be unpredictable, bordering on manipulative.

"How are you, Courtney?"

Hearing my name stopped me mid-throw.

I'd probably walked through life a million times without someone saying my name, but after three weeks with only myself to listen to, I suddenly wanted to hear more people say it. I dropped the airplane. My emotions roller-coastered. Dr. Maggie could be here to get me out. I didn't want to kamikaze swans for the rest of my life. I was ready to traverse hot coals to see the sun again. Take me to the surface of the earth.

"I hope you haven't been too bored." Dr. Maggie sat on the bed and picked up an origami swan from the floor where I'd toppled it.

"Get me out of here." My voice cracked and I cleared my

throat. It felt weird to talk to another human. Weirder when she answered. The mural people I created only had feet, no faces to pretend conversation with.

Dr. Maggie's voice was kind as she said, "You can't leave yet."

"Why not?" I took a deep breath through my nostrils and that's when I smelled it. The green aroma of soap and mint. I eyed her top to bottom. Clean clothes and a touch of make-up. She had to be kidding. I was stuck with a tiny cleansing bar and travel-sized toothpaste and this witch is taking a shower?

"That's what I came to talk to you about." She smiled. Her black ringlets bounced around her face. Her scrubbed clean face. The face I imagined smashing to bits. "We've been maintaining communication with the forest service, the fire ended yesterday."

"You talked to people above?"

"Of course."

Okay. I'm going to slug her for real now. "Then get me out of here."

"And send you where?"

"I don't know, anywhere." I dusted off my hands ready to leave this horrible grave behind me.

"It takes more than eight days to place a couple hundred inmates."

"Eight days?" I looked at the twenty-three soap-marks on the wall.

"Yes, the fire was intense," She nodded, smoothing her clean shirt, "The good news is the flames have been contained and they've begun clean-up."

"Eight days?" I repeated.

"Yes. The fire would have lasted longer, but The Center cabins were equipped with internal and external sprinklers.

It didn't stop the flames from destroying the trees and bushes but saved the structures."

"It hasn't been eight days. I've been locked up for three weeks?" My voice sounded shrill in my ears.

Dr. Maggie shook her head, "No, you haven't."

"Yes." I put my fist on my hip to keep from slamming it into her face.

"No," she said slowly, "We've been down here for exactly eight days."

"No way," I shook my head. "You're lying." I didn't start marking off days until after a week had passed. And I wasn't always consistent after that. But there was no way my count could be very far off. No way.

"Courtney, you're not alone in thinking you've been here longer. You're not. Human seclusion plays tricks on the mind."

"I slept here more than eight nights. There have been more than eight lights out." I challenged her, but I wasn't sure. I wasn't.

Dr. Maggie's voice was as calm as a hypnotist, "For eight days, the lights have turned on between 6:00 and 7:00 am depending on the section you are in. The lights go out 16 hours later."

"I'm not crazy. You want me to think I'm crazy."

"Courtney, isolation can play funny tricks on the mind. I promise you, you've only been in this cell for eight days."

I shook my head. It wasn't true. It couldn't be. "I counted the days. I counted the meals. We were fed three times a day."

"No, you were fed five times a day. The portions are too small to keep you healthy. We served you breakfast, a snack, lunch, a snack and dinner."

No way. No freaking way. I looked around the room. She

wanted me to believe I folded swans after my afternoon snack, not lunch. If she was right, it was early afternoon not evening.

Toppled papers litter the floor I'd been pacing for weeks. Weeks.

Right?

The soap marks on the wall couldn't be lying to me.

My brain didn't lie.

I'd rather believe my mind than Dr. Maggie. This had to be a trick. A game. A surge of vulnerability swept over me. Time trickled in this place. I couldn't be sure. Eight days, not twenty-one. Impossible. Could one day really have dragged into five? Insane. I couldn't stay here a minute longer. I had to see what was happening above. How could I have forgotten about the real world? I hugged my baby.

Even though I didn't want to believe her, I could have been wrong. I'd slipped into a delusion, painting horrible wall art and playing with paper. I crossed my arms and rubbed my biceps. And what happened to Dee Dee and Ángel and Jackson? I wanted to know.

"Tomorrow morning," Dr. Maggie continued, "A team will go through The Center's entrance outside and check the conditions."

I needed to be on that team.

"That's not going to happen."

I moved toward her not caring about the verbal slip. I'd let all the words from my brain leak as long as I could stand on the ground and not under it. I couldn't stay here another minute. "I want to be on the team. I have to go." I pushed against the tears forming at the back of my eyes.

"I can't let you do that." She put her hands on my shoulders and I jerked away. She raised her hands in surrender and said, "We can't risk endangering any inmates."

"I'm losing my freaking mind, and you don't want to endanger the inmates?" I paced to the door and back again. "You're unbelievable. You've showered and changed. You've spoken to other people. You haven't even let me see Dee Dee. Or walk the halls. You could have done that. You could have. But you don't care. You don't."

She straightened and said defensively, "Over five hundred youth offenders are in this place. It's taken time to determine where to place them. Organizing play dates wasn't a priority."

"Go to hell." I paced to the sink. The basin I used to brush my teeth and clean my underwear. The sink I might be stuck using for another hundred confusing days

She exhaled a deep sigh before continuing, "Look, I'm sorry. I didn't come here to upset you. I've actually come to offer you a chance to stay somewhere other than this cell."

"You said I couldn't go above ground."

"It's not above ground." She stacked the birds next to the pillow and cleared her throat. "With the aid of government grants and private endorsements, I've created a virtual town called Bunkerville."

"A town below ground?"

"Yes," she said with pride, "And within it is a rehabilitation program I call Reconstruction."

PART III

The Present

CHAPTER 7

Confusion overwhelms me. I've been in Dr. Baum's office before, but something on the edge of my mind makes me think of a different office in a different place.

The decorations on her wall had hung in another room. A room in a place my mind called The Center. A wooden giraffe stands on a table by the door, it used to be on a bookshelf.

Without thinking, I lift it to my nose and breath in the scent of smoke. "This came from your old office." I say, fighting to keep my voice steady.

"Yes, yes." She waves her hand at me and doesn't look up from her typing. "Please, sit."

I sink into the chair I'd sat in before. Both here in Bunkerville, as well as back in a different room before all this confusion.

A printer in the corner whirs to life. A printer. That's a lot of electricity, I think. The idea feels novel. Like it's an interesting thought.

Dr. Baum, whose first name might be Maggie, I can't remember, makes her way to the small device and brings the half dozen pages over to me.

"Here's what I need you to sign."

I stare at the only page she hands me. The last page.

"What is this?"

"It's permission to conduct the treatment."

"The surgery?"

"Yes," she says with confidence.

But I'm no longer sure. "Maybe I should sleep on it. My parents are coming, right? They can be here to help me make this decision, right?"

"Yes," my counselor places the page on the desk on top of the others. "No problem. That's a good idea."

Tension releases from my shoulders and I draw the shoe box into my arms. It's silly to be afraid, but I'm just so confused.

"You look anxious." She glances over the rim of her glasses.

"I am." I confess.

She sits in the chair across from me, taking my hands in hers. "How about a quick hypnosis session? To help relax you. It's been a confusing day." She tips her head and smiles. "Do you know I was the first person to go through Reconstruction."

"Reconstruction?" The word sounds familiar, but I can't place it.

The doctor continues, "I didn't call it that, of course, but it changed my life. My past wasn't worth remembering. My life was made of family members who didn't love or care about me. When I discovered I could change my past, I embraced it. I legally changed my name, my will, and my emergency contacts. I adopted my own people and found life could be lived in peace."

"Is that what we're doing?"

"Yeah, it's the basis of Bunkerville."

"So, this whole place is based on a lie?"

"What lie?"

"We're in a fake world."

She tenderly squeezes my hand. "What makes the real one so much better?"

"IT'S REAL." I don't mean for the words to come out harsh, but they do.

"So what?" Her tone and demeaner remains calm. "I bet you haven't spent more than an hour combined thinking about your little sister. Yet, I watched you walk through fire to save Dee Dee."

"Who's Dee Dee?"

"Exactly. You can't remember the one person whose life you were willing to save. How important can she be?"

Every blood cell in my body turns cold. Gritting my teeth, I let the words out. "I'm so confused. Honestly, nothing you are saying is making sense. Flashes of memory slip in and out of a fog. You say I have a sister. Is Dee Dee my sister?"

"No," Dr. Baum taps the shoebox on my lap. "No, Dee Dee is an inmate, like you. The sister from the biological family you've decided to divorce is named Kat."

"Wait, what biological family?" I rub my temples. Faces and names were blobs of gray in my mind. "I don't understand."

"It's okay. Transition is hard." She slows her voice. "You're reconstructing your history. We've found new parents for you. New parents for your new life. Unhealthy blood relations no longer have to bother you."

"In my new life, I get to choose what I keep, right?"

"I would never take away the best part of you."

"So, I can choose what stays and what goes?"

"Of course. That's what our hypnosis sessions are all about."

I find myself nodding. It isn't a voluntary action, just a simple up and down of my head. But I don't trust her. I don't trust any of this. How could I? There are so many names. So many different faces. None of them really clear. Except one. Jackson. His face I know more than the rest. Although why his name has stuck isn't as clear as the knowledge of his friendship and love.

"It will be fine." My counselor says, taking in a deep breath. She encourages me to join her. I do, matching the slow intake of air through my nose, holding it for a few seconds before the slow exhale.

"Good." She pushes a button, which releases the smell of grapefruit and lemon and ginger into the room. "Try to make yourself as comfortable as possible."

I wiggle on the cushions until I'm intentionally uncomfortable. Hypnosis requires a willing participant, and I'm still not sure I want to do this. Shutting out her words, I focus on trying to appear relaxed. My shoulders sink. My jaw opens slightly. My hands grow limp. All the while, I keep my toes curled like claws inside my shoes.

I wait for Dr. Baum to lift a watch and swing it in front of my eyes and say, "You are getting very sleepy." But she doesn't. She softens her voice and says, "Lift your left palm toward your face."

I obey, my heart racing. My fingers feel cold. I have to concentrate to keep my hand from trembling, fight to maintain control. If I only pretend to concentrate on what she says, I can keep my brain alert without raising suspicion.

"Do you see the lines in your palm?"

"Yes," I say, but my voice cracks.

"You don't have to talk. Just nod."

I bob my head, forcing myself to do it unhurriedly like a robot. I lick my lips, afraid I look too robotic. Could I do this? Fake her out as she tries to reinvent me into a fake?

"Now," Dr. Baum says in a monotone. "Study the line on your hand. Find a spot right in the middle."

I stare at the spot but don't focus on it. Which is crazy hard. As soon as I shift my attention to my fingers or the air around my hand, my eyes shift. Did she see that? I return my gaze to my palm, trying to do and not do what she's saying.

"In your palm is a very calm place."

Not calm, chaos.

"It's a gentle place."

Not gentle, harsh.

"It's a place of peace where you can relax."

War. Do not relax.

"Now, as you focus on that place, the palm of your hand will slowly get bigger. It will grow and open up to you as your hand moves closer and closer to your face. As you move in harmony, relax your body. Allow yourself to enter this quiet place. That's it, allow peace and relaxation to approach, embrace it. Yes, let go."

No. I shake my head. My hand is suddenly an inch from my face. I blink and bite my lip. How did that happen? I'd tried to remain distant, but somehow my body reacted. Vigorously shaking my hands from the wrist, I sit as straight as possible.

"That's okay." Dr. Baum's voice remains eerie and tranquil.

My toes are no longer clenched, so I tightened them again to prove I can.

CHAPTER 8

"Dorothy, wake up, your mother has arrived."

I stretch sore muscles and look around. I'm in Dr. Baum's office. "Did I fall asleep?"

"We had a session, remember?" The counselor places an old-style phone into the base. Cellphones don't work in Bunkerville and only a few offices have lines running to them. I remember a time when I carried a phone everywhere. The idea seems ridiculous now.

"They called me, your mother's in orientation."

My mother, that's right, she's coming today. "Oh my gosh, I didn't make it to the market."

"Don't worry, we'll go to the diner together, my treat."

"Okay," I say as my equilibrium returns.

"The shoes, don't forget your shoes."

"Oh, yeah." Cradling the box like a baby in the crook of my arm, a sense of calm rushes through me. I let Dr. Baum help me up. My tumor has become so big.

"That's why I want to move up the surgery."

"Did I say that aloud?"

"No one minds a slip now and then."

It feels wonderful to be understood. "Thank you."

We step into the bright lights of Bunkerville. It reminds me of my San Diego childhood, without the salty ocean. The creators built the self-sustaining city next to a fresh-water lake.

The entire town is an experiment. And one I'm proud to be part of. People have chosen to live in this underground city, like pioneers decided to go west. People seeking a world safe from drugs and war. A place helping to stop global warming and waste.

Bicycles and electric vehicles surround a small park. Two old men play chess at the picnic table. A family plays frisbee on the fake lawn. The creators have piped in the smell of fresh-cut grass and honeysuckle. Disney theme parks or Universal Studios have nothing on the quality of Bunkerville's illusion.

"I hope my mother likes it here."

"Most people do," Dr. Baum's voice echoes my pride.

Birds chirp through a soundtrack. Bunkerville doesn't have wild or stray animals. While I've never had a cat or a dog or a ferret, I've seen people walking theirs down here.

Dr. Baum and I enter the visitor's center. Three other people wait patiently on benches scattered along the wall. I don't remember what's on the other side of this room, but Glinda told me Bunkerville has one guarded entrance leading to the auditorium on the other side.

I find a seat. A video must be playing in the other room because I can clearly hear the narration. I eavesdrop as I think of my mother watching images I can't see.

"Food and other supplies," the broadcaster announces, "arrive through the same mine tracks you traveled in on. If there's something you need, and you can afford the processing fee, we can order it for you. In Bunkerville, patience goes a long way. We believe in living at a slower, cleaner pace. Not only internally, but within and without our planet.

"The founder designed this place to use only biofuel. Methane generators, hydro-electricity and selectively placed solar panels on the earth's surface provide all the energy necessary for a fully green city.

"Most of the electricity is used for the façade. People here live successfully without refrigerators or televisions. Appliances in our homes run off rechargeable batteries. It's the price we pay for the wall-to-wall and floor-to-ceiling flat screens which provide a stunning sky and breathtaking horizons. Most buildings use candle-lit aromatherapy to prevent seasonal affective disorder. It triggers our brains to accept the artificial.

We do have botanists working to on growing fruits and vegetables under the ultra-violet lights in the greenhouse. Simulating the sky is one thing, but we haven't fully mastered replacing the sun."

"I have some bad news," Dr. Baum places her hand on mine. "Your father can't get here any sooner."

"Really?" I have no idea how to react. I frown because she said it was bad news, but I don't know the man. In fact, I don't know the mother on the other side of that door. To be honest I don't really know myself.

"I can still try—" Dr. Baum continues, "—to move the surgery. I'm not sure, yet. I need to have a conversation with your mother, maybe we can remove the lump without your father present." Lifting her hand from mine she places her soft palm on my cheek. "I want you to have all the support you deserve. Soon you will have the best life ever."

"Thank you," I say, hugging my new shoes to my chest. I want to open the box to look at them, but I focus on the announcer instead.

His calm tone is gentle and reassuring. "So, whether you are here for a visit or have come to stay, Bunkerville seeks to support a greener planet and our citizens say welcome."

Music swells to a crescendo as the doors open and I hear the sound of a couple dozen people clapping. I straighten my shirt and stand.

Time to meet my mother. I swallow. According to Dr. Baum, this woman has chosen me. But that was on paper. I adjust my wig. She could change her mind after meeting me. She could leave Bunkerville if it doesn't work out. Couldn't she? I should have asked Dr. Baum if surrogates ever change their minds.

A thirty-something couple with two small children step into the lobby followed by what looks like three college students and their white-haired professor.

The curiosity on their faces must match my own as Dr. Baum says, "There she is, you see, the petite blonde."

I spot her. She's holding a handbag in both fists as if she's as nervous as I am. She doesn't really look old enough to have an adult child. Not that I've been an adult long. And she's really pretty. I search her face for any sign of me, but I can't see a resemblance. Maybe I look like my father.

"Dorothy?" She rushes to me and pulls me into an enormous hug. And suddenly the world feels right. All anxiety flows from me. I fold into her, relieved.

"Mom?" I speak into her straight golden hair.

"Yes, honey," she pulls me back. "Yes, it's me."

I laugh and set the shoebox on the bench so I can initiate an unrestrained hug.

CHAPTER 9

Jackson invades my dreams. His movie-star features and kind voice. He holds an art kit toward me. Charcoal, pencils, paint. I embrace the gift to my chest as he nods his head toward the cliff overlooking The Center. "I'm proud of you," He says.

In my dream, I recognize his pride comes from something I've released. Something big and important. The sunset glows in shifting colors, not stunning as much as authentic. My heart soars.

We stand side by side. He holds a book titled, *The Word of Truth*. I chuckle. Truth. Of course, he'd pick Ángel's side, Truth Sessions rather than Reconstruction. I cradle the art kit in my left arm and reach for Jackson's free hand only to have it morph into the calloused claw of Rowena. Dr. Maggie's laugh bounces against a false sky. Terror courses through me, powerful enough to wake me.

I rub my hand across my forehead at least a dozen times trying to release my brain. What a tangled mess of confusion. Laying back, I try to relax. Names, faces, and muddy memories surface as my eyes adjust to the darkness. As shadows take shape, I remember I'm buried in a prison undergoing voluntary hypnosis.

This isn't the first time my brain has reclaimed full possession of reality. The darkness surrounding me shuts down most of Dr. Maggie's hypnotic triggers. If she knew, she would probably make me sleep with the lights on. So, I don't tell her. Let her be Dr. Baum in the mock daylight. I prefer to hold tightly to what little reality I can.

I'm buried beneath The Center, not in the ugly yellow cell where I began my time in The Bunker. While I don't remember why I joined reconstruction, that part is very foggy, Jackson and our time on the mountain remains clear.

The soft bedding and comfortable mattress are part of the Bunkerville façade. The choice I made during a less clear part of my time here. Whenever I am awakened to thoughts of Jackson or life above ground, I'm gripped with an overwhelming sadness.

A person can never really run away from truth. All the hypnosis in the world hasn't erased all my past. In the darkness, My Truth sessions refuse to be silenced. Based on the size of my belly, I do have a tumor that needs to be removed, but right now, what comes to mind are the months of video sunrises and shoe shopping and toe-curling sessions of where I thought I'd avoided hypnosis.

My mind proved to be a weak vessel. In the invented light of day, I'm a puppet. I'd never mastered the fake in the fake. Told myself I'd chosen luxury for the sake of my health but had not given up my mind.

But I had. That's easy to know as the sleep and hypnosis to fade from my brain. Sitting in the black night, I allow the memories of my early days in The Bunker to return. I want to recall them. They belong to me and I want them. If I wait for Bunkerville's morning to dawn, Dr. Maggie will become Dr. Baum again. I will be pulled back under and something evil lurks in the light of a Bunkerville day. I force myself to think of my past because in this moment I'm missing something important. Some part of my mind is still captured and if I focus on where I've been, I can find that missing piece.

PART IV

The Past

CHAPTER 10

My Truth journey began the day Dr. Maggie told me I'd been in The Bunker for only eight days. I didn't trust her or her creepy descriptions of an underground world she called Bunkerville. The place sounded Orwellian. Who would ever choose such an option?

"Is it really worse than what you have here?" Dr. Maggie asked me on that morning.

She had a point, she did. The yellow cell with a hidden half-mural beneath my bed wasn't great, but it was real and that's what I wanted. Reality over lies.

When I told her that, disappointment laced with anger covered her face. Her Jekyll and Hyde flip told me I'd made the right decision. I might be a prisoner, but she didn't own me.

A few minutes after she stormed from the cell, Ángel entered. I hadn't seen him in weeks. "No," I whispered to myself, not caring about the Latino's presence. "Days, not weeks."

"How are you doing?" The kindness in his voice irritated me.

"That's a stupid question," I glared at him "I'm horrible." He smelled like the counselor. Mint toothpaste and green soap. "This isn't fair."

"You're right, it's not."

"Don't be condescending."

"I'm not."

"Oh yeah, well your clean clothes and washed hair are."

He rubbed the back of his neck, "I get it. But I didn't take my first shower until this morning. And you'll get one soon as well."

"Why not now? Take me now."

"Courtney, I have to brief you first." His tone matched my pissy attitude. "Will you cool it long enough for me to do that?"

"Whatever."

"Look, I've been locked up down here as long as you have."

"But you graduated from The Center and became a guard."

"An intern guard," he emphasized the title. "I was released from my cell within the first day. That's how I was able to help distribute food. Remember? It's been chaotic identifying where everyone would land."

"How many people are down here?"

"Down where?"

"Down here," I said, leaving the word *duh* implied.

"Sorry, I should have clarified. The Bunker is really broken into two large sections. The prison which we are in and Bunkerville."

"The fake place Dr. Maggie talked about."

"Yes, I'm not sure how many people actually live there,

but it has to be more than a thousand."

"What?"

"It's not only prisoners."

Shock stopped my words yet Ángel nodded at the question I didn't ask.

"Crazy I know, but Dr. Maggie's been building her world for years. Hundreds of people choose it as their home. Only a section of the population are inmates of some sort."

"What do you mean—" even though I hate air quotes, I signaled with my fingers when I said — "'of some sort'?"

"Not just criminals."

It took a second before it dawned on me what other kinds of inmates existed. "Do you mean insane asylums? Are there mentally deranged people down here?"

"Kind of extreme language, but yeah, or people going through rehab, et cetera."

"No freaking way!"

"Look, Courtney, I don't have time to get into everything wacked about Bunkerville. I'm part of the team who works with the prisoners from The Center evacuation who stay here. And there are about two hundred of you."

I wanted to ask more, but I changed my line of questioning. "Is it true The Center burnt down only eight days ago?"

"Yes, that is true."

The soap lines on the wall were a lie after all. My brain fooled me. The idea scared me as much as Dr. Maggie's fake world. I hated not being in control of my own thoughts.

"I'm here because I've been assigned to explain the alternative to Reconstruction." He picked up a swan. "The staff is fiercely divided over the two programs." He flapped the paper bird's wings. For a guy in such a hurry, he paused often. I tapped my foot. The rising anxiety made my stomach ache.

Without looking at me Ángel said, "In Truth, you will be released from your cell as often as in Reconstruction."

"Released?" I turned and faced him, my heart racing with optimism.

"Yes."

"I get to go above ground?"

"Oh, no, not that." His head shook hard enough to break loose from his neck. "No. You will be able to get out of your cell."

"To do what?"

He set the swan down and turned around. His serious expression squashed any lingering hope. "If you choose Truth, your release times will be in an open common area. It's a place where prisoners can exercise or read. Most of your time will be spent working or studying."

"You have textbooks down here?"

"No. It's not that kind of study."

"I don't get it."

"In Truth, you study truth."

"What truth?"

"Your truth."

"Come on, Ángel, you're talking in circles."

"It's impossible to explain, you'll have to see it for yourself."

I puffed out a breath. "Basically, you're telling me that if I don't choose Bunkerville, I still have to stay buried in these cement-walled caves. There's no option to go above ground."

"Right, your guardians preferred you be here rather than in an above ground detention center."

"But I'm an adult, I already turned 18."

"Yeah, but you agreed to serve your sentence in a juvenile detention facility and have your record expunged upon release. If you want me to see about having you transferred to an adult facility, I can do that. But I've been in one before. I don't recommend it."

"Are you really telling me it's worse than my options down here?"

"Worse in a different way."

"So, my parents," I used the horrible air quotes again, "get to choose until my sentence is over."

He nodded.

The ache from my stomach moved to my heart. "Of course, they do." Sliding down the wall, I let my head fall into my hands. Swans and airplanes had entertained me for a minute, but beyond that, I'd believed this place was temporary. Once the fire died, I thought I'd be outside.

"Listen," Ángel's voice was kind. "You're not alone. Lots of inmates have had their judges or guardians sign them up to stay in the experiment and serve their sentence here."

"Experiment?"

"Yes. Dr. Maggie has obtained grants and support and permission to use those approved applicants in her social experiment of Bunkerville."

"But I'm not choosing that."

"I know. But another social experiment is going on for those who remain in the prison section."

"So, my real choice is either go to an adult prison or become a lab rat."

Ángel squatted beside me. "No, there is one other choice."

"Oh really, and what would that be?"

"You can stay a prisoner in this cell. Some people do. Nothing will change. You will be fed as you've been fed.

You will be taken out alone to get showered, but that's about it."

"That's not a choice. Anyone choosing that would go mad eventually."

"Strangely they manage."

"Manage?" I mocked.

"While I don't know how long they will last, for now, some spend hours in prayer. Others read or write music. I know of one person who paints on the walls."

I shot him a side glance. Was he talking about me? I tested him by asking, "Where do they get paint?"

"We give it to them."

"Seriously? I could get paint?"

His reaction let me know he knew nothing about the feet beneath my bunk. "If you want. Of course, you'd only get a little each day. Not enough to sniff or swallow."

"I barely eat the food in here, why would I eat the paint?"

He chuckled and I thought. Deep inside I knew it wasn't something I could do without going crazy, but I allowed myself a few seconds to really think about it. Would time feel as long and stretched out if I knew this was my home? No. No way. Being a lab rat allowed me to interact with other people, and I'm not and never have been a nun.

"When would Truth start if I did choose that?"

He glances at the door as if someone might be listening. His voice isn't lower but feels conspiratorial. "Courtney, I think you should stay here. Keep working on this." He points to the wall mural I thought I'd hidden.

"And go crazy? No way."

"There are worse things than serving your sentence."

"Like what?"

"I don't know. But I don't trust the effects the Truth experiments will have on anyone. I've only sat through a couple and didn't like what I saw."

"Like what?"

"Like manipulation."

"And?"

"That's it. I can't really explain it. But if I were you, I'd stay here and finish my time."

"But you're not me, are you? You're not stuck like I am. You served your sentence above ground and have no idea how crazy this windowless world can make you. How do I know you're not trying to manipulate me right now?"

"That's not true or fair."

"Then let me decide without all the if-I-were-you nonsense."

That shut him up. I hate it when people think they know what's best for me without ever being me. "I have to do something other than this. If I chose Truth, when would I get out of this cell?"

"It's up to you, just say let's go."

A bitter chuckle escaped my lips. The illusion of choice didn't hold much weight. Those in charge could pretend a little paint might stop me from going crazy in isolation, but I knew better. With a shrug I said, "Let's do it."

CHAPTER 11

Ángel remained on the floor but faced me with his legs crossed. "Okay," he said once I made eye contact with him. "Both experiments begin with the same process. Rowena will escort you to Bunkerville."

Visions of crazed lunatics and psychedelic scenery overwhelmed me. "But I don't want to go there."

"You won't stay."

"This doesn't make any sense."

"It will when you get there. Bunkerville has equipment and resources to support the prison. I wanted to prepare you."

"Fine, I'm prepared, but why can't you take me?"

"I'm not allowed to escort inmates beyond the prison. We have to respect the rights of those who've chosen Bunkerville to live in their illusions."

"Does everything about this place have to be a circus?"

"After today, you never have to go to Bunkerville again."

"Fine, let's get this freaking madness over with."

I stood and Ángel joined me. Crossing my arms, I waited for him to unlock the door.

"One more thing," he paused in the open door. His voice took on a tender tenor, "Remember no matter how traumatic it is, you've got friends in here who care about you."

My fingers grew cold and I shook them to restore the circulation. "That doesn't help." I pushed past him into the hallway.

The unpainted gray cement outside of my cell had not changed in the days since I entered The Bunker. Locked doors lined up like guards with their single small mesh windows.

At one window, a freckled-face boy watched us. I thought about the times I stared from my cell. My perspective had flipped. How many of these lonely faces had chosen Truth like me?

"Hey," I yanked on Ángel's sleeve, "Isn't that Dee Dee's cell?"

"Yeah," he looked surprised. "How'd you know?"

"We came into The Bunker at the same time. How is she?" I wanted to run to the window and look in.

"She's good," he said, nodded, "working in garbage processing."

"Working where?"

"Remember people who stay in Truth have jobs."

"Processing trash?"

"That's one area."

This isn't good. I hated the idea of being locked up in this cell all day, but I wasn't ready to sign up for trash duty either.

"Not all jobs deal with garbage. There's the kitchen, janitorial, and laundry."

All menial work. All jobs my family paid other people to do. The Manchesters didn't own a single blue collar. While I really wanted to be someone who left my snobbery on the surface, three months in The Center hadn't eradicated all my elitist attitude.

"Do people in Bunkerville do this kind of work."

"For themselves, yes, but not for the community. Inmates in Truth do the dirty work."

"So, we're not lab rats, we're slaves to the lab rats."

"Yeah, you kind of are."

"And you're good with that?"

"No, I told you these experiments are extremely divisive."

"So why stay? You're free to work above ground."

"I could." We round a corner to find another long hallway of cells. This place is so big. I kind of remember stairs and ladders when we entered. One thing was clear, if I ever tried to escape, I'd never find my way free from this maze.

Ángel continued, "I choose to stay because I don't trust this place. I got my degree in criminal justice so I could advocate for prison reform. And while I've only ever been locked up in four places, this, by far, is the most controversial."

"So, you're studying us as well."

His face changed from proud to horrified. "Courtney, don't look at it like that. I'm studying the system, not the inmates."

"Inmates, system, what's the difference?" I countered, "You're still watching to see what we'll do." Back in The Center, the Latino guard and I had begun to develop a friendship. While in here, I couldn't see him that way. And even if he was low on the totem pole, he still held the key keeping me locked in a yellow cell.

We turned a final corner where Rowena stood in front of an elevator like a mythical creature guarding Hades.

"Hello Rowena," Ángel said.

"Hello Ángel," she nodded at him then at me, "Hello, Courtney."

I didn't speak. This woman and I weren't friends and we never would be. As Ángel walked away I thought I could have been nicer to him. But why? Solid lines separate multiple classes of people in this place and I belong to the lowest.

"So, you're taking me to Reconstruction."

Rowena gave me a curt nod as she pressed the elevator button.

"Why do you get to escort me to Bunkerville and not Ángel?"

"Because I don't work in the prison."

"You chose Dr. Maggie's fake world?" I didn't see that coming. In The Center, she supported harsh punishment. One more important piece of proof I'd made the right choice.

When the elevator doors open, the Neanderthal jerked her chin toward the inside. My journey to hell was about to begin.

CHAPTER 12

Rowena pressed the button for level four. My stomach jerked as the elevator moved. Memories resurrected of my first trimester nausea, which led to thoughts of my unborn baby. How horrible does life have to be for someone to forget a fact as important as being pregnant? Of course, since I'm barely past the three-month point I'm not large enough for it to be super obvious.

The thought made me wonder how Dr. Maggie would have created a new history for me when a living part of my past grew inside of me. The psychiatrist made it sound like she would do everything she could to blot out all of my mistakes. Erase my errors. Abort my problems.

My grip tightened on the elevator rail. The thought sickened me. Was that what she would have done? If so, what other experiments were conducted in Bunkerville on the mentally deranged?

A shiver forced its way through me. I would scrub every toilet in The Bunker before I chose Reconstruction. The car vibrated and my stomach dropped. Although the lights on the display indicated we were going up, I would have bet the entire Manchester fortune we were sinking deeper into the earth.

"How long will this process take?" I asked, surprised at the desire to return to my yellow cell. Origami swans and food murals might be the best The Bunker had to offer.

"Long enough," Rowena clipped off her reply.

I would have pushed her further, but the sliding doors opened onto what looked like the alley of a small town. Old-fashioned metal garbage cans stood next to wooden entries.

The smell of fresh-baked bread filled the air.

Leaning from the car, I scanned the ceiling. White clouds floated across a blue background. The scent of wilted lettuce and orange peels mixed with the smell of dirt.

Fresh dirt, not dust pushed out of air ducts. If I hadn't been told any different, I would have sworn we were above ground.

Cautiously, I followed Rowena through the shadowed alley into the bright light of a country day. To the left, a lush green park flourished with trees and chirping birds. Gravel streets and bicycle stands replace asphalt and cars. Rowena clomped forward and I followed, reaching to touch the brick and glass and wood.

Fake. I mean, it felt real, but it was all fake.

It had to be.

Dr. Maggie's Reconstruction wanted me to pretend I was outside. But I'd been above ground. The Bunker wasn't below a town, because The Center occupied acres and acres in the Rocky Mountains. Pine and aspen roots should dangle above me, connected to trees charred to a crisp. Stalactites and stalagmites would be less creepy than the deceptive world I stood in. Programmed illusions and

Stepford inmates.

Not that I saw people. The streets of Bunkerville were as empty as a post-apocalyptic movie. If thousands of people lived down here, I couldn't see them.

Glancing at the windows, I wondered if I was being watched.

Not wanting to have any watchers see me watching, I turned my attention to the fake sun. It glowed above the tree line. Heat generated from it, perfecting the pretense. Standing in the shade was cooler. White clouds floated on a breeze of fresh-mowed grass. My hand slid against a banister until a flake of wood embedded itself into my skin. Pain. The ache brought my finger to my mouth and I chewed on it.

"Stop that," Rowena scowled like she was my mother.

"I've got a sliver." I shoved my middle finger at her before putting it back in my mouth.

"Get over it and keep moving."

"Give me a minute," I squinted at the reddened area. Between two ungroomed fingernails, I attempted to capture the dark intruder.

Rowena crossed her arms and tapped her frustration with her fingertips. "You were the one in a hurry. Not me."

"Fine." I let my arm drop. The sliver can wait until I'm safely back in my cell. A strange souvenir to take with me from a strange place. And the word fit perfectly. Strange was exactly how Bunkerville made me feel.

As a child once, I'd entered an amusement park fun house, only to hurry past stretchy mirrors. Puffs of air had shot from the floor causing my heart and legs to jump. Nanny Bella had refused to come inside. My mother's laughter had scared me more than the bug-eyed clowns and spinning tunnels. Soon as we'd escaped into the sunshine,

I'd run to Nanny Bella's rosary bead-busy hands.

An involuntary tremble shuddered through me. The more I chewed, the more the sliver worked its way deeper into my skin. I wanted to return to my cell with my folded swans and painted mural. Nanny Bella wouldn't be at the end of this ride. Nagging the fingertip, I prayed for freedom.

We stopped in front of a small barbershop. An old-fashioned blue and white and red pole spun slowly beside a hand-crafted sign.

Rowena paused at the door and said, "It's up to you what you share with this barber. He has no idea you've chosen Truth, for all he knows you're entering Reconstruction."

She opened the door without waiting for my response. A cowbell clonked and a man with a handlebar mustache said, "Welcome."

Dr. Maggie had gone too far into the past with this guy.

"She's next." Rowena presented me to the man before moving into the corner to stand at attention. Her stiff posture relaxed me. She was still my guard. Good thing. If she had left me alone, I probably would've peed my pants. I needed something in this moment to be unchanged. I was a prisoner and I was entombed, those were solid facts. The rest was fantasy.

"Hello there." The old man smiled. "So, this is your first day in Bunkerville."

I nodded.

He gave me a crooked smile. His soft tone sounded as if he was sorry for what he was about to do. "You get a fresh start, are you ready for that?"

"Sure." The word came out limp because I wasn't ready for any of this. I lifted my finger to my mouth.

I heard Rowena grunt before she said, "Can you please help her remove a sliver from her finger."

"Oh." His voice dropped to a soft bass. "Yes, of course, I have just the thing."

I threw her a look as the barber opened a cabinet and grabbed a brown bottle of hydrogen peroxide. Ángel wouldn't have made a federal case over me nagging my small injury.

"Come to the sink." I followed the barber across black and white tile to an old porcelain sink with a neck rest. The H_2O_2 foamed over the opening but didn't sting. His soft hands made me believe he must be a grandfather or uncle. With a small set of tweezers, the barber delicately removed the tiny slip of wood.

"Now we've got it." He showed it to me before dropping the sliver into the trash. "Such a small thing can cause so much pain." He patted me on the shoulder, and I didn't hate it.

He guided me to my chair and pulled out a black plastic cape which he flapped with a magician's bravado. "Now, let's return you to your infancy."

Before I could comprehend his words, the chair swiveled around. The image in the mirror startled me more than the phony town. The posh girl with designer shades and straight blonde hair who'd entered The Center months ago no longer existed. The metal plates from my cell revealed little. The beauty salon-sized glass showed me everything. Evidence of The Center's demise covered my smoke-stained uniform. My hollow cheeks were clean, but not my neck or ears or body. I swallowed. Muddy red curls commanded half of each strand where the yellow dye had grown out.

Rowena stood behind me as the barber plugged in his clippers. Her tone was threatening, "You can do this the hard way, or the easy way. No matter which, you will leave this shop with the same amount of hair you entered the world with."

"Excuse me?"

She spun me around and leaned her hands on my wrists. Her grotesque face was close enough for me to smell her stale mint toothpaste. "I can either hold you down while he buzzes it off, or you can relax and get a nice shave." A smile cracked across her face as the realization made it to my brain.

The grandfather figure who removed the thorn from my flesh was going to shave me bald.

CHAPTER 13

When I was thirteen, I saw a lady with a buzz cut. The woman wore a pleated sundress. Her pale head looked naked and scarred and sick.

My band of bullies laughed, and Helen pointed while Ashley covered her mouth. We were loud. We didn't care when the woman looked at us like we were missing out. She was a joke. And now, I was about to become a joke as well. I didn't know about karma or Nanny Bella's reaping and sowing, but I was about to become what I used to laugh at.

My confidence broke.

My sentence won.

My head fell.

The barber tucked his knuckle under my chin and raised it, but he couldn't lift my shame. Ángel told me I'd have to study my own truth. Maybe this was part of it.

In the old-fashioned barber shop, buzzing clippers ran through the side of my head exposing my ear and part of my scalp. I'd never been mugged, but sitting in this swivel chair I felt the kind of violation I thought attack victims must feel. And I was way too buried to call 911. Not that it would help.

"Is this a medicinal patch?" The barber asked as he touched the adhesive strip behind my ear.

"Yes," I said. How right was the nurse back in The Center when she didn't believe I would remember my baby enough to take prenatals. She was right, of course. It took effort to remember the baby inside of me. This patch was good until the end of my second trimester.

The barber drew the clippers over my head to clear a new row of emptiness. The vibrating hum raised goosebumps on my arms.

Back in The Center, I was the one who'd told Dr. Maggie I was interested in self-sacrifice. Very funny. But if she thought this would break me, she was wrong. I never liked my red hair, anyway. It's not a sacrifice to give up something you hate. Nothing to cry over. I wiped my cheek and focused on the pathetic image of me in the mirror. I'd earned this shave. I wanted this shave. Nanny Bella said my hair was my crown, but the queen needed to be dethroned.

I swallowed.

Another row across the center of my scalp.

Don't turn away. Don't do it.

The clippers cut a fifth stripe across my head and the air felt different against my skin.

I glared at the freak in the mirror. Stop being a baby. You don't need hair. You don't. I lifted my chin as another muddy red curl floated to the black and white tile floor.

CHAPTER 14

The barbershop smelled of oil and pine, a perfect match to my forest fire soot-covered neck. I didn't want to know how many other areas of my body had been forgotten in my cell with no shower or mirror. My peach-colored face was clean, unbleached freckles reached right to my former hairline. My straight razor-shaved scalp was deathly pale. The contrasting colors made me look like a freakin' bird or exotic flag. So much for Reconstruction's promised luxuries.

The longer I stared at myself, the funnier the entire moment became.

Dr. Maggie knew what she was doing.

I laughed and Rowena frowned which made me crack up more.

"That a girl," the old barber patted me and smiled. An actor for sure. All the nervous energy I'd felt was being swept away with the barber's broom.

I was numb.

Numb wasn't bad. It didn't matter because the best thing

about having the worst thing happen to you was only better things lay ahead. I shook the barber's hand. "Thank you, marvelous job."

His broad grin indicated no one in his Reconstruction chair ever said thanks. "You take care." He patted my arm with his grandpa-soft hand.

"I will." Turning to the mirror, I viewed myself from side to side. My scalp had uneven dents no longer hidden by hair. I nodded with false confidence before wiping my hand against the smooth surface and said, "Yes, sir, fine job."

"Okay, enough jokes." Rowena grabbed my arm. "Let's go."

"You're not going to tip him?" I stumbled after her.

"Ha ha."

Rowena dragged me through the shop. I strutted the way the bald woman in San Diego had. The woman had brushed off my laughing back then. My cutting barbs didn't have the lasting impact I'd imagined. The joke was on me. Stupid to think my adolescent opinions demoted the woman. Can you say narcissistic, Courtney? I shook my head.

We stepped through the back door.

A less elaborate set design surrounded us. The smell of dust returned. Or maybe it was no longer overpowered by the fake world air fresheners they used. No more store fronts or parks and people. We were in cement hallways. I rubbed my arms in the chilly corridor.

We entered a small bathroom. The toilet and sink were porcelain rather than metal and, in the corner, behind a black, plastic curtain was a shower.

"I get to bathe?"

"Yes." Rowena's stern face couldn't steal my rising joy.

A shower, finally. The very idea had me giddy to the point of tears. This place had me on a jerky roller coaster of feelings. Horror to elation in less than thirty minutes. It wasn't right. None of it.

I pushed my emotions deep into the recesses of my soul. I could have a breakdown once I was back in my cell. But not here, not in front of this woman. No. I'd enjoy the shower, without becoming hysterical about it.

A deep inhale invited the smell of lavender soap. A fresh, outdoors smell.

Whatever. I peeled off my dirty uniform right in front of the guard. I didn't care. I was going to be clean.

Rowena picked up my dirty khakis and extended her hand in my direction.

I covered my underwear-clad body. "What?"

"I'll take the necklace."

"Oh no you won't." I clasped the pearl at my neck. "I'll wash around it."

"That's not allowed."

"Why?" I clung to the one tangible piece of Jackson I had. "Why can't I keep it?"

"Don't worry, you'll get it back." Her hand jerked toward me like the tongue of a snake. "Hurry up. I have better things to do than argue with you."

I contemplated my choices. Fight to keep the pearl and lose my right to a private shower. Or dig deep and trust this horrible person. Regretfully, I unclasped the chain and dropped it into Rowena's man-sized palm. She took it and turned without another comment leaving me alone in the room.

I whispered to myself, "Don't let her get you down. You'll get it back. You will."

I straightened and approached the shower. Behind a crisp plastic curtain, I twisted two old-fashioned knobs controlling the hot and cold water coming from a wide showerhead. Removing my bra and underwear, I climbed into the warm flow.

Oh my gosh.

Had warm showers had always felt so amazing? Sudsing up, I promised myself and God, if he existed, to never take shampoo for granted ever again. Not that I'll be using that for a while. Bubbles engulfed my hairless head. In the patter of falling water, the last remains of the world above slipped down the drain.

CHAPTER 15

Dry, clean, and happy, I felt like a new person. Heroic and superhero-strong and ready to wear the ugly green jumpsuit Rowena brought me. Pulling it on reminded me of days above ground trying on new clothes in mall dressing rooms. The fabric is a quick-drying blend of nylon. Easy to clean. A definite indication of my full indoctrination into prison thinking. And even that thought didn't get me down.

We re-entered the cement hallway and through the back door of a dark room coated in black paint. The Bunker's interior designers had a penchant for solid colors. From the floor-to-ceiling yellow of my cell to the wall-to-wall darkness of this place.

I stood in the shadows next to Rowena, squinting at the bright lights which illuminated a massage table. The girl lying prone with her face in the oval was not getting her shoulders rubbed. A tattoo artist was inking something into the nape of her neck. She had full sleeve tattoos over both arms. The only part of her visible skin not littered in ink was her recently bald head. A fresh canvas where her hair used to be.

The scent of rubbing alcohol overpowered the stink of sweat. An assistant prepped bandages while the ink machine hummed. The tattooed girl's hands reflexed into fists. The memory of getting a bird tattoo on my hip at sixteen caused my own fingers to clench.

Rowena pointed to a group of folding chairs where a petite girl wept while she waited. The tall guard approached the assistant. "She's the last one for the day."

The assistant nodded and I sat down next to the whimpering girl. The guard grumbled about needing a break and headed toward the door.

Before anyone could stop her, the small inmate had slipped out of the room and Rowena bolted after her.

"Stupid girl," the assistant muttered as she opened a locked cabinet and retrieved a syringe.

I eased myself into the chair, not wanting to agree with the woman. But where exactly was the young inmate going to go? We're not in a real city. This is a cave and even if you could get out of the set, you'd be stuck wandering around in the dark. Nothing could motivate me to run. Maybe I was still in shock from getting my head shaved, but I was too numb to worry about a professional giving me a tattoo.

The assistant prepped the needle before walking out of the same door the girl had hoped to escape. Futility surrounded the entire situation. Three of us in this room now. The girl getting the tattoo, the artist giving it and me. No guards. No one to stop me if I walked out. My soul screamed go. But where? Into the arms of guards or needle-wielding assistants.

As hard as it was, I stayed and watched the artist finish

his work.

He spoke to the girl with sleeves as he took on the missing assistant's role. "This is the lowest number I've ever inked."

The girl remained silent as she sat up.

"So, who did you kill?"

"Your mother," Sleeves said flippantly.

Her joke woke me as much as the question.

This guy knew he was working on inmates. And the girl getting a tattoo had actually killed someone. The Center was a high-tech prison intended for reform. Up there a person's crimes were secret unless they wanted to share. The only indication of someone being dangerous was the taser bracelet. I knew it was for violent criminals because I'd gotten one for fighting, but I honestly never thought I was sitting in classrooms and sharing a dorm with killers.

A scuffling sounded before the escaped girl, now wearing leg shackles, was dragged back into the room between two guards. "I'm not a murderer. I don't need a tattoo." She appealed to me. "I didn't mean to kill my sister. I promise, it was an accident."

"Someone's dead because of you. That makes you a killer, and we only tag the killers," Rowena said.

I looked at the other guard, then at the closed door. I hadn't killed anyone. The desire to flee rushed through me again. I shouldn't be here. Like the frantic girl, I hadn't killed anyone.

"Rowena, I think there's been a mistake."

"Courtney," she stood over me. "Let me make this clear. You are scheduled for a tattoo. You can get it the easy way." She pointed to Sleeves. "Or you can get it the hard way." She pointed at the limp girl now splayed out on the massage table. "You're choice."

"That's not a choice. Quit talking about choice."

"Get the meds," Rowena turned to the assistant.

"No. No. No." The words staccato from my mouth. "I'm good."

"You sure?" Rowena lifted her eyebrows at me. "Because I'm going to be sitting right outside of that door. And it won't be painless if you change your mind."

I didn't think I could hate this woman more that I had, but as she turned her monstrous body away from me, I could taste bile rise into the back of my throat.

The artist's machine hummed as I stared at the cement floor. The Bunker had levels of unfair impossible to comprehend. I had a sentence to serve, but this was inhumane. My conviction had nothing to do with homicide. I'd bought drugs on the internet in another person's name. I'd done illegal things, but I was not a murderer. Unless...

I'd given the oxy to another person. The Center and The Bunker staff would know about that. Nicole's name was written all over the papers I'd folded into swans and planes when I'd still occupied a cell. Maybe she'd gotten addicted. She'd been alive when I left Virginia, but she might have OD'd since. This place would've considered that my fault. I squeezed my hands tighter.

The assistant cleaned up the still incapacitated inmate while the tattoo artist bent over a sink to disassemble and clean the tattoo machine. Something about his demeanor indicated he wasn't proud of his position.

His assistant was rougher. She yanked the girl upright causing her head to wobble like a ragdoll. Without asking I jumped up.

"Do I need to medicate you?"

"I came to help you," I said grabbing the girl's other arm.

"I don't need you're help."

The tattoo artist cleared his throat before speaking in a calm deep baritone. "Let her help."

"Fine," the woman rolled her eyes. "But don't try anything."

I didn't answer. I couldn't. The levels of frustration taking over my body were hard enough to contain. I focused all the energy I could on making sure the girl was walked safely to the door.

The assistant knocked and Rowena opened it. She signaled to another guard to come help carry the girl away. The snotty assistant pivoted back to her position. I followed her. I don't think of myself as a violent person. Although Jackson had scars on his face from my battle with him and Rowena in The Center. I'd been in fights in both high schools I'd attended. My natural instinct says I should go out punching.

"Can you tell me something?" I said to the artist.

"I can try."

"Why are you giving me a tattoo?"

He picked up an electronic notebook and said, "Truth has calculated the number of people who have died because of choices you've made. They put this number under the hairline so that when you leave, it can remain covered if you want it to."

"Seems really cruel and pointless."

He didn't make eye contact which made me believe he agreed. "What's your name?"

I told him. As he searched thoughts of people like Ashley, and Lorry came to mind before the wheel of memories landed on one name.

Ribbon.

She was the one.

Ribbon's suicide could justify my tattoo. Ashley told me,

back in San Diego, Ribbon had killed herself because of how much we trashed her locker and tortured her. Death by suicide. I'd led the gang of mean girls before Dad moved us to Virginia at the end of my junior year. I was guilty. Like the limp inmate, it wasn't my intention, but it was the result of my actions. Truth was already showing its hand.

"Did you say Courtney Manchester?" His fingers paused on the screen. I rolled my shoulders trying to get comfortable. Thoughts of concentration camps came to me. Numbers. Permanent labels. Of course, those camps contained innocent people. I'd earned my sentence, so the comparison was stupid. But still. Tagging prisoners was barbaric.

"You have got to be kidding." The man gasped. He leaned the pad toward me. "Are you really Courtney Manchester?"

"Yes."

"Wow." He exclaimed again. "You're actually Courtney Manchester?"

"Yes." I said more annoyed than before.

"You have the largest number I've seen."

"What does that mean?" I squinted at the guy.

"The boss believes you've killed a lot of people." He pointed at tablet.

"No, I haven't." I pull away from him as the assistant walks over to look at the screen.

Her eyes grown wide as she leans closer. "Thirty-three." She spat the word at me. "You're the worst."

"That's enough." The artist boomed.

"Thirty-three?" The number tumbles out of my mouth. "Oh, hell no. I'm not a serial killer. I might be connected to the death of one girl I bullied, but that's it."

"Everyone here says their number's wrong." The

assistant mumbled.

"But I'm telling you, I didn't kill that many people."

"The boss is never wrong." The horrible woman growled.

The tattoo artist must have sensed how close I was to blacking this woman's eye because he physically placed himself between us. "Time you take a break."

She rolled her eyes. "Always a do-gooder, aren't you?"

He pointed to the door.

"I'm not going. You aren't allowed to be alone in the room with an inmate. The only way I'll leave is if you sedate her. Better safe than sorry."

"That's not going to happen."

A glance at exit where I'd carried the lethargic girl. I couldn't be her. My fist relaxed I had an unborn child to consider. It would be one thing to drug me, they'd done that in The Center. It would be another if my obstinance contributed to long-term effects on an innocent child.

"I'll do it. I will." I straddled the chair like a bucking bronco. My heart raced at the injustice I was volunteering for, but I had a child to consider.

I leaned forward and put my face into the oval pad. I heard the door close and fought back trembles as the assistant swabbed the nape of my neck. Her action triggered a distant thought of whether or not the tattoo itself was a risk to the baby I carried.

Sitting up, I lifted my hand in surrender and said, "Is this safe?"

The man with the machine gave me a calm, questioning look.

"I mean, is it safe to get a tattoo if I'm pregnant?"

The assistant huffed, "Just lay down so we can do our jobs."

"I'm willing to get the tattoo as long as it's safe for the child," I said as my hands trembled.

"Do you think you're the first person who's tried that trick?"

"I'm not lying."

The artist lifted his electronic notebook. "There' no record of a pregnancy."

"But it's true."

"Sure, it is." The assistant moved toward me and instinctively balled my hand into a fist.

"I can prove it," I said pulling my ear back, "Look at this, it's a prenatal vitamin patch. It's good for three months."

The artist tipped his head to the side for a better look.

"Please believe me, I'm not making it up. I saw the nurse while I was in The Center and was diagnosed within the first days of being there."

"HIPPA does limit medical record information. Did you ever sign a release?"

"No."

"That could be why it's not in the records."

"You can't seriously be considering not giving her this tattoo." The assistant turned to me, "This isn't going to make a difference, you have to know that. If you don't lay down, I will inject drugs into your arm and force you to get it."

"That's not legal."

"You agreed to Truth, didn't you?"

"Yes, but not at the expense of losing my child." I attempted to run my fingers through my non-existent hair. I no longer cared if these people thought I killed thirty-three people. Saving the life growing inside of me overshadowed everything else.

The artist patted my arm like the barber had earlier in

this nightmare. "Getting a tattoo isn't as dangerous for an unborn child as the drugs she's on right now."

I glanced at the dozing girl who'd been whimpering a moment before.

"The biggest risk with tattoos and pregnancy have to do with infection. And I keep an extremely clean shop."

"Are you sure?"

"Yes, have you ever had a tattoo before?"

"I have a small bird tattoo on my hip."

"Now you'll have the Roman Numeral XXXIII, on the back of your head." The assistant chuckled.

The artist turned on her, "You need to step back."

She pulled away from his rebuff before pressing her lips together in anger.

In a protective tone he said, "This time the pain will be worse because you have very little fat on your head." He opened a cupboard, "While it isn't necessary, I'm going to open a new bottle of ink. I never reuse needles. You can be sure, I will do this 100% clean with no risk of infection. If you think you can tolerate the pain, I'll make sure you're safe."

"Sounds like I have no choice."

"You said it before. You really don't."

I gave up. Being branded was certainly not as bad as whatever drugs this crazy place would put into my system. The assistant wiped the oval face holder with an alcohol swab. And the artist told me to lie down. It was hard to settle into the chair but focused on the safety of the baby I carried. A cold swab wiped against the base of my head, bringing the sharp tang of the rubbing alcohol.

The injustice made me want to scream. Moments later, I screamed from the intense pain. As he burned the ink into my skull with a needle, I screamed like I was dying.

Involuntary tears rolled down my face. I'd gotten my blue bird tattoo at sixteen in a seedy shop in downtown San Diego. The guy had asked my age. When I'd told him I was twenty-one, he hadn't asked for ID, just cash up front. But the small open wings had gone on the fatty part of my hip and I'd hardly felt it. This time it felt like the machine drilled right into my bone.

CHAPTER 16

My fingernails dug into the chair until the humming stopped. It wasn't long. No color to add. I couldn't see the XXXIII, but it burned my flesh at the nape of my neck.

My fists tightened as the tattoo artist rubbed ointment onto my sore skin and placed a section of Saran Wrap over the top. "All done."

The assistant grabbed my hand and I yanked it away.

She snatched it and said, "Hold the bandage."

I put my hand on the cloth she'd placed over the already covered tattoo. "What's the point?"

"We like to keep it covered until you leave Bunkerville." The artist said.

I winced as the pressure burned against my inflamed skin as she taped it down.

Rowena re-entered the room right as I sat up.

"Thank you," I told the tattoo artist and meant it. While I had been sarcastic with the barber, I really did appreciate how kind this guy had chosen to be. He had a job to do and he decided to do it with empathy.

We all had roles in this place.

The tattoo artist had to clean his equipment.

The assistant had to sterilize the chair.

Rowena had to take me to the next horrible step in this crazy experiment. There would be no going backwards. The bandage at the back of my bald head wouldn't be there forever. People would see it and think I'd killed thirty-three people. A serial killer. So much for Truth.

I stared at my clean, green jumpsuit. I shouldn't have compared my tat to concentration camp prisoners. When I was free, I could grow my hair and cover my label. This number was as temporary as my confinement. Which made it more psychological than purposeful. What was the point?

"Excuse me?" Rowena asked as we exited the black room.

"Nothing," I said not caring about my thoughts slips. Futility hung heavy on me.

"The tattoo isn't there for others, it's there for you."

"For me?"

"Yes, by the time you finish Truth you will acknowledge, accept and confess to every death you contributed to. That's what Truth is all about." She pointed for me to take the next corner.

I did.

All of it was about torture or humiliation. The Center, The Bunker, Reconstruction, and this so-called Truth, they were all a bunch of ridiculous mind games.

Taking the elevator back to my cell, I wanted nothing more than to escape this place and live my life. But my life, will never be the same. I'll never escape my past, unless I give Dr. Maggie a shot at erasing it. It would be stupid to leave now that I'd been branded, but if life in Truth gets any worse, I will definitely give the false world a try.

PART V

The Present

CHAPTER 17

The Bunkerville news wakes me.

"Good morning citizens, I hope you enjoyed a good night's rest," the announcer's voice beams like the fake morning sun. Sleep didn't pull me back into hypnosis like I thought it would.

"It's Wednesday and we are blessed to receive a free morning. For the next three hours, enjoy your breakfast, a good book, or roll over and hit the snooze because we are enjoying our periodic sequester."

I sit up. Memories from my recent past flood to me. Previous sequesters were done while I was under the influence of Dr. Maggie's hypnosis. Then I believed the rest was a gift, not the unsettling feeling I have today of being universally lied to.

While the radio spits out deceit, I tip-toe barefoot to the window, an action I never felt compelled to do before. I know the front door is locked. Even if I wanted to, I can't leave my room. No one can. A town stipulation. We aren't prisoners. It's for the greater good. And it's never for more than a few hours.

What made sense before, has me wanting to confirm my thoughts. I pull the curtain back enough to peek down at the street. The barber shop is not within my line of sight, but the path to it is.

My heart races with the desire to see and not see what might be happening. It would be nice to have The Center and The Bunker be the dream and for Bunkerville to be the reality.

It doesn't take long for the confirmation to come: This is a glorified prison.

Rowena escorts an inmate through the empty streets of Bunkerville. The girl from The Bunker studies the windows for signs of life as I had months ago. Ángel said people could stay in the cell if they wanted. Obviously one of those holdouts has made a choice.

The clattering of dishes in the kitchen yanks my attention away from the window. If Rowena is down on the street playing guard, she can't be here pretending to be my roommate Glinda.

Dishes clank

Pans clatter.

Water splashes.

The last person I want to encounter is Dr. Maggie. Yet, she's the first one who jumps into my head. Of course, because this is a prison, for all I know, she's given me a new roommate. Maybe the girl with tattoo sleeves decided to step into hypnosis and I could be living with a straight-up murderer.

Not only living with but locked up with. No one can leave, which means no one can come in and save me if I scream.

Blankets make poor shields, but I race back to my bed anyway. Huddled against the headboard with the linen to my chin, I turned my neck to hear better. The sounds definitely come from inside the apartment. Not next door, but right outside my bedroom. Someone is here and they aren't afraid of me finding out. Reconstruction has already messed with every part of my psyche, the sound of kitchen activities raises every hair on my arm.

This is not a timid troll or ghost or ...

Before another crazy thought can invade my brain, I notice a small hairy animal laying flat on the floor beside my bed. It doesn't move and I'm pretty sure it must be dead, or I would have startled it when I got up. A shudder runs through me.

Stepping along the wall, I reach for the lamp on the nightstand. It won't budge. Seriously? They nailed the freaking thing to the table?

I lean against the wall. I have to think. I could try to shoo at it, see if it moves, but I'm not ready to see who's in the kitchen. Maybe I could smother it with the blanket. If it moves, I could sprint to the bathroom to avoid rabid teeth.

With shaking hands, I inch closer to the bed to get the blanket. The creature doesn't move. Bending as close as I dare, I study it and realize it isn't breathing. Not alive. Not an animal.

I drop my hands from where I placed them on my cheeks.

The hairy mass on the ground is the cheap wig. I rub my bald head, hating how stupid I feel. Yesterday's mind games have me seeing danger around every corner.

I bend over and scoop up the wig and toss it on the bed. How long ago had I promised myself never to drop my wig on the floor next to the bed? Rowena rattled me. I can't go backwards. I'm over this fear. If a killer washes dishes in the other room, I'll deal with him when he appears.

"If I am going to die," I tell my irrational brain, "then let's do it with some dignity. The anticipation and worry isn't worth it." In my polyester pajamas, I walk to the door barefoot.

I press my ear against the wood to hear better. Someone is cooking. And humming. A woman with a deep alto voice. The inviting smell of frying bacon reminds me of the days when I believed Rowena was Glinda and she was a friend.

No matter who's on the other side of this door, I probably should pretend I'm Dorothy, not Courtney. Best to be safe until I can assess the situation.

I twist the knob slowly to silence the click.

I peek through the doorway.

The humming grows louder, as does the sizzling of breakfast.

A wall separates me from a good view of the stove. I creep across the carpeted floor. A blonde woman moves into my view as she sets dishes on the dining room table.

I step out of her line of sight.

I know her. She's my new mother. She's here to help me get the surgery to remove the tumor… No it's not a tumor, it's my baby. I slip into the bathroom only to be stunned by the size of my belly. Holy crap. I'm huge. I put my hands on the sink to keep from falling.

How many months have I been down here? I turn sideways as a distant memory climbs into my consciousness.

My real mother had been tiny when she carried my sister Kat. Smaller when she carried me. Uncle John showed me a picture of her pregnant with me.

"Can you believe she was 8 months along in this

picture?" He had said it with admiration. And rightly so. My mother was gorgeous, not bloated. Her small belly could be hidden under loose clothing. Not that she was wearing loose clothing in the picture. My 8-month pregnant mother was in a swimming suit and glowing. "She was so happy." He told me. "You have to remember that."

"No, I don't."

"Yes, it's important."

"Why? It doesn't help me when she's not happy now."

"Courtney," He palmed my cheeks. "Remember one thing, you were not an accident."

"Unplanned is a synonym for accident," I threw at him. "Buy a thesaurus."

"True." His crooked grin let me know he admired my answer. "But unplanned doesn't mean unloved."

I jerked away from his tender touch. "Tell that to my dad."

"My brother loves you in his own way." I let him hug me. He was my confidant. I could tell him anything and he never made me feel stupid for asking. He didn't judge me when I told him how I wished they were dead. Both of them.

Sitting in the buried bathroom, my memories aren't perfect, but I know one thing, My surrogate mother is cooking me breakfast as if she isn't here to help Dr. Maggie remove this baby from my belly.

Standing up I look directly into the mirror and allow regret to surge through me.

I wish I would have listened to Uncle John all those years ago. I wish I would not have tried so hard to change my life. And more than anything, I wish there wasn't a woman in the other room who wants to replace the woman I most want love from. My fight isn't over. Looks like it's only just begun.

CHAPTER 18

The smile fades from my fake mother's face. "Dorothy?"

She looks as if she's having a hard time remembering me. Maybe she's feeling regret at her decision to be my mother. Sounds stupid and insecure, but when your own parents don't fully love you, you forever wonder why anyone else in the world would.

"What happened to your gorgeous hair?"

"I left it on the floor in the bedroom."

"Excuse me?" Her shocked look means she didn't know I was bald. Dr. Maggie should have told her that. It should have been an important part of orientation.

Unless...not all residents of Bunkerville get their heads shaved. I rub the inch-long curly stubble. I don't know how long it takes for hair to grow but my developing baby provides more indication of time passing than my hairless head. Obviously more than Truth items have been shaved from my memories. I'd love to have a private moment to think, but my surrogate mother stands there looking awkward.

"I thought you knew I'd lost my hair."

"Oh my gosh, I'm so sorry, from the tumor, of course," the words fumble from her mouth.

"Yeah," I lie. She and I both know pregnancy doesn't cause baldness, but this is all an act, isn't it? For a brief moment, I miss being hypnotized. I could have walked into this woman's loving arms and received possible real condolence about a fake situation. But what kind of stupid selfish thought is that?

Hypnosis means the death of my baby. And I need to focus on what I can do to stop the surgery. But that means time and trust. Two things I'm not super equipped with.

"I'm gonna go get dressed so we can start this day over."

"You don't have to, it's okay, I didn't..." she trails off.

"It's fine," I snip at her, then regret it. While she doesn't deserve my trust, she might be my only hope. Maybe Dr. Maggie had convinced her it was a tumor as much as she'd convinced me. Maybe I shouldn't be mad at her but at Dr. Maggie's mind games. This woman does know she's not my real mother.

She takes a step toward me and I involuntarily take a step back. Her face drips with maternal concern and I fight the desire to roll my eyes.

From a safe distance I say, "No worries, how about I go get dressed and we start again in five minutes." A statement not a question. I'm not looking for her permission, but I'm also not looking for a fight. I really want to run to my closet and find solace in my shoes. But that feels like a denial drug as well. No, I'll pull something from the hamper.

The woman in front of me crosses her arms and squeezes her biceps as if she needs the hug. "Yeah, sure, okay."

I offer a smile, glad for a moment of peace between us.

The reprieve is brief because as soon as I pivot, she utters a gasp of fear.

Reflex pulls my eyes back to the woman who has her hand pressed against her chest. Her eyes are wide as she points a finger in my direction.

"What? What is it?" I jump to get away from whatever scary thing she's sees.

Everything around me appears unchanged. No spiders or killers with knifes ready to attack.

She slumps into a chair and whispers, "What have I signed up for?"

I have no desire to comfort her. My frustration grows into anger. She's a stranger and her rejection shouldn't hurt but it does. Balling my hands into fists, I decide I'm not going to fight it anymore. The anger and the frustration melt into mellow at the thought of climbing into my closet. I'd like to rush out and slam the door, but I can't because I smell burning food.

My fake mother's shock keeps her planted in a dining room chair while whiffs of smoke rise from a frying pan.

I hurry to the stove.

Cubed potatoes rest in the brown residue of burnt butter. I don't remember the last time I ate fresh potatoes. She must have brought them with her. I slide the pan off the flame and stir the hash browns, hoping desperately to save them.

An unexpected memory of Nanny Bella standing in a large kitchen sneaks into my brain. I've had a surrogate mother before. Someone who was paid to take care of me, but never made me feel that way.

"I'm sorry," the woman says before blowing her nose on a napkin. "When they asked me and my husband if we wanted to foster an adult through rehab, I had no idea what I was getting into. Maybe I romanticized what being a hero would require."

Turning off the flame, I notice the flowers on the counter and fresh fruit cut into neat squares and arranged in a glass. This stranger might be paid to be here, but that doesn't have to make it bad. Feeding a person is a way of showing love. The treats on the counter are for me.

Anger and frustration melt away as I reach the table and give her what I seldom give to many people. My attention. It's the least I can do for someone who wanted to meet me, even if she regrets it now.

She stares at the linoleum floor as words tumble from her mouth. "It was my idea to come. I didn't know a lot about this place. A casual dinner conversation with some friends of ours. My husband and I don't get many opportunities to hang out with our friends."

She pauses to correct herself as if she thinks I might be questioning the quality of her marriage.

"He's an actor and often can be gone for long periods of time on the set, but we really try to have weekly date nights whenever he's shooting in Los Angeles. We were double dating. I can't remember the name of the couple we had dinner with that night. Double dates are fun, they help prevent the stilted conversations that happen after you've been married for a long time."

Of course, I really am doubting their union, so I ask, "How long have you been married?"

"17 years, yeah, college sweethearts that whole thing. I've known him my whole life. He's really truly the only man I've ever been with." She shifts in her chair, "Sorry you don't want to hear all of this."

"No, I'm curious, I'd like to know how you got to Bunkerville."

"Are you sure you don't want to go get dressed."

"We have all morning."

"True," she pauses before continuing. "As I was saying, this couple we had dinner with told us about Bunkerville. She said it was a mix between The Truman Show and Stepford. It all sounded creepy at first." She glances around her. "But after I got here, I could see the charm. Although I will tell you I do not like the news this morning. What if those potatoes would have caught fire and we're locked in this room? It's not safe. Too controlling."

She has no idea.

"But," she continues, "I am not a citizen here, so it's unfair to judge. My stay is temporary. I came to help you and I want to. I'm afraid I'm not qualified to do it."

"I don't need you to care for me. I'm an adult."

"I didn't mean it that way. The woman, Kathy, I think her name was, had a brother who came here for rehab. I told her I'd never heard of the place. Bunkerville isn't advertised. You cannot google it. People allowed in here must be vetted. And it took a couple months of background checks and interviews before we were chosen. We wanted to help someone through rehab, like you."

I fight back a chuckle. I entered The Center to gain rehabilitation, not from drugs, but from crime, but she doesn't need to know that. If Dr. Maggie didn't share with her this information, I shouldn't. Besides, I think that might send this woman through the probably unbreakable windows.

"From what I understand," she continued. "Four different kinds of people live here, not counting the doctors and scientists running the place." She taps her right index finger on her left as she counts. "The first are rehab people like yourself who are trying to change their lives. Reinvent themselves if you will." She taps a second finger. "Next there are surrogates, like myself, who step into the role of healthy family members. My husband and I have fostered children before."

"So, I'm your new foster child?" I chuckle.

"No, we're your fictional family. Successful rehab programs require successful social circles. We're acting in the role until you're strong enough to set boundaries in your life to reengage with your real family."

"Is that what Dr. Maggie told you?"

"Who is Dr. Maggie? I work with a woman named Dr. Adeline Baum."

Oh yeah. I nod my head and rub my mouth to keep my thoughts from jumping out. To this woman I'm Dorothy. Faking this is going to be harder than I thought. Unless…

I relax and tell her everything.

No that's stupid. She thinks I have a drug habit, not a drug conviction. "Who else lives here?"

It's the wrong question, I can tell because her expression turns suspicious. "Why don't you know all of this?"

A little bit of truth can't hurt. "Because Dr. Baum uses hypnosis in our program. Part of my memory is missing."

She places her hand to her heart as if she's about to have an attack.

"It's part of the surrogate process. I thought you knew. How else would I think you were my mother?"

"I thought you were acting."

"Acting?"

"Yes, another segment of this population is actors."

"Actors?"

"Yes, it's a great place to practice a new personality. According to the woman's brother, you can sometimes see Hollywood elite vacationing here. No paparazzi. From what I heard they relax on benches reading scripts and will engage in regular conversation if the situation is right."

"Oh, I get it now. You didn't come to help me, you came to see the famous people."

"No," she sits up straight. "Not only is that not true, it's unkind. I'm married to an actor and to be perfectly honest, they're not all they're cracked up to be."

"Fine, okay. I didn't know. I don't remember much of what I've done since I've been here."

With her chin still elevated she says, "Fine, I forgive you. But honestly, if we are going to continue in this arrangement, we might as well treat each other decent."

"Absolutely," I say. "I really am sorry." And she believes me because it's true. I have no beef with this woman. "So, who's the fourth population?"

"Preppers and ex-pats. People who want to believe utopia exists."

"And you don't?"

"I don't know. I think I did. When I first arrived, I was super impressed with the self-sustainability of this place. The views, although fake, are stunning. The apartments are comfortable. And all the people have been kind. Clean streets, soft sounds, sweet smells. All a human soul craves."

"What has you unsure?"

"The fact you have a tattoo on the back of your head for one thing. It doesn't look like something you choose."

I reach back and rub the smooth surface of my skull, unready to explain the brand's meaning. How to I tell this woman The Bunker not only labeled me a serial killer but proved it through Truth sessions.

Ironic how concerned I was when I woke up worried about living with a murderer, I lean back in my chair. We have at least two and a half hours left in the sequester and I don't have the energy to keep secrets from this woman anymore. I believe her when she says she came to help a person through rehab. And the least I can do is be honest with her.

"How about I go get dressed, while you rescue breakfast? We have plenty of time to talk." I want to be as comfortable as possible for the long conversation. Besides, she should eat before I give her reasons to lose her appetite.

CHAPTER 19

Alone in the bathroom, I wash my face and brush my teeth studying myself in the glass. In The Bunker, they didn't have mirrors. Not in my cell or the shower room or the work rooms. Self-reflection only happened in Truth Sessions. A shudder runs through me at the revelation of my kills.

Lifting the hand mirror, I turn my back to the vanity positioning myself until I find the bold, black XXXIII spread three inches wide and one inch high above where my hair would grow. It occupies a larger portion of my head than I imagined but remains hidden by the wig or a future head of hair.

All the desire to race to the closet and find peace leaves me. I've not been a kind person. It's not in my upbringing. Today, I'm going to be kind. Setting the mirror onto the counter, I smooth out the wig I grabbed from off my bed. I secure it to my bald head, ready to play the part of a decent human being.

Back in the bedroom, I avoid the closet. I'm still unsure, but part of me believes Dr. Maggie has put some kind of post hypnotic suggestion on me with footwear, because the pull is so strong.

Sorting through the laundry basket, I find the freshest pair of pants and least wrinkled t-shirt in the bin, remembering another aspect of Bunkerville's inequity.

This laundry won't be done by me, unless I choose to wash it by hand in the bathroom. Water is in large supply down here, but not electricity. One job in the prison area is the laundry room, and what can be hand-washed or quick dried is done manually. The job requires hard work, I should know because I used to do it.

Truth is, dirty jobs aren't done by Bunkerville citizens. Something I hadn't really thought about much. Seems like every time I move towards being a better person, I find another selfish aspect of my personality. The Center's goal to reform me has been effective. Obviously, a person can't get better if they don't know what they suck at.

Smoothing the wrinkles in my shirt over my baby bump, I return to the dining room, ready to talk about Bunkerville over burnt potatoes, crispy bacon, and cubes of fresh fruit.

My new mother begins the conversation by telling me I look very pretty and then apologizes, "Not that you aren't pretty without the wig." She shakes her head to fix what could have felt like an insult.

"No problem, it's okay."

I sit and our chat remains simple. I discover my new mother's name is Faith. Appropriate for the role. I openly share everything I know about Bunkerville until my plate is empty. Together we clear the table and wash the dishes through superficial conversation. I think we are both waiting until we're seated to get into the ugly stuff. I'm impressed she doesn't dive right into questions about the tattoo.

"I saw a few boats in the Bay." Faith puts the last clean dish into the cupboard as I wipe the table. Maybe she's as uncomfortable about going too deep as I am.

"Yeah, nothing bigger than a rowboat. All man-powered." We move to the living room sofa. "We even have fishermen."

"Yeah, I saw in orientation how they populated the lake with trout and bass. Any fish swimming in Rocky Mountain fresh water can survive in this lake."

I curl one foot under me as I sink into one corner of the couch. Faith mirrors me on the opposite side. I tell her about the fish market. About canned and dry goods. "Fresh produce, red meat and dairy are luxuries. Most people go for canned chicken and condensed milk. Parmesan is the easiest cheese to get because you can keep it on the shelf.

"But not for long."

"No, but we don't keep as much food around as my spotty memory of the outside world." Nanny Bella and her pantry come to my mind, but I don't say it. After a moment of me staring out the fake window, Faith shifts the subject back to the lake.

"So, I understand from the orientation film, the lake is made up primarily of melted snow from the mountain above us."

"Yes, there's another entrance than the one you came through. It's on the mountain top." I'm careful with my words, wanting to gradually introduce the prison area of The Bunker. "It has heated sidewalks providing runoff into natural and man-made fissures..."

"Oh, yeah, they didn't tell us about the other entrance and the forced melting of snow, but they did show us the flow of water channeled into waterfalls feeding this lake. The dam on the far end of town supplies the hydro-electricity."

"See, you know more than I do." I press my lips together. The mass scale of the work put into Bunkerville has me suddenly feeling uncomfortable. Powerless. Dr. Maggie couldn't be doing this all by herself, but the fact she has all the political and physical power to lock up free people for three hours to keep her secret going has me terrified. She's a bigger threat than I've really ever allowed myself to believe.

"Faith," I look at her and hope she understands as I say, "I have to admit, I don't like everything about this place."

"I think we're going to be okay, Dorothy." she says as she places a hand casually on my shoulder.

I wonder for a moment if her real name is Faith. That could be as fake as Dorothy and Glinda. I think to ask her, but the baby moves, and my new mom yanks her hand away from me.

"What was that?"

Looking at my stomach. The pressure of my child distorts my belly out of a normal shape. The movement used to freak me out when I thought it was a tumor.

"That's the baby," I say pulling my foot out from under my butt and placing it on the floor.

"What baby?"

"The baby I'm carrying."

Her mouth gapes.

"You didn't know I'm pregnant?"

She shakes her head, "No, I was told, you have a malignant tumor."

"Yeah, that's the story Dr. Baum told me as well." I say, confused. "But I honestly thought she would have given you the truth."

"She did not." My new mother uncurls her legs and gets up from the flowered sofa.

"What's the problem?" Here comes the rejection. I should have known. I should have kept my mouth shut. "You were willing to help a drug addict, but not an unwed pregnancy?"

"You know you're pregnant?" She stands in the kitchen using the tone of a judge.

"Yes."

"And you want to have it removed."

"Removed? What?" My brain cells light up. "Oh, I would never agree to an abortion. What I'm trying to say is I don't know what the truth is. Dr. Baum has mentioned a C-section."

Faith shakes her head, "You're not full term, people don't get C-sections early unless there's a risk."

"I don't know how far along I am."

She lifts her hands in surrender. "I can't do this. I don't believe in abortion."

"But that's not what's happening. Dr. Baum told me. I signed the papers."

"What papers?"

I'm too embarrassed to tell her I was too focused on my new shoes to read what the counselor had put in front of me. "I'm pretty sure they were adoption papers."

"No, no." She paces the floor the way I did in the yellow cell. "I was told you were having a tumor removed in seven days. This doesn't feel right. Why would your doctor lie to me?" She walks to the door and tries the handle, but it's still locked. "I can't do this."

My eyes follow her movement as my train of thoughts catch up with hers. "Do you think the doctors here would really kill my baby?"

"I don't know. But I'm not about to stay and find out. I'm sorry."

"But you can't leave me, not if this is true." Rising panic cracks my voice. The idea of fear floods me more than the memory of why I should be afraid.

"We have to ask her." Faith resumes her pacing. "We have to know. As soon as this door opens, we are going to talk to her. I need to look her in the eye and find out."

Thoughts of Rowena materialize. Her desire to inform me of the truth. "I don't think she wants you to know."

"Why not?"

"Because someone else tried to tell me and the next thing I knew she pulled me back into hypnosis."

Faith returns to the couch. "You told me earlier Dr. Baum doesn't know you're no longer under her spell."

"Right, I'm not ready to be completely lost."

"Then we can't tell her, can we? If she stopped someone who works for her, she won't tell me."

"I know. There's only one thing we can do."

"Which is?"

"I need you to help me escape."

"Escape, you make it sound like you are a criminal. Escape from what? When these doors open, we'll exit the door we entered through."

"Well…" I pause and stare at my bare feet. I have to come clean. I have to tell her of my conviction. She has to know this is more than just walking out of a voluntary program. If she helps me and my baby, she will be helping a juvenile offender escape from a detention center.

Based on the time left on the clock, I've got a couple hours to tell her what I know, as well as remember what I don't. Including the fact that I am a criminal.

"Do you want to know everything?" I ask her, giving her one last chance to leave without knowing.

"Yes." She doesn't hesitate. "I realize my reaction hasn't been respectful this morning. I'm not a person who does surprises well. If Dr. Baum—if that's even her real name—had told me the whole truth, we both could have had a better morning."

"The name she uses outside of Bunkerville is Dr. Maggie."

She relaxes. I can see how important knowing the facts is for this woman as a light goes on in her eyes. She nods her head saying, "That's what you called her before."

"And funny you should mention Truth. That's what they call the other part of this place."

Her puzzled expression is justified.

"You might as well get comfortable, because what I'm going to tell you will definitely make you uncomfortable."

Faith grabs a throw pillow and hugs it to her chest. She squeezes it tighter when I tell her the other entrance to The Bunker is connected to a prison. I have to stop looking at her or I won't be able to get the words out.

In the corner, the lamp has a curved edge. It's probably bolted to the floor. The random thought of Dr. Maggie's ultimate distrust for the Bunkerville citizens helps my words flow. I start with my first trip to Bunkerville, explaining why we are sequestered. By the time I get to the tattoo, I no longer have a reason to not reveal what it means. "The XXXIII represents the thirty-three people who died because of me.

"Whoa, wait a minute."

I love the doubt in her voice.

"That's not possible, what are you 18 or 19 years old?"

"I turned 18 this year."

"It takes years for a killer to kill that many people."

"Do you still want to know the entire story?" I make eye contact with her. It is her choice to know or not. She has enough information to leave Bunkerville.

To my surprise, she nods her head, so I tell her about the return to my yellow cell after receiving the tattoo. "When I first got it, I didn't believe the number was right either."

PART VI

The Past

CHAPTER 20

When Rowena and I left Bunkerville, she dropped me off in my yellow cell where I ate dinner before lights out. All night I curled in a fetal position. Anytime I tried to lay flat, the bandage at the back of my head pressed against the freshly inked and searing skin.

XXXIII.

Crazy.

Ángel told me this place was all about Truth. But I refused to believe I'd killed that many people. One maybe when I was in high school and bullied that girl. But I honestly don't know about any others. I kept searching through my brain for more intentional or unintentional harm I could have done to kill someone, but nothing could ever reach the magnitude of thirty-three.

Somehow I slept, because before I knew it, the lights clicked on down the hall until the wave swept through my room. When breakfast came, I decided to ignore thoughts of the tattoo. Trying to find some sense of normalcy, I made paint from the raspberry jam and ketchup packages. The condiments didn't highlight the red hair on my female villain as much as I would have liked, given the limitations of my canvas, but it felt freeing to paint. A distraction I hoped Truth wouldn't take away from me. When the guard arrived to get me, she didn't say anything about the wall.

I silently put my paint containers in the sink and followed her into the hall. Every door in the section was open and girls stood at attention in a straight line down the middle. No one turned to look at me, their statue-like frames stared forward. I spotted the back of a young black girl's head. She was three inmates ahead of where I joined the procession. That must be Dee Dee. The single letter "I" contrasted boldly against her hair-less head. Roman numeral one, that must be nice. Of course, Dee Dee had always been kinder than me.

Rubber heels slapped in rhythm on the cement. I joined the procession. Standing straighter, I swung my arms in matched step. The action wasn't intentional. It happened naturally after about ten steps. Hypnotically, the desire to stop was not as strong as avoiding getting trampled. After about fifty paces, we rounded the corner and arrived at the group showers.

The guard turned to me. "Try not to get the bandage wet, we don't want the Saniderm to peel too early."

I remember from my first tattoo how the plastic wrap stuck to my skin for a few days before coming off. One other girl had a bandage against hers. The rest of the tattoos were exposed. As I undressed with the others, I never saw a number higher than ten.

The splash of water and the squeak of faucets mixed with the mint of soap and toothpaste. The water turned off at the same time for all of us. As much as the group movement frightened me, I was glad I'd hurried with them or I'd still have suds on my hairy legs.

On a shelf, neatly folded towels waited as each girl retrieved one in smooth order. I glanced at Dee Dee who raised her eyebrows at the sight of me. I gave her the first sincere smile I've had in this place. She sent back a silent wink as she retrieved her green jumpsuit from a hook. She was dressed and gone before me. A guard pointed to the hook with my new outfit on it as the rest of them left me alone. The female guard remained silent as I flattened the Velcro on my green jumpsuit as well as the boring shoes.

She pivoted on her heels and I followed her to an office where Ángel sat at a desk waiting for me. With her duties done, the female guard left as quietly as she'd entered.

"How'd you sleep?" he asked.

"Horribly," I said because it was true.

"Sorry about that, do you want me to look at your tattoo?"

"No." I pulled away from him. He has no right to know the number. "You should have told me about what was going to happen to me in Bunkerville."

"I didn't know all the specifics. I never know until after you leave when they give me your file. And if you think I'm afraid of your number, I'm not. Truth Sessions reveal unintentional deaths as well as premeditation."

I thought of Ribbon. While I didn't intend to kill her, I did intentionally bully and harass her. I'm guilty of that. Nothing more. Whether he knows I have a thirty-three inked on the back of my head or not, I'm not ready to talk to him about it.

"I only wanted to see if it was healing okay. I care more about your health than a stupid number. If you feel it's good, then I'm good."

"There's nothing good about any of this. It doesn't hurt if that's what you're asking."

"Why are you mad at me?"

"Because you might not know my number, but you knew it was coming. You knew they'd shave my head. You knew they would give me a tattoo. You knew that."

"I did."

"And?"

"I'm sorry."

"Not good enough."

He knew it wasn't. He wouldn't have liked to be surprised like that. "Now I don't know what to believe."

He didn't respond. Probably couldn't.

He shuffled the papers on his desk. And I felt horrible as I remember he was a convict not so long ago. Six weeks tops. Nervousness edged his voice, as he read from a document. "Because of Courtney's unique transfer, the boss believes communications with this inmate would be best coming from someone she knows and trusts."

"Someone I trust?" I huffed. Not sure why I needed to stay mad at him. But I did. Former inmate or not. He was part of the *them* now, not the *us*. He wasn't going to get on my good list any time soon. "Someone like you?"

"Someone like me." His voice was low.

I wasn't as mad as I could have been. Not mad enough to rage, but trust is a very difficult gift for me to give, and he has crossed a line, by allowing me to ever enter that place unprepared.

"You have two job choices," he continued. One is in the laundry room, where you would wash, iron, and deliver clean clothes to the distribution center. The other is with Dee Dee in the inferno where you would sort recycling from trash to be burnt. I can tell you, one girl wants to switch jobs and she'd prefer laundry over trash. But the choice is up to you."

"Does everyone get a choice?"

"Yes, to begin with. The boss selected these two options for you."

I had to wonder more and more who the boss was. I couldn't imagine my case was unique enough to make the big boss care. Unless. My uncle was a Senator. The place did have some government funding. But I couldn't think of that. He wouldn't have wanted me to stay here if I was in danger. Sure, my parents signed me up to be in here, but I refuse to allow myself to believe the one member of my family who ever showed me love has anything to do with the decisions to make me an experimental monkey.

"Lucky me," was all I could think to say.

Ángel didn't answer. Standing, he wiped his palms on his pant legs and said, "So which is it? Laundry or Trash."

"Laundry, of course."

"Okay." Leaning over the desk, he wrote a note and returned the file to the drawer before turning and asking me, "Are you ready for your first Confession Session?"

"Do I have a choice?" I asked sarcastically.

"No."

"Are you going to tell me about what's going to happen next?"

"I can't. I've never been in a session before."

"Convenient." I said, worried about what I was about to see. I knew I'd injured Ribbon. Knew I'd bullied or beat up others, but there was no way in hell I'd killed thirty-three people, intentionally or not.

CHAPTER 21

When we reach the room, I squint at the blizzard of white covering every surface. It had been so long since I'd seen white walls, my anxiety didn't diminish. Everything in The Bunker was so dirty, this room screamed false.

"You know, Ángel, an honest room would have stalactites or stalagmites. Bats should be sleeping from the ceiling."

"Maybe the color represents purity."

"I don't buy it." The scent of baby powder tickled my nose. My fingers stretched across my belly hoping Truth didn't require pain. I could recall ancient articles about torture. So do Jackson's long-ago warnings about being sent to The Bunker while The Center still existed.

Something not great was about to happen to me. A couple white folding chairs in the corner blended into the brightness. And in the middle of the room a leather barber chair waited for me. The people who run this place must have stock in paint and leather. The worn brown cowhide in the barber shop and the black, leather massage chair for the tattoo.

"Why does it look like I'm going to be strapped to that thing?"

"Maybe it's the positioning."

"You think?"

His attitude had shifted from shrinking at my harshness to ignoring it the way an older sibling would. That helped me respect him a bit more. As much as he could have helped me back there, he wasn't to blame for my situation. If I was a bigger person, I would have said it, but I held my tongue as he walked to a white chair camouflaged in the corner. He picked up what looked like a remote control and read from a document. "According to this, you can start anytime."

"Can I sit over there?"

"No, you need to be in the chair for the video to work."

"But I don't want to be strapped down." Memories of The Center when they attached the taser bracelet to me rushed forward.

He flipped through the pages. "It doesn't require you to be strapped down. This says the video will play as long as you are seated in the chair facing that wall." He pointed to the open white concrete in front of the chair. "If you get up or close your eyes, the images will stop until you return your attention to them."

Ángel crossed his arms as I thoroughly inspected the beast. I would kick and bite and claw my way out of this room if I found a single strap, needle, or control device.

Nothing on the sides.

Nothing underneath.

Nothing at the head.

No cabinets or shelves lined the wall where torture tools could be stored.

No hooks or chains on the floor.

Above me, high in the ceiling a large projector pointed its cyclopic lens at the wall directly across from the chair.

"You good?" Ángel asked.

"I guess." My checking felt pointless. I couldn't have stopped them from doing whatever they wanted. As much as Ángel or Dr. Maggie used the word "choices", all free-will decisions ended when I got sentenced. Those mistakes were made by a different Courtney in a different life. One in which I'd apparently be playing the witness.

Ángel extended his hand toward the chair without coming closer. He aimed the remote control at the recorder. Nothing happened. I leaned one hip on the chair with my opposite foot firmly on the floor. The projector whirred to life. The lights dimmed and the white walls grayed as Ángel sat in the corner, his finger moving over the device in his hands.

"Are you taking notes?"

"No, the device only has two buttons." He showed me. A large green one which he'd pressed down. "It says to press the red one right before we exit the room. Other kinds of motion devices must run the videos."

"Of my family? Of my childhood?" I wiggled against the chair until I found the least uncomfortable position while keeping one foot on the floor.

He flipped some more pages before staring at the wall where the projectors beam got brighter as the rest of the lights went black. "Says here," his voice was apologetic again, "the videos will be of your crimes."

He looked at the floor as flickering images appeared before me. Images of Ashley and Helen from the high school in San Diego. I'd never seen this film before. I had no idea who would have taken it. But the constant bullying from the clique I controlled in San Diego played in sequence. Of all our victims, Ribbon suffered most.

The one death I knew I'd have to face.

The awkward girl had worn outdated clothes and untamed hair. All my disgust for the misfit flared up within me while I fought to suppress it.

The girl was dead. Dead because of me. I should have felt remorse. My brain drifted to the countless days in high school when she'd annoyed me. Clompy shoes. Dirt in her fingernails. Not a stitch of makeup on her face. And what fueled my hate most was the stupid, open smile on her face.

Truth.

Ángel had said I'd have to face it.

Truth was, I was a bitch. I'd gotten a gang of girls to torment and torture Ribbon simply because I couldn't stand her independence. Throughout junior high she'd held the kind of happiness that ignored the crowd. Strange outfits and a bright smile. She'd celebrated every event with an awkward dance. Her whole persona had felt like a cold slap to my dysfunctional home.

Rubbing my belly, I wondered how much I'd actually changed. The privilege of being a Manchester flowed so thoroughly through my veins, I wondered if I ever really be released of my sense of entitlement. Wasn't I thinking about free will moments ago? Wanting positive outcomes although I deserved to be here. I did commit this crime. Turning my face from the screen. The white wall turned gray in the dark light.

Sensors must have recognized my movement because a computerized voice boomed from a speaker and bounced against my chest. "Are you ready to confess?"

Truth had its own technology. The intimidating voice sounded like a Darth Vader version of Microsoft Sam. It didn't impress me. I had no problem confessing. This crime happened years ago. I was guilty. Even now, I still lacked the proper feelings of remorse associated with the death of Ribbon. I didn't know her well enough to trigger tears.

"Are you ready to confess?" the voice asked.

I looked at Ángel. He shrugged as he scanned the papers they'd given him.

"Are you ready to confess?" the voice asked again.

"Sure. I killed her."

"How?"

I didn't know how to answer so I responded with, "Humiliation?"

"How?" The voice grew louder.

Not wanting to drag this out any longer than it needed to be, I rambled. "I bullied her, okay? Tormented and teased and crushed her. Her suicide was my fault. I was the leader. I did it." The words stung. "I admit I haven't given Ribbon much thought beyond the inconvenience her death had on me. My Father had to give up his school board position and we moved to Virginia." I paused. The screen focused on Ribbon's smile. In a more respectful tone I said, "Back then I blamed everyone but me. My crime was destroying the only girl who had the one thing I couldn't buy. Joy."

"One death confessed out of thirty-three." The Bunker deity announced.

I shivered. This wasn't fun, but it failed to meet the terrifying standard Dr. Maggie had hinted at. As the lights came on, I did wonder what they might show next. While there was no way I'd killed anyone else, they'd gotten this one right.

CHAPTER 22

With the white room bright again, I turned to Ángel. "Is that it?"

He nodded. "I guess. The only orders I had were to bring you here. The boss did mention he wanted you to process this crime in Isolation before you see the rest."

"The rest," I scoffed. As much as I wanted to be less bitchy, I really was over this idea of thirty-three kills. "I'm not a great person Ángel, I get that. But you can't really believe I killed thirty-three people. I was definitely a high-school bully, but I'm not a serial killer."

"I believe you."

"Then show me the rest, I want to get this over with." I missed my mural and the friends I was painting there. I missed my swans and paper airplanes. I missed being nothing more than a prisoner.

"I can't," he said with too much pity in his voice. Typical anger flared up within me instinctively, tightening my fists. I had to resurrect images of Ribbon knitting purses out of plastic grocery bags in order for me to recognize how much the desire to hurt someone still reigned in my veins. While I could unclench my fists, I couldn't prevent my feet from stomping as I stormed from the room. If I could return to my cell, I could have time to cool down. To process the memories without witnesses.

"Go ahead and press the red button," I commanded as if I had an ounce of power in this place.

Ángel complied and I followed him through the halls, to another guard. "Take care, Courtney." His face was sincere. Too sincere for me to look at him.

"Yeah," I snarked. "You too."

I didn't watch him leave. Didn't trust myself to want more from his friendship than I knew how to ask for. Wanting usually leads to being let down. Quietly, the new guard escorted me to another all-white room. It contained the same toilet and sink as my yellow cell. The cot looked the same. The only addition was a notebook and pen sitting on a white table in the corner. A matching white chair was tucked in ready for me to pull it out and get to work. But on what? The space gave off major insane asylum vibes. Part of me was surprised when the guard closed the door without wrapping me in a straitjacket.

"Maybe later," I chuckled to myself, "Plenty of time for crazy in this place."

I approached the chair and picked up the pen. Twirling it I read "Amends Journal" across the white cover. I didn't know exactly what it would take to escape this awful room, but I could guess.

Document ways to make amends for my crime.

Write how I could repay the universe for destroying someone as innocent as Ribbon Barber.

What I didn't know was how many amends it would

take. A life can't simply be replaced.

The thought sent a pang of guilt through me.

When I set out to persecute Ribbon, I never considered how permanent the damage was. She was inconsequential to me until now.

The chair scraped against the white cement floor. Sitting, I wrote without thinking about it. Black ink bled onto the page as the amends journal accepted my confessions. Ribbon was dead. As much as I hadn't liked her, as a human being she'd deserved better than she got.

I paused, suddenly realizing how selfish this moment was. I hadn't written anything about the girl or her death, but wrote to appease myself. This was not about me. This was about Ribbon. And no matter what I wrote in the stupid notebook, I couldn't bring her back to life. No restitution in the world could return a child to her mother.

My own son kicked, and I wondered if giving my unborn child to Ribbon's parents would help or hurt. That would be ironic, wouldn't it? I imagined myself deciding to step so far away from my dysfunction as to give my boy to parents who ate granola and powered their house with poop. I'd found that out from my father, that part of school gossip was true. They'd had some kind of methane generator. Would it be fair to sacrifice my son to a life of bullies like me? No.

"No," my voice echoed against the lonely walls, "There are other ways."

I drew a line under the last selfish sentence I'd written. Then I created a list of amends.

"Donate to charity."

"Speak at schools."

"Work at the Barber family's co-op."

All of it seemed hollow and empty.

It was impossible to make amends for the death of a child. You can never pay back such a debt. The Barbers required something truly sacrificial. And nothing felt right except the idea of giving my child to Ribbon's family. But I could never write that. I could never do that. I wanted my boy to have a better life, not just the opposite end of the spectrum.

I turned to a blank page and tried to sketch what I could remember of her face. With thin blue lines, I contoured cheeks and a nose fully aware I'd failed at step two of Truth. Tomorrow and probably the next day and the next week would be painfully long. I couldn't be sure if Ángel's boss wanted me to sign away my baby, but I wasn't going to do it. The child growing inside of me was my only true hope of redemption. The only chance I had to learn to love someone other than myself.

CHAPTER 23

For hours I wrote and drew until someone brought lunch. Standing, I offered the guard the notebook, but he ignored me and left without speaking.

Did they know? Were they somehow reading what I wrote while I wrote it? I wanted to be a better person. The kind of person who could give away the only chance I had of love. At least the only chance I felt certain of.

Sitting, I wrote a list of those whom I knew for sure loved me.

Nanny Bella.

If I was honest I could count my sister Kat. While I hadn't shown her any real love, she was still young enough to want a big sister.

Uncle John. Although, I hated how he didn't pull me out of The Center when I asked. But I couldn't be mad at him about that. He wasn't my father or mother. And he had a point back then when it came to how much better The Center had been compared to an actual detention center. I wondered what he knew now. Did he realize the lengths Dr. Maggie had gone to beneath the earth? Had his tour of the above ground facilities extend to life down here?

I couldn't think of that.

Those thoughts would crush me.

Tapping the pen against my lips, only one other being besides the baby came to mind.

Jackson.

But I couldn't be sure his professions of love were real. They could have been done in haste. Too many men had said they loved me and as soon as I had sex with them, the love got swallowed by their desire. And when their desire faded away, so did they.

But Jackson was different. We'd never had sex, but I think he loved me anyway. Of course, now I'll never be sure that if we had that he wouldn't have left.

I scribbled out his name.

This is stupid.

I'm supposed to be thinking of Ribbon. Of her pain and the pain of her parents. I need to figure out what the boss wanted from me.

I wrote Ribbon's name.

I wrote every word and act of cruelty I'd inflicted on her. I wrote what I encouraged others to do to her. And as much as I wanted to keep my thoughts on Ribbon and what I'd done to her, my mind wandered back to my own comfort in less than a minute. My mural. My routine.

I had to get out of here. This wasn't working. If I knew what they wanted, I'd do it. But honestly, I'd be doing it for myself because I suck. Dropping the pen, I plopped on the bed. Staring at the ceiling I begged sleep to come.

CHAPTER 24

I woke to find the lunch tray had been replaced with dinner. The long drag of time had begun. Putting my feet on the floor, I pushed myself off the cot and staggered to the door. Muted silence joined me. No human howls or squeaky wheels of food carts. I laid on the floor next to the door. No footsteps.

They wouldn't keep me here.

They couldn't.

Ángel told me I'd get a job.

He inferred I'd be living in the yellow cell.

How quickly I'd gone from hating the place to wanting it. The sense of isolation overwhelmed me. I desperately wanted to cry, but my eyes stayed dry.

The pain in my heart wasn't for Ribbon. It was for me. This white room wasn't working. Instead of making me feel more for others, it forced me to focus on myself. My needs. Instead of building empathy, thoughts of my comfort possessed me.

Ribbon's death was so long ago.

Her connection to me wasn't specific enough.

They should have made me write for a few hours and then showed me more deaths. They weren't teaching me what they wanted me to learn.

"This isn't working," I screamed. "I don't know how to think about others," I shouted to the walls. But no one came to help me.

No one came to teach me.

When the lights went out no one howled or wept. The eerie silence could mean the walls and door were soundproof. By the next morning, I waited for what seemed like hours before a guard brought me a tray.

"Please," I pleaded, "I'm ready to go, I've written all my regrets and the things I would do to make it up to the world for what I'd done."

"You can't leave yet," the guard said placing the tray on my table.

"Then when? When can I leave?" I ran to the desk and grabbed the journal. "Look, it's practically full. Is that what you want? More words? A full book? Tears? What?"

"Isolation ends under one of three conditions." His voice wasn't robotic, but it was monotone. "One day of Isolation for each kill."

"But I came here yesterday."

"A day is equal to 24 hours and you still have two more left before you're done."

My heart hurt, what could I possibly do to pass the next two hours? "You said three things, what are the other two?"

"A request to be transferred to Bunkerville."

Of course, Dr. Maggie would try to get me one way or another. But she wouldn't win. "No, I don't want that.

What's the third?"

"Death."

My mouth dropped. "Are you freakin' kidding me?"

He answered by closing the door on me without a response. He was joking, he had to be joking.

A shudder pained its way through my heart.

Had people died in here?

At the sink, I splashed water on my face.

Stay focused on the positive.

I leaned against the door, willing a noise to squeak through the metal. The mausoleum was quiet. Images from the psych class documentary about prisoners in solitary confinement forced their way into my memory. One inmate bit into his wrist and used the blood to paint the walls.

Don't go there.

No. This is temporary. Two hours isn't forever. I tapped on the wall hoping to hear someone return a tap to me. Nothing. I rubbed my belly. The inside of my mouth felt dry. Licking my chapped lips, I walked to the sink. The small plastic toothbrush with a travel-sized toothpaste lay next to a hand towel and bar of soap. After I loaded the brush, I scrubbed every tooth.

The movement of muscles exercised my brain as I tried to push away thoughts of bloody inmates. The images darted in and out of my brain on fast forward.

I rinsed and spit moving from the sink to pace.

My legs fought to keep up.

"Two hours. Two hours. Two hours," I chanted when the walking didn't chase the thoughts away.

This was temporary.

"Temporary. Temporary. Temporary."

As I paced back and forth, back and forth, I understood tigers better. Once while at the San Diego zoo, I'd watched a big cat do the same. I hadn't understood it at the time. I wished I still didn't.

Remembering my first days in The Bunker, I realized two hours can feel like two days with nothing to do. The idea of scratching my own eyes out joined all the other crazy thoughts, including giving in to Dr. Maggie.

"You have to be careful, *mija*," Nanny Bella's words entered my thoughts. "If you let your brain catch hold of an idea, it's really hard to let it go. You see that man? He's thinking of his family." She loved to watch survivor shows. Not just the social ones, but those where people are left alone for long periods of time. "If he doesn't stop soon, he will be going home without the money."

"Thank you," I said to the memory of my caretaker. I pushed away all thoughts of living in Bunkerville. And fought to remember what the wilderness survivors did. Laying back on the cot, I sang the words to every song I could recall. I was finishing the last line of "Jingle Bells" when the guard opened my door.

CHAPTER 25

I wasn't taken back to my cell, but to the shower room. As I bathed alone, the evidence of others having been there elevated my mood.

Dressing quickly, I smiled at the guard, happy to see another face. Any other face. She ushered me to a stairwell where we descended two flights. Cement walls surrounded us like those in tall buildings blocking the view of flights above or below. Possibly a couple dozen stories stood between me and the exit, and if I could, I'd take them all.

One day.

I nodded.

One day.

The guard entered the gray corridor. The doors in this hallway weren't as close together as the cells. I was going to work, so maybe they led to other work areas or classrooms. Ángel said something about study or learning, I think.

The guard stopped at the fifth door and opened it.

Smells and sounds escaped with a blast. I learned the

word cacophony in school, but I never really experienced it until that moment. The explosion of voices crashed against my chest like a wave of air on a fast ride. The moist smell of detergent blended with dryer lint. An amusement park ride smile stretched across my face. I was going to work, and I'd never been more excited in my life. As much as I had missed my cell, isolation made my soul crave human contact. Out of character, I smiled at another inmate who only gave me a mean-girl glare.

Whatever, I'll take it. Her adolescent attitude couldn't bring me down. I wasn't above ground, but I was no longer alone. Maybe about twenty girls occupied the room. The noise got louder when the door closed, as if the sound was as trapped in this space as we were.

At the front, inmates worked at wide basin sinks. They chatted with each other as they scrubbed clothing in sudsy water wearing long sleeve gloves.

To my right, a long row of clothing hung on movable racks. On the left were long white tables where inmates folded towels, jumpsuits, and linen.

I'd never done laundry before The Center, that was Nanny Bella's responsibility. One thing was for sure, if I never learned anything else in this place, I'd grown to love that woman more and more.

"The attendant in charge will give you instructions," the guard said as a very, short lady with round glasses and a blonde bob approached.

She eyed me up and down before pivoting on her heels, saying, "Come with me."

I followed her to the back where two industrial sized washers loomed next to four large dryers. Sheets tumbled in them. As we moved toward the machines, noisy conversations grew quiet. Inmates slowly turned toward me and my petite escort. No one spoke at first. They just stared. It wasn't until someone shouted, "No f-ing way! She's tagged with the number thirty-three."

The woman beside me took a step back to look.

"Wow," she said as if she were impressed.

Stupid thing to be impressed about.

Some girls took a step toward me as if I were the only caged animal in the place. My joy at being with other people was beginning to fade.

A girl with dark hair and pale skin shouted, "Her tattoo, dudes, she's killed thirty-three people."

She'd said dudes, even though the room was full of females. All of whom were trying to get a glimpse at the back of my head.

"Ladies," the attendant said sternly, "Get back to work."

The inmates complied, but the noise welcoming me into the room had settled into the biting sound of whispers. I had no opportunity to see the tattoo on anyone else as they'd resumed their tasks because no one turned their back to me.

Whatever. I don't care what these people think. Who were they to judge me? An inmate was an inmate. Not so long ago we were all above ground learning to hold hands and sing kumbaya. Now, everyone had the hardened look I'd seen on TV criminals. All of them are inmates. All of them are guilty of some crime. Lifting my chin, I follow the guard to the back wall where she pulled a clipboard off a hook on the wall. "Best to start at the rollers." She wrote on the board and hung it back up. "You can join the other new girl. She can show you how it works."

She pointed to where the sinks were. We paraded past the others again. Some still pointed, others refused to make eye contact.

The clothes on the racks shifted. Above me, a pully

system took the wet clothes on a ride across the room. I looked behind me to see what happened to the clothes at the end of the line, but the rack turned at such an angle, I couldn't see.

The clothes on the racks jerked forward as if a person rather than a machine moved them. From my perspective, all the shirts, pants and towels were made from the same quick drying microfiber. These clothes wouldn't need much more than a dehumidifier to dry them out.

After passing the racks of drying clothes, we headed to a section I didn't notice when I entered. Ten aluminum basins lined up before me. They contained the old-fashioned rollers used to ring water from clothes.

At the washing basins, a girl whose freckled face didn't match her bald head looked down her nose at me. Her back was to the white plastic utility sink to keep me from seeing her tattoo. Keeping eye contact, she scrubbed suds over wet clothes with her hand. In the sink, I could see an old washing board as well as what looked like a broom handle. Without taking her eyes from mine, she dunked the wet garment into the water and dropped it into a large bucket next to her, causing the clean water to splash against my feet.

"Oops," she sneered. "Sorry about that."

"Get back to work," the attendant pointed at the girl as if she knew she'd done it on purpose. "And if you keep it up, you'll spend an extra day in Isolation."

The inmate returned to hand-washing a pair of black pants while smiling the fakest smile I'd ever seen at the woman in charge.

I sloshed away from them, trying not to think about how uncomfortable my feet were now. The entire interaction brought two thoughts to mind. One was how unnecessary the whole thing was, the other was about how much the girl reminded me of the images I'd seen in the white room yesterday of myself and my friends in high school. Maybe people exist in this world who don't learn from their mistakes.

We approached one of three girls who had similar buckets beside them. The girl closest to me swirled a green jumpsuit around in the water. She then lifted the garment and wrung as much excess water into the bucket with her hands as she could before folding it in half. She fit the garment legs-first into the rollers and turned the crank. Another girl was ready to receive it. She shook the jumpsuit a couple times passed it through a second set of rollers. The third girl in the row would then take the outfit and put it on a hanger before pulling the cord to move the jumpsuit in the same way I'd seen all the other clothes go. From this angle I could see five to seven empty moving clothes racks ready to receive more laundry.

Hundreds of hangers waited for clothes to dry. Some garments surprised me. Dresses and shirts, shorts and tops in bright colors hung next to dozens of green jumpsuits. The assembly line moved quickly considering how my appearance had interrupted the work. The miniature attendant and I approached a different girl who was tucked away in the back corner by a faucet.

Water flowed into large, wheeled buckets. The girl next to it waited for it to fill. She was the only girl who kept her back to me, exposing the VI tattooed on the back of her bald head. She paused long enough for me to think she wanted to show me not only her number but respect. When she turned around, I recognized her from the tattoo parlor. Her jumpsuit covered her fully inked arms.

In her eyes I saw admiration. Stupid. Not just because I

didn't do it, but stupid even if I did.

"Please." From the attendant's mouth the word sounded like an order. "Show her how to do your task. Once she's got it, you should be able to give one of the roller girls a break."

The inmate nodded and the guard left us. She returned her eyes to the bucket and turned off the faucet.

"Our job," she said without a hello or anything, "is to make sure the washers always have clean rinse water." She rolled the bucket over to one of three washer girls. "Choose the bucket with the most clothing in it." She passed the girl who'd splashed me. "You'll notice," my instructor said, "some people don't work as hard as others."

The freckled girl dropped an f-bomb loud enough for us to hear, but too quiet for the supervisor in the back.

The tattooed girl didn't flinch and continued as if she hadn't heard the additional unkind words the angry washer spat at her. "Once you find a full bucket, swap it with the clean rinse water. Simple as that."

We turned toward the roller station when the troublemaker kicked over the bucket next to her. The girl with the sleeves didn't have time to catch herself and landed on her bottom in the wet suds.

"Oh," the culprit feigned regret, "I'm so sorry. Are you okay?" She reached her hand toward her victim, but the tattoo girl was smarter than that. She pivoted away from the fight and was standing by the time the guard made it over.

"What happened?" The guard posed her question to me, but the freckled girl spoke first.

"It was my fault, I knocked it over." Which wasn't a lie. The lie came when she said, "I'm so sorry."

"You're going to have to wash those again." She pointed to the floor and the girl groaned.

The tattoo girl might have slipped, but the instigator didn't escape unscathed. Reap what you sow and all that. What I didn't understand is why this girl would risk Isolation.

The guard looked at me. "Is that what you saw?"

The question felt like a huge test and I wasn't sure I was going to pass it because no matter what, I wasn't going to open my mouth. I lifted my shoulders as the inmate assigned to teach me repeated, "The bucket got knocked over." Her voice was calm, "I slipped in the sudsy water." She made eye contact with the perpetrator and said, "I accept your apology."

Red flashed across the girl's cheek.

Sleeves grabbed me by the arm and we returned to the rolling station and away from the supervisor and her obnoxious charge.

I resisted the temptation to look back at the guard and the inmate who angrily splashed clothes into the sink. "It might be better to spend my time in Isolation."

"Don't say that," my companion hissed. "Nothing is worth staying in Isolation."

My comment had only been sarcastic and dishonest, but her tone reminded me of what I had left less than an hour ago. At the sink, my teacher pointed to the faucet. I dumped the remains and rinsed the suds from the side with the hose. When it was free of soap, I set it under an open tap to let it fill.

"Tell me something," the tattoo girl leaned against the wall as the water ran. "How are you going to do it?"

"Do what?" I said, glancing at the sink, thinking she wanted to find a way to get back at the girl as some sort of initiation. Who knows, maybe the spilt bucket was meant for me.

"Isolation," she leaned close to me. "How you going to endure thirty-two more days of it."

The water in the bucket had reached the red painted line inside. Instinctively I turned the water off. She stopped talking as we wheeled the bucket toward the sink. Watching the next step in the process, the fullness of what was said dawned on me.

Isolation.

I have thirty-two more days of isolation broken up or not, the number was daunting.

An invisible knife pierced my heart. In the day-to-day activities, I hadn't taken the time to process what the tattoo on the back of my head really meant.

Ángel or the supervisor or the inmates around me could think it means I killed thirty-three people. And real or not, that's not what it meant in the long run. While I regretted Ribbon's death in ways I never had before, it was the past and the past was dead and gone.

No. What the tattoo really meant for me was thirty-two more days in Isolation. I could try to kid myself into thinking I would get better at it. But that didn't work when I had a window and mural friends. Eight days had felt like weeks. What would thirty-two feel like with even less stimulus than in the yellow cell?

The girl's demeanor solicited an honest response, "I don't think I can."

"But you have no choice," she pointed out as the roller girl selected a pair of wet pants. I watched as a crank squeezed all it could from the unsuspecting garment. I wondered if the pants knew they weren't done. Another roller waited for them before they'd be hung to dry.

CHAPTER 26

I couldn't do it. I couldn't.

As we quietly sloshed buckets from place to place, I knew I had to think of a way to get out of Isolation. A small part of my brain imagined escaping, but the smarter lobes said, don't be stupid. I'd be either caught or die of starvation trying to wind my way out of this maze.

No.

I seriously doubted persuasion would get me anywhere with these people. Which left me with two serious options: the first, they were flat out wrong. They would take me into the white room, and we'd all discover the freckled-face washer made me do it, like in the stupidest movie ever made, when it was obvious who did it from the first scene.

The second thing I had to do was find out more about Reconstruction. It was my solid plan B, so solid, it should be plan A, but I knew curiosity would kill me if I left for Bunkerville without seeing what they accused me of.

In the middle of my contemplations, a loud whistle

pierced the room. I pressed my finger against my ear until the short woman stopped blowing it.

"Line up for lunch, ladies." She swung the whistle around her finger on a string.

"Already?" I said more to myself than anyone else, but the tattooed girl answered me anyway.

"You came in halfway through the shift, remember."

I didn't, but it made sense. I'd spent the morning locked alone in a cell. It wasn't like I'd forgotten, it was more like I'd been there for much longer.

Faucets were turned off, folding stopped and inmates began to line up. I followed the crowd, not really hungry for more than knowledge. And the best person to get it from might be the girl with the tattoo sleeves. While I knew Ángel from our days in The Center, I trusted this girl more. She had less reason to lie to me.

We ate in a room down the hall with twenty other girls on our level. A couple of them gave me skeptical looks after seeing my XXXIII brand, but I didn't pay them any attention. I picked up a tray from the counter and ignored them.

Folding tables littered the room, each with matching chairs as if this place waited for a women's bridge meeting. Sleeves picked a place, but before she could sit, the freckled-face girl pulled the chair away.

This time my companion righted herself before landing on the ground. "This is our table. Find another." Three knuckleheads joined the girl as a guard eyed us more closely.

I stood stunned at how little the thought of Isolation had on this set. They had to know they'd be sent there or worse for behavior like this, but they taunted me. "Go on, thirty-three, follow your ink-covered friend."

I knew how quickly defensive adrenaline could rush

through my veins. As a person always ready to fight, I wouldn't have a problem putting this girl right.

"Let's go, she's not worth it." The inked girl said.

We turned and walked away. As I went to take my second step, I felt someone's foot lock against my ankle and pull. I would have hit the ground if Sleeves hadn't caught my fall.

"Oops, I'm so sorry," the girl next to freckles said. "Are you okay?"

My cheeks warmed as I bit back a curse.

"Don't do it," Sleeves said, "These hard heads don't care about isolation." She yanked me by the arm to the furthest table possible.

"What in the heck is going on?" I set my tray down. "I feel like I'm in high school again."

"Different people respond to cages in different ways. Those girls are hungry for trouble, that's all."

"But she acts like it's personal."

"It is," she said, sitting. "We got in a bit of a scuffle while in The Center. It's because of her I got a taste of The Bracelet. You remember those taser days, don't you?"

I nodded and left it at that. This wasn't the time to revisit the details of how Ángel got zapped when he tried to stop Fisher from raping me. The story wouldn't get me any closer to what I needed to know. As much as I'd love to talk trash about the girls at the other table, I had more important information to gather.

"So," I asked directly, "You mentioned I would have to spend thirty-two more days in Isolation based on my brand. Are you sure about that?"

"Yeah," she bit into her tuna sandwich. After chewing a bit, she continued, "I finished my 24-hours this morning before breakfast." Wiping her mouth with a paper napkin she said, "I asked the guard about alternatives to Isolation."

"And?"

"He offered Reconstruction."

I decided not to share the darker option the guard mentioned to me. "You must have been in the video room right before me."

"I guess," she swallowed. "All I know is I'll take time with that idiot over there and her attitude all day long before I add one more day of solitary to my list. It might make girls like that angry, but I'd probably hurt myself if I stayed in that place for long. I have no idea how I'm going to make it through five more days," she indicated the number six on the back of her head, "and to think you have thirty-two more." She pointed to my tag this time. "I honestly think it would kill me."

I stared at the plastic table while I told her how the guard who brought me breakfast said some people had died in Isolation.

"Figures." She sat her sandwich down. "So, what you going to do?"

"I don't know. I've been thinking about Bunkerville. What do you know of the place?"

"Not much more than you, I think. It sounds too much like brainwashing for me to show an interest. But then again, I'm not facing as many days alone as you are."

I bit my lip. Like her, I wasn't hungry anymore. I pushed my tray away.

Back in the laundry room, I worked quietly next to the tattoo girl until dinner and ate without a word. When I returned to my cell, I sank onto the cot and stared at the soap marks that had lied to me. It felt like I'd been buried for months.

Not that I'd be here to count for much longer. Using the sleeve of my jumpsuit, I scrubbed hard to wipe off the soap marks wondering if I'd be around to clean my dirty uniform.

How many days had it been? This was a truth I wanted. Counting on my fingers, I began with eight, based on what Ángel and Dr. Maggie had said. One day to get tagged. Another day of Truth, which took me into 24 hours of Isolation where I finished day ten in the Laundry room. Impossible to believe, but I'd only been buried in the ground for ten days.

Above ground, summer wasn't over. The forest fire hadn't cooled down yet. Three months and ten days since I got knocked up while living free.

Can a life really change this drastically in a hundred days?

And now I was about to experience Bunkerville and start a whole new life. Become reinvented yet again. Become the mother my child deserved. Part of me wondered how much Truth could do me good. Help me accept what I did wrong. But I didn't kill that many people, and I would never survive thirty-two more days of Isolation.

Unless they break them up.

Maybe I could do one day at a time, maybe once a month. But that would leave me here for over two years. Crazy. My sentence was only for two years and I've served three months. No, I couldn't break them up like that. The best I could expect was to rip them off like the biggest bandage in the world. Endure some consecutive days in Isolation. I might survive. Remain the person I was, only more self-aware. Nanny Bella used to say, "The devil you know is better than the devil you don't."

Rubbing my belly, I said aloud, "Maybe your momma's stronger than she thinks. Maybe all these hard lessons can prepare me to be the mom you deserve."

CHAPTER 27

Choices raced through my head like rats all night. Give up my past and become someone Dr. Maggie designs, or suck it up and own my mistakes. Of course, the second could destroy me worse than the first. Could drive me mental. But so could the intentional delusions Dr. Maggie offered.

By morning, I'd decided brainwashing held too many unknowns to dive into. I wanted to be strong. To grow. For several weeks, I'd believed the child growing inside of me was a boy. And if hope of gaining the respect of a grown man existed, he was it.

When Ángel came to take me to my second Confession Session my nerves were fried. While I'd made a firm decision in my mind to pass on Bunkerville, I still wasn't sure how I'd survive Isolation.

I didn't like the unknown and hated the dark anticipation of scary movies or haunted houses or The Bunker's Truth Sessions. Sitting on the leather chair, I gritted my teeth as the lights dimmed.

The boss, or whoever was in charge, changed the timeline. Gone were the soft beaches of California. An aerial drone captured the thick green wall of trees next to the weaving Potomac River. I leaned forward, recognizing my father's house. The camera captured the commute along the George Washington Parkway into Alexandria, into Crystal City until it stopped above the Pentagon City Mall.

The scene changed from distant shots to security cameras at the food court.

I knew what was coming.

Shock burnt memories into my brain the way XXXIII scarred the back of my head.

The Starbucks had a line of people. Anticipation scraped against my nerves as I found myself in the scene. I'd expected cameras in The Center. I'd expected surveillance in The Bunker. But this was of my regular life. The events of my past.

"Where'd you get these?"

Ángel shrugged, "Who knows." He leaned toward me and whispered, "All the videos they've shown you so far seem like a violation of your civil rights." He leaned toward me and showed me a paper he had hidden in his sleeve. He was taking notes. With the tiniest shake of his head, I knew he wasn't supposed to be doing that.

He moved to the corner and I turned to see Nicole from Master's Elite. It was the day I accidentally knocked her into the escalator. This had to be video from cameras in the mall.

She bought her tea and a different me hid behind other customers. Less than a year ago, I was free to make horrible choices. My plan had been to bump into her, feign an apology and build a fake friendship. Back then, I didn't have this aerial perspective. My view was limited. As Nicole neared the escalator I turned away. I didn't need to see the gash in her head. My memory replayed the cracked skull and splashed blood of my rival. The images froze. The sensors knew I'd turned away.

The computer asked, "Are you ready to confess?"

"Is Nicole dead?" I asked, knowing I would have to confess to her death as I did Ribbon's.

No answer from the speakers.

Pressure rose in my heart. This event felt much closer to me than Ribbon's. I'd never seen the broken body of the girl I'd bullied. I'd never touched her flesh. But Nicole was different.

"I didn't mean to have her fall into the escalator. I only wanted to spill her drink, apologize. That was it. I didn't mean to hurt her." I swallowed. "Not like that."

The silence continued as I study the screen. The video commenced. People came to help and blood from the broken girl's head leaked from her opened scalp.

"Is she dead?" I asked again.

The images shifted from the Pentagon City Mall to the library a couple blocks away.

My hands trembled.

The library where I bought the oxy I gave to Nicole. While my goal wasn't to get her addicted, I knew it was a risk. Everyone knows how addictive painkillers are.

"I'm ready to confess. I'm ready."

Lights went up in the room. The white walls blinded me. Ángel came from his quiet place in the corner.

"If Nicole is dead," I told him. "I did it. I accept it."

The room remained silent.

"I'm guilty," I shouted, "Okay? She didn't deserve what I did to her. She was as innocent as Ribbon. She had something I wanted so I tried my best to destroy her."

Ángel returned to his corner and rested against the wall. "Maybe it doesn't want me standing next to you."

I shrugged.

We waited silently for further instructions. I adjusted my seat and stared at the wall, but the images didn't come. I could feel it the way a nerd knows they are about to be humiliated in a high school lunchroom. The anticipation. The dramatic pause. I might have lasted less than a minute, but Ángel and I were so focused on the mock screen we both jumped when the door opened.

Pressing my hand to my heart to help slow it down. The guy handed Ángel a stack of papers and left the room.

"What was that?"

He flipped through the papers without answering.

"What's going on? Is Nicole dead?"

The room remained silent. Ángel sank into the chair he'd been occupying. He didn't look at me but focused on the screen. He shook his head, "This isn't fair," fell from his mouth.

I turned on him. "What?" I pointed to the papers. "What does it say? I'm ready to spend my day in Isolation if this is about Nicole. That's the entire reason I got committed to The Center in the first place. If they want to pile on her death, I get it, I understand."

"This isn't only about Nicole." He looked at the ground.

"Then who else could it be about?"

"Nicole's addiction led to the death of thirty-two people."

"What? How's that even possible?" I stood because I literally couldn't take what he was telling me sitting down. "If Nicole killed people, what's that got to do with me? I get it if she'd died. I'd be guilty. But I can't be blamed for her choices. I refuse to confess to her crimes. Get her in here. Let her confess."

"It's not that simple."

"What's not that simple?"

"She killed people trying to kill you. It was you she was after. If you hadn't given her those pills, thirty-two people would still be alive."

I stared at him. "What are you talking about?"

"Revenge. She killed for revenge."

"But how? She never could have gotten to me. I've been in The Center the whole time."

"I know." He paused before saying. "Nicole set the fire."

"What fire?" I asked.

"The one that burned down The Center."

She what?

I blinked.

My brain spun.

"The boss is saying you are the reason The Center burned. You were her target."

CHAPTER 28

I lowered myself onto the seat without fully comprehending what I'd heard. Ángel didn't move as the lights dimmed again.

The flickering scene on the wall shifted from Virginia to the Colorado Rockies. The majestic wooden buildings, the sun shaped chapel, the dorms, and stone office of Dr. Maggie. The Bunker's pyramid entrance. The aerial view stirred nostalgic emotions.

The Center, the way it had looked when I'd arrived. Snow covered land contrasted against dark pines. Jackson's face was the first to appear and my stomach tightened. His silent laughter filled the room visually, wall to wall. Even without sound, I could hear his joy from deep in my memory banks.

He bantered with a group of guys, Ángel included.

"Jackson's alive, right?"

Ángel didn't answer.

On the screen, the Latino patted Jackson as his bright

eyes shone over me. Three other inmates approached. I didn't know their names. The group of about five guys mouthed silent conversations as the projector whirred. The camera froze on an unknown inmate for the count of about three seconds.

When it unfroze, the image changed to a couple girls sitting on a random bench in The Center. Again, the scene stopped in the middle of one girl's gentle expression. I counted, three seconds passed.

It switched again to Dee Dee and the girl Vicki who wore dreadlocks, hiking past The Bunker. I remembered that day, but not from this view. The image froze on the face of the hippie girl who'd hated me so much. I still remembered her dying screams as The Bunker doors locked her out.

Dee Dee's alive. I saw her a day ago. But Vicki. Vicki was dead for sure. She died trying to get into The Bunker. Vicki was one of Nicole's victims. One of mine.

Three seconds later, the edited film scanned the cafeteria, stopping and pausing on faces. Most of them I couldn't name. But the stop and pause happened at least ten times before I realized I should be counting. I mean, the intent was obvious. The Truth group meant for me to know and see specific people.

A skinhead laughing.

A former prostitute talking.

Inmates studying.

I started counting, estimating I'd seen a dozen frozen faces so far. At least one of them—dreadlocked Vicki—dead. Dead because Nicole wanted to kill me. The first face they showed me was Jackson's. Had it been frozen? I hadn't noticed.

The idea stabbed through my heart. This couldn't be. Jackson couldn't be dead. Could he? I stared harder at the images. The small field of dirt and grass next to the gym. A pick-up soccer game commenced. I recognized some faces from the cafeteria scene. Ángel kicked at a ball but was bowled over by Fisher. The jerk who tried to rape me stole the ball and kicked a lucky goal into the net. The image stopped on the goalie's face as he jumped to deflect the ball.

Three seconds.

What number was he?

The image moved again. Ángel high-fived a short girl on his team and the camera stopped on her face.

Three seconds.

A heavy hiccup came from the guard in the corner.

My lower back ached. My breathing felt labored. Guilt and fear and loneliness rose within me as ghosts smiled from the screen.

I got up and paced. The video stopped. I hated this place. Hated it with everything in me. I'm not built for deep empathy. I'm not. It's too much. I was ready to pay for Ribbon's death as well as Nicole's, but the idea Jackson might be dead stirred a deep need to reject everything on the screen.

Blame my heart.

My brain understood how shallow that was. It did. I'm a horrible person. Thirty-two people died in a forest fire and all I can focus on is one.

Jackson.

The guard who professed his love to me.

It shouldn't mean anything. It wouldn't if he was alive. But if he's dead he will forever be the one who could have been. "I want to go back. I want to see the beginning of this video." I rubbed my muscles.

"Are you kidding me?" Ángel rose and pressed two fingers against his chest. "How is this not killing you?" His breathing shuttered. "I knew these people too. Probably knew them better than you. Everyone buried here did. This is horrible. I don't want to see another face and you want to go back?"

"Yes. This is my truth not yours."

"You're unbelievable." He turned on me. "This truth—" he jabbed a finger toward the wall. "—is about every person buried here." Disgust radiated from him. "Can you really be that selfish? Can you? Tell me, Courtney, do you even know their names? Do you? Because I do. I know them. I spent time with them." Tears choked his throat.

He was right. I was selfish. The whole time I watch the image I wasn't thinking about anyone but Jackson. And what did it matter now? My heart knew. Jackson was gone. I sank into the seat and the video began again.

Silent tears rolled down Ángel's face as we watched the damage Nicole had done because of me. When the happy images of dead people stopped, the camera panned down to the fence surrounding The Center. A couple deer jumped about two-hundred yards from the lens. A moment later, a person appeared along the fence line, too far away to recognize. Based on the pink parka, I could only guess this was Nicole. She had a bright-red gas can and poured its contents along the dry grass.

A scream boiled from beneath my skin.

The girl lit a match and dropped it with a burst onto the fence line.

I'd seen that fire.

Jackson had seen that fire.

At the time, I'd thought it was a random camper.

The camera followed the figure into a jeep traveling along a service road to the Northern Parameter. The pink parka repeated her actions at all four points of the compass.

More gasoline. More matches. More flames.

Nicole got into her jeep and drove away.

My brain flipped through the faces.

The deaths.

Nicole burned down The Center because of me. Thirty-two people died because of me and the only one I feel concerned about is Jackson. An avalanche of guilt and disgust tumbled over me. In this moment, I'd never felt more self-hate in my entire life.

With my fists clenched, I tipped my head back and pushed a primal scream through my lips.

CHAPTER 29

I couldn't stop the howls coming from my heart.

Hating myself hurt more than I could have ever imagined.

They had to sedate me in order to calm me down. With my arms over the shoulders of Ángel and another guard, I was drag-pulled to Isolation. Laying on the floor next to the cot where I'd fallen, I stared at the single bulb in the ceiling. Thirty-two people were dead because of me. Dead because I decided to fight for a dumb boy in high school who didn't want me. Dead because I didn't care what I did to Nicole to get him. Dead because I didn't stick to dating older men. Men who knew enough to at least pretend they cared about me. Dead because I was a selfish, worthless bitch who twisted love so tightly in my fist I destroyed it.

Rolling over on the stone floor, I stared at the wall and stared at the dark blotch left on my retina from the light bulb. The gray circle would fade, but my guilt wouldn't. And it wasn't only about the deaths. Ángel was right. My reaction had been equally bad. I'd figured out pretty early in the film which faces represented the dead, and only one stabbed me with regret.

Not Ribbon.

Not Vicki.

Jackson. Only Jackson.

He was still the only victim driving my desire to cry. Well, not only him. I desperately wanted to cry for me. For my loss. That's how much I sucked as a human being. To lay on the concrete floor hurting for myself more than the others I'd injured. Something was horribly wrong with my heart. I didn't feel what other people felt.

Based on my high school psychology class, that meant I was a sociopath. A human unconnected to other humans.

That was the real problem.

The real sentence.

I rolled over and curled into a ball, rubbing the small child who had the misfortune of being related to me. I had nothing to write in the amends journal. Nothing to say about myself. Thirty-two days couldn't change the monster inside of me.

My son kicked me in the ribs, too small to really do any damage. When he kicked again, I shifted my position. I'd like to think I did it for his comfort. If I really cared about him, I would give him to a family who can't have babies. Unless, of course, my mental condition was hereditary. Neither of my parents cared much for me. This could all have come from the twisted strands of my DNA.

"Sorry, buddy," I said aloud. "What do you think? Should we give up this place and disappear into a world of illusion?"

No doubt Dr. Maggie knew all about Nicole and the fire. Yet she didn't seem to think it would stop her from fixing me. Maybe she really could get to the part of my brain that only took and couldn't give.

Maybe the problem had nothing to do with my family. My issues had been obvious since birth. The best thing to do was protect this child from me. Maybe my father had seen something in my infant eyes telling him to stay away. Maybe my mother had a reason to be so cold and distant toward me.

I sat up.

If I chose Bunkerville, I'd have to make sure Dr. Maggie fixed my heart as well as my brain. This boy deserved a mother who would sacrifice anything for him. I rolled over and pushed my selfish butt up and washed my face.

I was tired, but I was going to get up.

I wasn't hungry, but I was going to eat.

I still sucked, but the best and first thing I could do to make amends for the lives I'd injured was to take care of myself until the baby was born. And when the guard came to take away the dinner tray, I told her I was ready for Bunkerville.

PART VII

The Present

CHAPTER 30

"Stop, please," Faith lifts her hands as if she has the power to change what she heard. "I can't listen anymore."

My words end.

My head lowers.

I understand.

Dr. Maggie had not only erased my past, she had erased my guilt, but as I tell my story the full weight of who I am returns. I can't blame Faith for her reaction. I'm not what she signed up for.

As the ghosts from my Truth Sessions linger in the room, I'm disappointed. In myself. In the unnecessary deaths of Jackson and thirty-one others. The horror of who I really am.

My surrogate mother stands and rushes to the door. "We're getting out of here." She grabs her purse from the hook and turns the handle.

It doesn't budge.

Glancing at the clock I see we have at least an hour left

of sequester. "We can't go anywhere."

"They can't do that. I'm a free citizen."

"Yes, you are, but I'm not."

She studies her toes for a half second before hanging her purse again. In a firm, but quieter tone she says, "This isn't right."

"Look, I'm sorry you're stuck in here. I am. Once that door opens, Dr. Maggie will let you go."

I can't read the look on Faith's face as she sinks into the sofa beside me. She reaches for my hand and I let her. "Do you think for one moment I plan to leave this place without you?"

Her sincerity disarms me, and I pull my hand away.

"Courtney, look, this place is crazy. Really crazy and I couldn't leave you here. No way."

"You still want to help me knowing all I've done?"

"What have you done? I mean really. Nobody is one hundred percent innocent in life."

"You can't believe that."

"I do. The way I see it, each person is a single drop in a huge ocean. However, every drop creates a ripple. Our existence will always impact the people we love as well as hundreds of people we don't even know." She sits back against the sofa and stares at the wall as if a video of her life was projected on it. "I'm sure I've injured people I've never met. I've made bad choices. I have."

"Did those actions lead to the death of thirty-three people?"

"Who knows? For all I know if they put me in that room, I might have the number one hundred on the back of my head. The longer we live the more likely our actions negatively impact others unless we make a conscious effort to remember. To live intentionally."

She makes sense. A lot of it.

"Look, I believe what they're telling you is true. But I don't believe the way they're telling you is right. They are making it seem as if yours is a unique case ,as if Ángel or Dr. Maggie aren't equally guilty."

"So, you think the whole world is full of criminals."

"I never thought of it like that." She lifts one shoulder in a half shrug. "I guess I am. Look, can I tell you a story?"

I point to the locked door to remind her we have all the time in the world.

She tucks her leg underneath her and begins. "The summer before I started college, I dated a guy who treated me like gold. To this day, he's still the sweetest guy I've ever known." She laughs and says conspiratorially, "Don't tell my husband."

I laugh too, surprised at how open this woman was being with me given what she heard. There has to be a catch, something I'm missing.

"Anyway, we dated the entire summer until it was time for me to go to school. A week before school started, he asked me to marry him. I loved him, I really did, but I didn't want to get married. He wanted me barefoot and pregnant, I wanted to get my degree and travel the world. The break-up was amicable. He began dating someone else and I dove into my studies."

She pauses long enough to prompt me to say, "Is that it? What does that have to do with Truth Sessions or Bunkerville?"

"About two months after we broke up. I got a late-night call from a friend. She wanted to know if I'd been watching the news. I hadn't. At that time in my life, I didn't really like the politics and stuff the news was all about.

"She asked me if I'd heard about the guy who had been arrested for killing a woman while her child slept in the next room."

"What?"

"Yeah, I couldn't believe it. The sweetest guy I'd ever known had been arrested and taken into custody."

"Did he do it?"

"The trial took a long time, but eventually he was convicted. We had one phone conversation during this time, and I asked him."

She exhales deeply before saying, "He said he didn't remember doing it, but after sitting in the court and seeing all the evidence, it could have only been him.

"He's serving a life sentence. He's been locked up for 20 years."

"Wow."

"You see, that was the moment I knew every single human being on this planet had the capacity to kill. The sweet guy I dated had been in combat. It's possible an injury from his past triggered the reaction. I don't know. I stopped looking for answers long ago. I believe we all have the power inside of us to really hurt other people. And we all have the power inside of us to really love other people. It's a choice we all have to make day by day."

I lean back and consider what she said. This woman isn't afraid of me, I can be sure of that. She also doesn't hate me. She believes I have a chance at a better life.

"Thank you," I finally say. "Thank you for coming here and thank you for trusting me."

"You're welcome. Now we need to talk about how we get out of here."

"I don't think that will be so easy. You can still leave when they unlock the doors, of course. Dr. Maggie can't keep you here. But as for me, I have to stay. I am a convicted criminal, and I haven't yet served my two years."

She offers another half shrug and says, "I'm not so sure about that."

CHAPTER 31

Faith stands after making the statement. In the kitchen, she calmly runs water into the tea kettle as I comb my fingernails across my scalp, trying to dislodge any logical thoughts. What did she mean?

Looking at the door, the only reason I can come up with is escape. But that's impossible. If she did that, she'd be guilty of a prison break. There's no way she's that kind or that crazy. No one in their right might would help someone they just met escape from prison.

"This is more than a prison," Faith says over her shoulder from the sink. "The people running this place are as guilty of breaking the law as you are. Trust me."

It takes me a minute to get up from the couch. My hip is sore from having remained in one position so long. Once I'm up, I waddle to where Faith makes tea.

With the kettle on the flame, she turns to me with a huge smile.

I don't smile back. I'm over it. The last thing I need is for her to stir false hopes. "Don't do that. Don't. Don't stand there smiling as if the comment you made makes sense."

"Life always has options."

"You can't be serious. I lost my options when I broke the law."

"Not all of them. Look, I came here to help you and that's what I'm going to do. And from what I can tell, the best thing would be to get you above ground."

"Why? What then? I'll end up in a detention center somewhere else."

"Yeah," she crosses her arms and glares at me. "You would, but at least you'd get to keep your baby."

Protectively, I place my hand on my distended belly. "What are you talking about? I don't want to keep him. I want to give him a better home. Better than me. I can do that down here."

"Really? Are you sure? Based on what I've heard so far, no one in this place cares about your baby. And if I were to guess, Dr. Maggie is planning to abort it."

"The surgery is a C-section," I say, not thoroughly convinced. I hadn't yet told her I'd thought the same thing at one time.

"When did you conceive? Do you know?"

Her questions sound like an interrogation. Without telling her about the one-night stand with the piano man, I say, "Yes."

"Month and day."

"First week of May."

She counts off months on her fingers. "June, July, August, September, October, November, December." She holds up seven fingers at me. "Babies take 40 weeks of gestation. That means you would be due on the first week of February. Today is January 6th. You still have one full

169

month to go."

"But that's not possible." At the window, the sun shines bright from a blue sky. The trees have leaves and the grass is green. I'd never really spent time in the snow until I entered The Center, but the mountain we are buried under must be covered in snow.

"The entrance I came in did have snow," she responds to my slip. "We needed chains to navigate the pass."

"But not a snowcat."

"No. You would definitely need one on the mountain top, but old mining entrance is hundreds of feet closer to sea level. But I can see with Bunkerville's like-spring all year climate how you can forget about weather."

"Like San Diego." I say the name of my hometown with nostalgia. Sinking into the chair, I hold my child close.

"I was directly informed by the doctor of her plans on doing the surgery as soon as my husband arrives tomorrow. She might have planned a C-section, but it's been pushed forward. And while babies can survive an early birth, they do it in hospitals with incubators. Not where electricity is scarce. Besides, if she wasn't planning on aborting the baby, why not tell us as your surrogate parents? We could be there for you, no matter what decision you made. Why lie about a tumor?"

The tea kettle sings a low whistle and Faith gets up to remove it from the flame before it can really start to scream.

January. Unbelievable. While the time I'd spent in The Bunker cell dragged, time here had sped past me. Months of my life are gone. And I'm not ready to have a baby. I'm not ready for the decisions motherhood brings.

Faith places a cup of tea on the table next to me and I cradle its warmth. She sits in the chair and sips from her cup.

"My husband should be here tomorrow. And your surgery is planned for the next day."

"So much for options."

"I haven't told you the best part." She takes another sip before putting her cup down. "I think the three of us can walk out of here together when he comes."

"How?"

Faith gets up and approaches the locked door. She reaches into her purse and retrieves a folded document. She brings it to the table and lays it before me.

"This is a parental guardian form."

I pick it up and examined the pages. My fake name Dorothy has been drafted across the top.

"It wouldn't be legal. That's not my real name."

Faith leans over and points to a line with "Dorothy Williams (aka Courtney Anne Manchester)" written on it.

Faith turns the page. "That's my signature and the notary in California who witnessed it. Next to it is my husband's signature." I look at the rushed script of Stanley J. Williams. My eyes move to my own name. My full name, my real name, and my real signature. And below that was a court stamp and the scribbled script above a judge's name.

"I signed this?"

"Didn't you?"

"I must have."

"Then this is a legal document. My husband and I are your legal guardians. We are responsible for you until you turn twenty. We'd been told you asked for guardianship during your rehabilitation. I assumed you were getting over a drug addiction."

"No. Not an addiction, a conviction."

"Yes, I can see that now. But what this paper means is my husband and I have the power to take you from this place whenever we like."

"Even though my sentence hasn't been completed?'

"I think so. Didn't Ángel tell you your guardians chose this place for you?"

Thinking back, I remember he did.

"So, if your previous guardians had the power to assign you to this place, your new guardians should have the power to release you."

Hope tingles at the edge of my nerves. And it isn't a welcome feeling. "Dr. Maggie has invested a ton of time and thought into this program. She's not one to give up so easily. There must be a loop hole."

"I didn't say easy. I said possible." She places a warm hand over mine.

"Possible." I repeat.

"Yes, but in order to do that, I need to know everything you know about Bunkerville and Dr. Maggie's methods. You said you entered The Bunker in July. Tell me all you can remember about the last five to six months."

PART VIII

The Past

CHAPTER 32

Rowena was the one who came and got me from Isolation. Her smugness made me immediately want to change my mind. Every cell in my body screamed, "This is a humongous mistake."

But I had a baby to consider. A child who had a right to be well fed and have a comfortable place to sleep. The Truth session showed me all the selfish decisions I'd made in my past. I really wanted this to be more about the child than it was about me.

I followed the tall guard to an elevator which was surprisingly close to the Truth rooms.

The door opened as soon as she pressed the button. She smiled, bowed, and extended her arm, inviting me in. I'd never seen her smile. Her lips cracked like a scar over a perfect row of teeth.

"Nice dentures." I snarked.

"Want a pair?"

"Maybe later." As much as I wanted to think I could take

this behemoth, she had the power and the equipment to run the show. I slipped past without touching her.

My stomach growled.

Truth wouldn't satisfy food cravings.

Reconstruction might.

Truth wouldn't offer a soft bed.

Reconstruction should.

In fact, Reconstruction might give my baby a crib, although I had months to worry about that. In the end, Truth was harder than I could endure. I was not made of tough stuff. My bad girl behavior came from a place of privilege, not grit like the inmate with the tattooed sleeves.

The elevator moved and I could have sworn the car descended. Although the lights on the display indicated we were going up, I would have bet the entire Manchester fortune we were sinking deeper into the earth.

Up, if I watched the lights.

Down, if I closed my eyes.

Nothing in this world matched what I knew. Dr. Maggie had spoken about changing my past, changing me. I still worried about how Reconstruction would feel. The idea of living in a made-up town wasn't exactly encouraging.

I decided to ask the guard. Maybe she could clue me in. Trying to sound casual and cool, I asked, "Are we really going up?"

"Yeah, it's a very slow elevator, but Bunkerville is four stories above the prison." Her voice wasn't harsh or condescending. I decided to ask her more.

"What's Bunkerville like?"

"You saw it when you were shaved."

"Yes, but I didn't stay."

"It's fine," she said unconvincingly.

"But not great."

"What do you want me to say? It's a place where you get to start all over."

"And you approve of that."

"Look, Courtney, you might have thought I was too hard on you in The Center. But I believe in rehabilitation. I believe it's better than stuffing people into a prison and never letting them out."

"But Bunkerville is different."

"Maybe."

"You're not sure."

"No, I'm not. Some memories from our past are worth keeping."

I thought about the Truth Session. I wondered what she knew. She had been close with Jackson. Did she know I was partially to blame for his death? Did she know he was dead? No. She was as bad at hiding her feelings as I was. If she knew, she wouldn't be so nice to me now. She would be happy for any torture coming my way. Like the HIPPA law keeping anyone from knowing I was pregnant. Truth might tattoo the back of my head, but it didn't tell the world the specifics. Details were for me and Ángel and probably Dr. Maggie to share or not. "Let me ask you this. Do you think we should keep the memories of awful or painful times?"

"Yes, I do. I believe the painful stuff makes us stronger. Teaches us."

"So why do you work in Bunkerville?"

"Because it's a job. Unlike you, I don't have a wealthy family to run home to."

I wanted to say neither did I, but I knew that wasn't true. If I were to abandon my pride, I could return home once my sentence was over.

Rowena continued, "I've put in for a transfer, but that can take time. I don't know much about where you came from. I've heard you're shown parts of your history no one in the real world has access to see. To me that's just as fake as Bunkerville, where you volunteer to eliminate everything from your history."

"What do you mean by everything?"

"Far as I can tell, Dr. Maggie removes anything connecting you to the life you lived before Bunkerville."

"Not everything." My hands moved from the rail to my stomach.

"Absolutely everything."

"No way." I opened my mouth to grab deeper breaths. The car vibrated and my stomach dropped. This was bad. They couldn't take my child from me. He was from my past, but not the parental or criminal part. Of all people in The Bunker, he was the most innocent.

The elevator stopped.

"I've changed my mind."

"Too late." Rowena didn't look at me. When the doors opened, she exited. I didn't follow. As fast as my fingers could move, I pressed all the buttons on the panel as hard as I could and prayed it would close.

Wishful thinking.

The guard's size ten plopped down to stop the elevator door from closing.

"What do you think you're doing?" she growled.

"I don't want to erase my past. I don't. I've changed my mind."

"I shouldn't have said anything." She yanked hard on my arm and dragged me from the car. "You are still an inmate, which means I can't keep taking you back and forth on a whim."

"No. I don't want to go." I sank like dead weight to the ground.

"For crying out loud, you act like I'm taking you to an executioner." She opened a door in the dark corridor and hauled me through it.

My feet slipped from the frame as I kicked to stop the forward progress.

The door clicked closed.

Rowena dragged me on my butt for another foot or so before loosening her grip.

Turning on my stomach, I scrambled to my feet. I had to get out of here. I hurried to where I thought she had pulled me from, only the door was no longer there. I mean it was there. It had to be, but I could no longer see it. Before me towered a two-story brick wall. I patted and tapped what I thought would be fake stone, but the bricks were rough and real, not a magician's image.

I pivoted again. My eyes and brain and soul confused. The entrance had disappeared. Rowena sighed as I patted the wall looking for a door. "You're wasting your time." She looked at her watch. "And mine."

I gave up. Whatever gateway the big guard had dragged me through was gone.

CHAPTER 33

I no longer wanted to be the girl who fought my way through life. I wanted all the raging violence inside of me to stop. But I didn't know how to get my way without either manipulation or violence. Although, I couldn't really say in the end either had gotten me what I wanted, or I wouldn't be here. I'd be spending the summer with friends by a pool waiting for college to start.

Too late for that. A person couldn't go backwards. All I could do was be ready for whatever happened next in Reconstruction. One thing was for sure, I would never consent to killing my unborn child. And as soon as I saw Dr. Maggie, I would tell her. She'd let me choose. She'd have to. After all, she wasn't a monster, was she?

We passed the barbershop as well as the front entrance of the tattoo parlor. It was odd to see it from this angle. In the window were pictures of detailed inked images, not the horrible Roman numerals I'd experienced. The streets were empty, as if this place didn't open until the afternoon. Like an abandoned amusement park.

Rowena opened the door to a gym. Free weights and yoga mats lay unused around the space. To the right was a climbing wall. No treadmills or exercise bikes. We entered the ladies' room with a decorated sitting area as well as three doors, which led to large private shower rooms. "Go ahead and get cleaned up."

She shut the door and left me alone. The fact I wasn't in a wide tiled room with a dozen other girls was a good sign. Removing my shoes, I decided I would think positive. As long as Rowena brought me to safe places I would comply. If they tried to take me to a hospital or clinic, I'd fight like I did back in The Center. As much as I didn't want to be that person, I couldn't see another option.

I pulled back the shower curtain and turned on the water. Warm. Comfortable. A bottle of Johnson & Johnson baby wash sat on the wire shelf. Better than soap on a rope. This was a good sign. Everything was going to be okay. I'd take a bath and smell fresh and think positive.

Maybe I'd get hot food. The kind I could eat with a spoon or fork. I was not delusional enough to think they'd give me a knife to cut a fillet mignon, but I'd love some tomato soup with warm grilled cheese. Or fried chicken with mashed potatoes. Yum.

And a bed.

Yes, that would be great. No more thin-mattress cots for me. Bald and exhausted, soon I'd be clean and taken to a room where I could sleep on a bed with sheets and soft pillows. Comforts I had ignored in my old life were now the most glorious indulgences imaginable.

Water dripped down my face as I imagined clean clothes. Jeans or dresses or a cozy pair of sweatpants. No more green jumpsuits. I'd get to be a person again. Still an inmate, but a human one. And Dr. Maggie would give me the kind of past that would best benefit my unborn child.

I turned off the tap.

Steam escaped the shower curtain as I pulled it open. Rowena must have returned because my clothes were gone. On the wooden bench was a clean white towel. Only one, but as a bald person I wouldn't need a separate one to wrap my hair in. I dried off, looking forward to getting dressed, but the only article of clothing in the room was a dressing gown with yellow ducks on it. The pattern was infantile while the style was hospital. I could live with that, what I would never do was wear the pair of adult diapers the awful guard left as well.

CHAPTER 34

A chilly blast from vents above me trickled chills over my arms and legs. I pulled on the ducky gown and tied the strings. When Rowena said erase everything from my past, I'd thought I'd have some choice in the matter.

Huddling in the corner, I wasn't so sure.

I glared at Rowena as she entered. "Where are my underwear?"

Her friendly tone was gone. "Put the diaper on."

"That's not going to happen."

"You will either put it on, or I will."

"I think it would look better on you."

Rowena moved toward me and I slid along the wall to keep away from her.

"I don't want to, I don't. But I fought you in The Center, and if I have to, I'll fight you here."

"You are so predictable," she said with a small head shake. "You seem to forget, if it wasn't for your temper tantrums in the past, you might be above ground now."

"I haven't forgotten. That's the whole point. Don't you understand? I don't want to be here, and I don't know any other way to make you understand that." I raised my fist toward her only to find myself caught in her tight grip. Before I knew what was happening, she had my arm around my back twisting my wrist in the process. I wanted more than anything to struggle, but the angle of my arm made it nearly impossible to move without the monster snapping small bones.

"Listen, I don't make the decisions, my job is to enforce them. So, please put this on." She lifted the adult diaper and put it in my free hand.

"No, this is humiliating."

"You should have thought of that before you asked to come here."

"But I didn't think you'd make me wear a diaper," I said, tossing the offensive garment across the room.

"Do you honestly think that's the worst thing that could happen to you?" Her tone was layered with an accusation of entitlement and privilege. It made me wonder for the first time about who Rowena was as a person. Not the gruff guard, but the life that forced her to work in a place like this.

As if she sensed my softening, she released the hand from behind my back. "Have it your way," she growled and dragged me from the room, snatching the disposable underwear with her opposite hand.

Her vise-like grip stopped me from pulling away. I kept pace with her down the hallway and into an adjoining room painted red from top to bottom. Not a burnt sunrise red, but the color of blood when it first escapes a vein. A warm blast from vents covered me, but it didn't stop my chill. A soft whoosh, whoosh whispered through unseen speakers. Positioned in the center of the room, a black leather dentist chair rested, with metal straps at the wrists, waist, and ankles. I was never into horror movies, but I'd seen enough trailers to recognize danger.

"This isn't funny." I turned to confront Rowena, but she only held me tighter as she ushered me to the chair.

I dug my feet into the cement floor, but my bare skin only skidded with the more powerful force behind me.

"In the long run," Rowena snarled, "You'll wish you'd worn the diaper."

"Why are you doing this?" I trembled.

"You chose this, not me."

"But I changed my mind."

"We're beyond that point. Besides, I'm not talking about a rash decision you made this afternoon. You've made stupid rash decisions your whole life, it was all bound to catch up to you."

Rowena loosened her grip on my wrist long enough for me to pivot and swing my fist as hard and fast toward her jaw as I possibly could.

For a giant she was strangely nimble. The momentum from my missed punch propelled me into her ready arms. She bear-hugged both of my arms and lifted me onto the chair. I kicked, connecting with her shin. She ignored my attempt and flipped me onto my butt. I tried to kick her again, but her free hand grabbed my ankle and shoved it into an ankle cuff. The metal clicked closed like a handcuff mechanism.

"No. No. No. No." I did not want to be tied up. Couldn't be.

Rowena didn't answer. She pushed my head backward into the headrest, metal clinked around my neck. I reached to loosen it.

"The more you move, the tighter it gets."

She slammed my wrist onto the arm rest. I shifted to look. A click tightened around my neck choking me. A further struggle was pointless.

Click. Wrist number two was imprisoned. A buckle tightened around my waist. Rowena pulled the diaper up my free leg and clicked the cuff on the leg. She freed my other ankle and pulled the other leg into the cloth. She clicked my ankle into the metal before asking me if the restraint on my neck was too tight.

"Go to hell," I rasped.

"This didn't have to be this hard." She twisted a knob and the pressure around my throat lessened. "You haven't changed a bit. Always have to put up a fight." She clicked her tongue at me. "Dr. Maggie's going to have to be a miracle worker to change you." And with that she left me strapped to the chair, alone in the red room.

CHAPTER 35

From my prostrate position, I couldn't see much but the blood red ceiling. Squinting I could see the room wasn't only red. Someone had painted blue veins and flesh pink spots. The thumping sound I'd heard earlier continued. It wasn't hard to figure out what Dr. Maggie was about to do.

Bald head.

Diapers.

Thumping heartbeat.

I'd heard about reenacting birth before, but that didn't explain the diaper. Babies were born naked. I laid back, worried I'd be forced to eat baby food. I couldn't reach my belly to rub it. I'd become as frightened and vulnerable as my unborn child. He didn't ask to be imprisoned in me and I didn't ask to be strapped to this chair.

A nurse dressed in white scrubs came into view as she tightened the belt at my waist.

"Why am I tied down?" My voice squeaked.

She moved out of sight. "To protect you."

"I don't need protection. I'm good, I promise." Back in The Center, I was restrained because they thought I was suicidal, and those bands were made of cotton not steel. I was in a bed not a chair. Jackson was my guard not Frankensteina.

"I don't need protection." I repeated.

A metallic click.

Soft padded leather pressed against my cheeks.

"Please, I don't need protection."

She held my bald head with one hand as she clipped a strap under my chin. She released my head and laid a band across my forehead. The padding at my temples tightened as the restraints held me firm.

"I DON'T NEED PROTECTION!"

"Stop screaming it only makes it worse." Her voice was monotone.

She brought another belt across my chest. My heart raced.

"Please, why are you doing this?"

"We are prepping you for your rebirth." I felt her attach straps across my thighs.

"Do I have to be strapped for that?" Panic surged through me. "I didn't sign up for this."

"Yes, you did. This is step one to your new life." She walked from view and I heard the door close.

The whooshing increased while the scent of lilac the nurse carried with her faded.

"Hello?"

My voice bounced off the blood-red walls.

"Hello?"

I was alone. I made an unsuccessful attempt to move my legs. The bands tightened. Stupid. I should have stayed in Isolation. The straps against my chest prevented a strong inhale. The tips of my fingers felt like icicles. I watched the wall wishing for the ugly yellow paint from my cell. I missed my swans and my airplanes and my mural friends. Reconstruction was not luxurious. Reconstruction was not comfortable. Reconstruction was insane.

The door opened again.

"Hello?"

An arm raised a syringe and squirted a couple drops of clear liquid from the needle's tip. That would be inserted into my veins. I tried to lift my head as the needle disappeared.

"Wait. Stop!"

"It's okay." The nurse's voice. "It will help you through the transition period."

"I don't want help."

"That's not an option."

I could smell alcohol. A cold swab rubbed across the crook of my arm. Whatever help they were injecting into me wouldn't affect only me. My blood didn't belong to me alone anymore.

I screamed, "Stop! You will hurt my baby."

The nurse paused before saying, "Nice try."

"I'm serious. I'm pregnant. Ask Dr. Maggie."

"If you were, she would have said something."

"I am. I tell you, I am."

The needle remained frozen in the air barely in view. I couldn't see the nurse, but I could feel her thinking.

"Doctor?" Her question lifted to the ceiling.

"I'm coming." The angry voice of Dr. Maggie cracked through a speaker, sounding like Mr. Hyde. I'd only ever heard her that mad in The Center. Her flip-flop from Dr. Jekyll scared me then and she terrified me now, but I couldn't let the nurse inject me. I held my breath. The restraints dug into the side of my face as I attempted to see anything but the ceiling. I'd done a ton of stupid stuff in my life, but my decisions used to only affect me. Now I had a baby to take care of. A life other than my own. Making sure this kid was born safe and sound was critical. This was my chance to break the Manchester chain of control. I'd make sure this child ended up in a simple, middle-class family with a father who didn't travel. A mother who put dinner on the table at six o'clock. Parents who played family board games as a soft sun set.

I closed my eyes.

Bedtime would be announced.

And curfews would be enforced.

When the door opened, I wasn't surprised to see Dr. Maggie's head peering at me, rage seething behind her eyes.

CHAPTER 36

"What kind of game are you playing?" The doctor spit as she spoke. Restrained like a serial killer in an electric chair, I resisted the urge to spit back. This wasn't the time to fight, I had too much to lose.

With swallowed pride, I tried to convince her. "I'm not playing a game."

"We can get a urine sample."

"Yes! Yes! Do it." I'd pee in the diaper I was wearing if it proved my son's existence.

"You'd better not be lying to me."

"I'm not. Honest. I thought you knew."

"How could I know?" She paced away.

The restraints offered me no view of the psychiatrist. I had no ability to judge her intentions. The chair was designed for torture. My helplessness amplified with the sound of my oppressor's deep breathing and pacing.

"They did a blood test in The Center. It was positive. I'm pregnant. It's in my files."

"Your medical files are private." Resentment laced her tone. More shifting and pacing and breathing.

"Look, check behind my ear. There's a patch. Prenatal vitamins."

I winced as she jerked my ear forward to look.

This was my life. Dr. Maggie didn't really think she owned me, did she? Up until now I thought I'd get a new name, a fake ID, and a regular pair of clothes. But this was more. Dr. Maggie was trying to change me. Torture me. Control me. A smart woman would recognize a rejigged life would still belong to me. Reconstruction was only play-acting. Not real.

"Stupid HIPAA laws," she mumbled.

The story and scene she'd planned weren't working. I had become an uncooperative mannequin, the new dress she'd intended to put on me didn't fit.

A person this unstable shouldn't be in a position of power. But they were, weren't they, the nut-jobs, the sociopaths, the control freaks. They gravitated to the top like a dead body to the surface of a lake. Congress was full of them. Not my uncle, of course. The senator knew about The Center, but he couldn't know it all. He wouldn't let them perform these horrible experiments on me. Dr. Maggie had probably painted a pretty picture of her twisted reality. She'd misled him like she'd misled me. Of all the people in my family, Uncle John loved me. He'd always told me the truth. He'd always supported me. Once I got out of this place, the world would know everything. I smiled at the thought of her in front of a congressional hearing subject to the court of public opinion.

"What are the drugs for?" I stared at the red ceiling, wanting to gather evidence. Wishing I'd done more asking.

"They help the process, that's all." She said it offhandedly which meant she was still thinking. Still trying to decide what to do about me.

Surely other inmates had chosen Reconstruction days ago. I pictured people prancing around with fake smiles, drugged, and lost. I remember Jackson telling me about someone who'd come here as punishment from The Center only to return above ground like a zombie.

"You should have told me about the baby."

"I thought you knew," I said emphatically. A flutter tickled the inside of my belly. Whether it was nerves or my child kicking me in the gut, I didn't know.

A door opened.

Papers shuffled.

A foot tapped.

"Release her."

Relief should have overtaken me, but as the nurse loosened the metal bands from my head and chest and limbs, I felt more helpless. Unprotected. With my arms free, I crossed them over my stomach and sat up, thankful I wouldn't be choked again.

Dr. Maggie's hair frizzed chaotically around her face. Her eyebrows furrowed and she stared at the floor. She leaned against the wall, tapping her index finger on her bottom lip until she asked, "Why did you choose Bunkerville?"

I wondered for a moment whether I should be completely honest with her and tell her I wanted to escape thirty days of Isolation. But nothing in her demeanor made me believe I was safe in her care. Stuttering, I lied and said, "I, I, I want the dream."

"What dream?" She didn't shift her focus.

"A better future. A family with a loving father and mother. A safe place."

She rubbed her chin and said, "It's hard for me to get you there as effectively without the drugs."

"I'm not talking about me."

Her eyes narrowed. Distrust oozed from across the room. She blamed me for her ignorance about my condition. Let her. Right now, I needed to make sure she didn't do anything to hurt the baby.

"I want the dream." I repeated before adding. "But not for me, for my child."

"This isn't about the fetus."

"You're right." I said, knowing I was really ready to give the baby up for adoption.

"You should have told me about the pregnancy. You should have trusted me." The doctor pulled herself off the wall. Her face relaxed. Whatever she was struggling with before was gone.

"I honestly thought you knew."

"Well, I didn't."

"Sorry." Another lie. I couldn't be sorry. Her unpredictable personality could have been triggered by anything. If it wasn't the life inside of me, it could have been my choosing Truth first, or making friends with Jackson. I'd made a huge mistake assuming this was a safe choice. And while I chose this path because I thought it better than Isolation for the baby, it only put him at more risk.

I hadn't become his savior at all, the reverse had happened. My child had saved me from the invasive drugs and possibly worse. Dr. Maggie had to do more than inject a person in here or she wouldn't need the straps. The child might be my ticket out of Reconstruction. And once I was safe, I would take over the role and find a way to be his hero.

Dr. Maggie's face suddenly relaxed. Mr. Hyde retreated as her features softened to normal. She tipped her head as she spoke. "We can fix this problem."

"Wonderful, so no drugs."

"I didn't say that."

An involuntary shudder trembled through me as she smiled. "What are you saying?"

"I'm saying–" She held my hand as if to comfort me. Her creepy grin widened while my heart broke at her next words. The most gruesome words in the world. She stroked my hand when she said aloud, "–no more baby."

CHAPTER 37

Dr. Maggie turned and left me alone in the room before my brain could register her plan.

She wanted to kill my baby. Her matter-of-fact tone made it sound as if she were removing a wart, not abolishing a person. In my former life, I believed in abortion. A fetus had been nothing more than a lump of cells. Then I'd gotten pregnant and discovered how long term a one-night stand could last. I realized an abortion wouldn't erase my cavalier actions. Being pregnant would forever be part of my history. Discovering I was with child had been scary enough, I didn't want to add another traumatic event on top of it.

I scrambled from the chair and huddled in a corner of the red room. They were not going to easily restrain me again. Dr. Maggie wanted to kill my child as she sought to reprogram me.

Placing my hands flat against the wall, I wish I could go back. It was stupid to want to start all over. While getting pregnant wasn't intentional, staying pregnant was. Surrounded by red paint in a fake world, I couldn't force my mind to erase my history. I couldn't. Bunkerville wanted to reinvent me, to give me a better life than the one I'd had before.

Impossible.

The whole program was delusional.

My left leg shook involuntarily, so I rocked back and forth from one foot to the other. The best chance for my son's future would be to find the adoptive parents of my dreams. They could make it happen for my child.

I bounced my back against the wall.

Dr. Maggie would have to kill me before I'd ever let her kill this child.

On cue, the crazy psychiatrist returned.

I slid along the wall and made sure the horrible chair remained between us. I would battle her in the ducky-covered gown and diaper if I had to.

She didn't approach me. Her hair and lab coat had been smoothed, her voice calm. "I'm sorry about earlier."

I shrugged. I couldn't say, "no problem," because if she still wanted to erase my child, we would have a big problem.

Dr. Maggie occupied the chair I'd been strapped to earlier. She'd softened into her friendly counselor act. "I didn't mean to make it sound like I wanted to take away your choices. Your pregnancy surprised me, that's all." She smiled at me. I didn't buy it. "This isn't your fault at all. With all the high-tech record keeping we did in The Center, of course you would have thought I knew."

She'd have to hold the conversation herself. I wasn't about to help her out. I wasn't about to help anyone but my son at this point.

"I don't want you to think I'm trying to force you to do anything you don't want to do. I have no desire to hurt anyone. Honestly." She fingered a strap. "I got into this business to help people, not to hurt them. If you want to keep the baby I understand."

I remained still. She mentioned choices, but I wondered if life really offered any. I wondered if destiny or God or whatever made all our decisions for us. I didn't choose my parents. This baby didn't choose me. Where did choice really begin? One thing was sure, if I had a choice, it began long before my baby was conceived. And if Dr. Maggie wanted to offer her help, let her find him a better home than the one I grew up in.

"Look, I don't want to keep the baby."

She raised an eyebrow.

"I've decided to put him up for adoption."

She straightened. "I see."

I couldn't be sure what that meant.

She rubbed her chin.

I decided to take her calm as a good sign and said, "I'm sorry I let you down. I'm ready to go to my cell."

Her eyes darted up to my face, "Cell? What cell?"

"I want to return to Truth."

She shook her head and chuckled. "No, that's not going to happen."

"What do you mean? I want to go back."

"You've seen too much to leave."

Pinching my lips together, I nodded. The nerves on the edge of my skin tingled. Dr. Maggie opened the door. A guard waited for me. I was glad to see her, ready to get away from this place with its drugs and delusions. Nothing here represented birth–the blood walls evoked death more than anything else.

A shiver ran through me as I followed the guard away from the red room. I might be leaving but that didn't change the fact I was stuck in a series of unbelievably bad decisions.

CHAPTER 38

The guard took me down the gray cement halls to an office. Rowena plunked away at a typewriter. Without looking up, she pointed to a chair with her pencil and I sat.

The room had three desks and some old-fashioned filing cabinets, something I'd seen in dusty government offices my uncle took me to. Above ground, paper might have been replaced with electronic filing, but not in Bunkerville. This only added to my lack of equilibrium. My nerves felt like elastic bands pulled tight, waiting for something to snap hard enough to send me flying across the room. I'd done a ton of cruel things in my life and I deserved to be locked up. But nothing equaled the extent of punishment in this place. And while I might be guilty, my unborn child was not.

The sound of Rowena typing triggered memories of my mother tapping away on her computer keyboard. I didn't need a Truth projector to see Kat and my father playing tag in the yard. The sun's reflection glistening off the Potomac. Nanny Bella making homemade tamales. Uncle John in his

New York apartment. Would I ever get back there? If I did, how changed would I be?

Senator Manchester couldn't be fully aware of this place. He couldn't. He loved me. I had to hold onto my belief in his support. He was on my side.

Rowena pulled the paper from the roller and placed it in a folder and filed it. I tapped my foot, trying hard to be patient and aware.

The guard turned and looked at me. "You're not drugged."

The disappointment on her face annoyed me. "No, I'm not drugged."

"That's never happened before. What did you do?"

"I didn't do anything."

Her eyes narrowed.

In that moment, I had a choice to make, I could continue to fight with this woman, or help move this process along. "Not that it's any of your business," I snarked, "I have a medical condition."

"Dr. Maggie bought that?"

"Obviously."

"This will be interesting." She chuckled pushing the chair under the desk with a scrape.

A violent urge to get even surged through me, but I pulled it back. Be patient and aware, that's my goal. Punching and kicking hadn't helped me once in life and I needed to step deep into that knowledge. I had to be stronger and better. I bit the inside of my cheek to control the words I might say as she led me through the open door and through dungeon-like corridors to a dim wardrobe room.

Normal street clothes hung limp from metal rods or lay lifeless in bins.

"Undress," she barked.

"Here?"

The door clicked closed with Rowena on the inside with me. "Are you going to watch?" My slack-jawed stare didn't move her. Her eyes drilled me as she blocked the door.

"You're sick, you know that? Even if you didn't invent this place, you sure seem to enjoy watching people suffer."

She didn't answer.

"Whatever." I couldn't worry about the ugly guard right now. Ignoring her stoic frame, I weeded through the thrift-shop leftovers. The racks did not contain haute couture, but anything was better than this duckie robe. I climbed from the adult diaper and slipped into a pair of cotton briefs. I found a bra and tank to replace the hospital gown. From a stack of sweats, I grabbed a yellow hoodie to match a pair of jeans. As I zipped the fly, Rowena pointed to a suitcase.

"Load that up with whatever else you'll need for the next week. You won't get to go clothes shopping until then."

"Shopping?"

"Yes." She dragged the word out to make it sound like I was stupid.

I gathered a second pair of jeans as well as a cute summer dress and an extra bra. Some pajamas, tee-shirts, tanks, and underwear. "What about socks and shoes?"

"Socks are okay, but shoes are only available in the store."

The idea of stores gave me a glimmer of hope. Without drugs, maybe I could find a way to be calm in this place. Calm would be a nice change. Calm would help my growing child. Calm could come from doing the one thing I excelled at above ground, shopping. Hoping I hadn't fallen into some delusional thinking, I grabbed about ten pairs of socks, and a pair of slippers, zipped the bag closed and dragged it through the door Rowena held open for me.

We crossed the hall and entered the room opposite. As soon as Rowena flipped on the lights, I found myself face to face with the bald version of me.

Not good.

It would take a while to get used to such a look. My forehead was way too short. My shoulders sagged as my confidence melted. I'd thought I was tough, but I was only an oppressed inmate trying to fake it until I made it. This clown show held all the eerie falsehood of a painted grin and unmoving eyes.

Overhead lights exposed a long, thin makeup room with shelves of wigs and trays of goop.

"Choose a wig," Rowena pointed toward a wall of brownish-red tresses. "Stick as close to your natural color as possible."

"Why'd you shave my head if you planned on giving me a wig?" I wanted to keep her talking. I wanted her to play the gruff guard.

"The hair is for trips outside, that's all."

"Outside?" Hope surged through me before I had a chance to stop it.

The ugly guard smirked.

Witch.

She was messing with me. Her idea of outside meant Reconstruction wonderland. The phony country town. The fake sky. Rowena had obviously referred to the pretend outside with its props and televised landscape. Piped in birds and smells. I knew better. Behind all the scenery loomed cave walls. Within those walls, worms writhed. Slimy, nasty, disgusting worms and bat-pooped cave walls had been whitewashed in Disney designs.

I grabbed a wig without looking. Whatever. It didn't

matter whether I was a lab rat or a circus clown, I had to suck it up. I shoved the hair piece on my head, barely straightening it in the mirror. I would survive their crazy game. I bit the inside of my cheek. I could do this. I could.

Wearing hand-me-downs and synthetic hair, I followed Rowena deeper into the dank hall to an elevator. Inside she pressed the up button.

The ride was short, probably only one level, and I hurried from the freaky, fun house ride as soon as the ride ended.

My feet sunk into a swath of thick carpet as I stepped into a plush lobby. Under my feet, the shag throw rug covered a dark, hard-wood floor. At the reception desk, a smiling clerk worked at a typewriter. When Rowena opened the glass door, I got a whiff of an ocean breeze.

The smell carried me to my hometown of San Diego. But that couldn't be. I hadn't lived there since my junior year. Besides, an elevator couldn't transport someone from the depths of the earth beneath the Colorado Rockies to an ocean town.

Yet, beyond the glass lobby doors stretched a wooden deck. Beyond that, sand. Beyond that, waves. I sniffed again. Moist salt and seaweed overpowered a remnant of grit and dirt.

We stepped onto the wooden walkway. Stores on our left. A crashing ocean to the right. I shouldn't say ocean, it had to be an extra-large wave pool. Palm trees reached beyond the height of a ceiling. They had to be fake because real plants would need to have sunlight. The cry of a seagull or, actually, the soundtrack of a bird. People strolled the deck dressed in regular clothes, no one paid attention to us as Rowena took me a half block and into an apartment complex.

"You'll get your mail here." She pointed to twelve metal boxes.

"Mail?" That's nuts. Nobody was going to send me letters here. Nobody real anyway. I had stubbornly ignored all my family's letters when I was above ground, so they had to be too frustrated to send me letters down here. Besides, I had no idea how much anyone in Virginia or my uncle the senator knew about Bunkerville.

Rowena didn't answer my question about mail. I followed her up two half-flights of Mexican tile stairs. We walked down an open deck to apartment number nine.

"You have a doctor's appointment in the morning. Someone will be here to escort you." Rowena turned to leave.

"Wait."

She pivoted. "What?" she growled. I'd never seen the guard look tired before, but she did. Fatigue hung under her eyes in dark bags.

I wanted to ask her to stay. A crazy idea, but there it was. This place creeped me out. I didn't want to be left alone here. I wanted my cell. I wanted to have my own hair, not this stupid wig. I wanted to cry or scream, but after a moment of staring at the fake sea, nothing came out of my mouth.

A smile tugged at the corner of Rowena's mouth before she turned and descended the stairs, leaving me alone with two brass keys on a Mickey Mouse key chain.

CHAPTER 39

The small key was for the mailbox and the larger one fit the door. I unlocked the deadbolt and the knob and entered fully aware of the irony of being a prisoner who could lock others out of my cage.

The Center was the same with the dormitory rooms. The concept of being able to protect myself while bigger locks on thicker doors kept society safe from me didn't go unnoticed. The purpose of my being able to lock myself in was to make sure I was safe from other—possibly violent— inmates.

Looking over my shoulder, I hurried inside the apartment and twisted the deadbolt. Dropping the keys in a bowl by the door, I took a couple of deep breaths feeling safe for the moment. The memory of a Ray Bradbury novel I'd read in high school emerged. The girl in the story hurried through a ravine at night feeling sure she was being chased. She struggled at the door with her key, happy to feel safe inside her locked room only to have the bad guy grab her while inside.

No. No. No. Don't think like that Courtney.

Inside the apartment, I leaned against the door for at least five minutes. Listening for sounds of other humans. Maybe a neighbor. Maybe an intruder.

But nothing came but the sound of waves from outside. A soundtrack with birds. I took a handful of deep breaths as my legs grew tired of standing. If a bad guy lurked in this place, he wasn't breathing. I pushed off the wall and scanned the room for hidden cameras. My ugly yellow cell didn't have eyes, but in this place, I fully expected surveillance.

I thought The Center with its 20,000 cameras, taser bracelets and GPS shackles was high-tech, but this place upped the game. High-tech sound, smell, and image machines. If Dr. Maggie had gone to all this trouble, she was definitely watching. I tried to appear casual as I surveyed my environment. The small kitchen-dining-living room had Ikea-type furniture. Nothing special. To be honest, it looked like every other small apartment I'd ever been in. And most of those were in San Diego when I'd dated older men. But I didn't want to think about those days let alone digest one more drop of this insanity. I was tired. Seeing no obvious blinking red lights, I allowed exhaustion to sink my shoulders. I scanned the open floor plan, narrowing in on the hallway. Fatigue dragged me toward the door I hoped led to the bedroom. Camera hunting could continue tomorrow.

I opened the door.

A bed.

A place to sleep.

A place to dream.

Only, Dr. Maggie might try to control those too. A

butterfly kicked below my stomach. I rubbed the spot. "No problem kiddo, we'll be fine." I couldn't let that mess get into my head.

I scanned the room. The incredibly cozy looking bed was positioned opposite a dresser with a mirror on top. Small end tables flanked the bed with a lamp on each side. A plush area rug warmed the floor.

Furniture better suited for life above ground, not buried in make believe. The wall had a window. I was on the second floor of some kind of movie set. I shook my head. An enormous monitor with a setting sun hung across from a gigantic wave pool which lay beyond the window's wire screen. What was the point of the screen? They wouldn't have mosquitoes or flies underground. Unless they'd imprisoned those creatures as well. I slid open the window. The sound of surf greeted me. Well, fake surf with a fake breeze infused with moist salt. When I shifted from one side to the other, the horizon shifted with me like those creepy portraits with eyes following you as you move.

I shut the window.

Closed the curtains.

Keeping the real separate from the unreal would be tough.

Even the bed, pillows, and duvet with purple flowers made me leery. I crawled under the bedding, wondering if it would dissolve into rough burlap. A strange thought, but I came to question everything my mind saw. I remembered a Modern artist who painted a picture of a pipe and wrote "this is not a pipe," in French. The Modern movement was all about paint not pretending to be anything but paint.

I scratched my head and the wig shifted. I yanked the fake hair from my head and threw it on the floor. I curled up and touched the wall. A wall with no window. This wall, like my cell wall, wasn't pressed against real earth. The cavern containing this madness must be vast and empty and terrifying.

Loneliness crawled in beside me as I wondered who might be suffering in an apartment next to me in a drugged haze. Beneath the soft sheets, I missed my painted friends. With my hands curled in fists at my chin, I sank into an unsteady sleep.

CHAPTER 40

A soft light, mimicking the morning sun glowed through the window. The piped-in, seagull squawks replaced the cries and howls of other inmates.

Crashing waves replaced broken dreams.

"Just pretend," it all called to me. "Consider yourself blessed."

Only I couldn't. I wasn't.

An occasional daydream was one thing. Creating an entire fictional life was another. I was an inmate. This dressed up room was a cell.

Stepping from the warm blankets, I picked up the wig I'd dropped the night before and vowed I would never leave it there again, it looked too much like a dead animal. In the bathroom, I found not only a mirror with a sadly accurate reflection of my bald head and freckled face, but also a wig stand.

The mannequin's face head stared at me from the vanity. Poor thing was bald as well. I plopped the mop of hair on her head, covering her unblinking eyes. I spoke to the bust as I uncovered her face. "Don't get too comfortable."

The face stared at me.

"We've got to stay strong. Stay focused. A child's life is at stake."

As the hair smoothed out, the painted face appeared happier.

"What are you smiling at? We're below ground, not above."

I shook my finger at her.

"This is a set. Designed by people, not a real place."

I picked her up and made her face the mirror. Her puckered smile didn't change

"We are locked in a prison with a bunch of crazy people. This is no place for a baby."

She didn't argue with me, so I set her on the vanity. "You and I are only props and we need to remember that." I could tell from her eyes she understood. "I'll need this." I removed the wig. "But I'll give it back at the end of the day. Deal?"

She remained mute, so I removed the wig. "Deal."

Rubbing my belly, I left the bathroom, glad to have made a new friend. This entire escapade could be endured. Besides, I'd evaded the worst of it, and I would evade the rest. The disheveled bedding drew me closer. I straightened the flat sheet. As I fluffed the comforter, I remembered I'd never made my own bed before living in The Center. Nanny Bella cleaned up after me. If I visited Uncle John, he didn't care if my room was clean or not. He had a weekly maid who took care of my dirty clothes and linens as well as his.

But that was the old me, I'm a better person now. Someone who's really trying to think of others, not just myself. I straightened the covers and fluffed the pillow.

If I was going to survive, I had to hold onto the best of what The Center taught me and reach towards release. Not just for me, but for this little guy. I patted my still-small bump.

Within an hour, I was dressed and the clothes I'd gotten were hanging in the closet. I spent the next couple of hours searching for hidden cameras. I didn't care if Dr. Maggie could see me searching, my goal was to find them. But nothing. No lamps with a lens or false fire alarms. Every book on the shelf was a book. No bugs existed either. Nothing could record what I was doing or saying.

Rowena arrived as I'd finished making a peanut butter and jelly sandwich. I wiped the bread dust into my hands and threw it away.

"So," I decided to ask the guard directly. She'd shown she was willing to share her opinion about this place. "Tell me, do you know if this room is bugged or recorded?"

"I do know." She smiled as we exited the room and she clomped down the steps for me to follow her.

"And?" I hurried after her.

"There aren't," she said, marching quickly up the sidewalk. "Electricity in this place is worth more than gold. The only way someone knows what you're doing is if someone sees it and reports it."

My morning wasn't horrible up until this point, but the comment about town gossips reminded me of the book "1984." The Center had posters about Big Brother watching. But monitoring was only effective if the townspeople like to report subversive behavior. Up until now, this new world had tried to drug me. And Dr. Maggie had made it clear that she didn't want me to be pregnant. This baby wasn't in her plans for me. Would my neighbors lie for her? Kill an unborn child for her?

I wanted to run but didn't. A pointless plan. I had no idea of the consequences of trying to get out. Dr. Maggie said I'd seen too much. As a smart person, the best thing I could do was play nice. Keep my cool. Maybe Dr. Maggie would understand that I was already a better person than when I entered this place.

"So, Rowena," I said, "How was your night?"

"Very funny," she said as she marched along side of me.

"What?"

"Look let's not pretend we like each other. This place has enough illusions, you and I, we're clear on where we stand. Let's keep it that way, okay?"

"Sure." I shrugged. What did I care. It was Dr. Maggie I had to convince, not this grump.

The smell of grass and sand was bottled. Everything in this place came from something thrown away. A discarded past where people I loved lived in memories. The creators were doing their best to fool me. Including the uneven sidewalk.

We headed in the opposite direction from the barber and tattoo parlor. I stepped over a crack like an eight-year-old trying not to break my mother's back. The bench on my left had scratched paint. In the sky, no, in the ceiling, artificial clouds floated. I wondered how much of me could really relax.

The thought of Jackson popped into my brain and my step hesitated for a second. The kind guard dead because of me. Ribbon dead because of me. Thirty-one others dead because of me. I had no right to relax, no right to find peace. No, if I was going to become a better person, I needed to remember Truth. Needed to find my way back to serving my sentence.

And when it came to this child, I needed to give him a

better life. And Bunkerville was not it. I'd been selfish to want to keep him. Possess him. My only hope was to live up to Jackson's view of me. I could be a decent person. I could offer this child more than I'd had, a loving home with two parents who would give him all the love I never felt.

And as much as I was ready to sign adoption papers, I would never trust Dr. Maggie to do that. No. I needed to get word above ground of his existence. If a letter can arrive inside, maybe a letter could go out.

"Hey," I addressed Rowena in a chipper voice, "Remember you mentioned about getting mail?"

"Yeah," she huffed back.

We passed a deli. Garlic and onions and fresh-baked bread aromas floated in the air. I didn't hate it.

"Does that mean I can send letters to those outside of Bunkerville?"

"Sure, I do it all the time. The mail is super slow because it comes through with the weekly shipments, but it does get here and there eventually."

We turned into the lobby of a small clinic. A bell hanging from the door rang as we entered. Corny. They knew we were coming. No need to be announced. The nurse at the counter acted on cue.

"Can I help you?" She smiled.

"She has an appointment," Rowena pulled some papers from her back pocket.

The nurse finished typing the form in her IBM Selectric. Finally, she said, "Follow me."

I hadn't spent a ton of time in Dr. Maggie's cabin in The Center. But I'd been there enough times to recognize the pictures on the wall in this room. Marching elephants and African women painted on cloth. Pictures from a safari. Souvenirs from the surface of the earth.

But how?

Dr. Maggie made it seem like no one was allowed above ground. Yet here were her mementos. Parts of her above ground life. It was clear no matter what I said to this woman, she wasn't going to be honest with me.

Sitting on a different chair than the one above, I knew one thing. This wasn't going to be easy. The best way for me to survive was to remember this woman wasn't to be trusted.

Nothing down here was.

CHAPTER 41

The first time Dr. Maggie hypnotized me, I dreamed of Jackson. He gave me art supplies, told me he was proud of me for letting him go. I thought back then it was about the baby. I didn't know he was dead.

I sat up trying to determine where I was.

Not in the ugly yellow cell.

Not in the fake apartment.

Not alone.

Dr. Maggie didn't speak as I wiped drool from my mouth. "What happened?"

"You did great."

"What do you mean?" My legs tingled as I shifted on the couch in her office. I pushed my hand against my heart hoping to slow it down. I'd succumbed to hypnosis.

"You went under after only the second attempt. Impressive. I like having someone who hasn't been through the rebirth process and drugs. It validates my findings."

"I went under?"

"Yes, and you showed me what is important to you."

"Like?"

"Jackson."

I bent to pick up the wig, hoping to hide the blush burnt into my cheeks. My hand trembled as I smoothed the crumpled mop. This wasn't good. It wasn't. I had no idea how long I'd been hypnotized. The fake sun no longer shone through the office window.

"What time is it?"

"It's late. But don't worry. You've been alert through the process. We had deli sandwiches for lunch and pizza for dinner."

An empty box sat between us. The doctor probably meant for the words to comfort, but they terrified me. An entire day gone. Food and time unremembered. I had no idea what the mad doctor had asked me or what I'd said.

"As promised, I will not remove the memories about Jackson from your brain."

"No." I shook my head and waved my hands in surrender. "No. You've got it wrong." She'd told me I could keep the memories of one person, but as much as my heart was crushing on the cute guard, he wasn't the person I needed to remember.

"The subconscious doesn't lie." She closed her notebook and stood.

"Wait, yes. Yes, I think it can. It's my uncle, not Jackson." I appealed to her. "Uncle John is the most important person in my life."

"Is he?"

"YES!" Pulling a loose synthetic strand from my face, I made eye contact with the mad doctor. I couldn't have the only memory from my past be of a passing flirtation.

"Dorothy," she said in a calm voice, "You don't have an

217

Uncle John.

I rubbed my forehead and discovered what I thought was true only seconds ago seemed ludicrous. I did have an uncle and he was the senator from New York.

Or was he?

Vivid images of Jackson's face remained strong in my mind, but I couldn't for the life of me remember where we'd met.

Dr. Maggie calmly tapped a thick stack of papers on her desk before stuffing them into a manila folder. "Look, Dorothy..."

"Wait, why are you calling me Dorothy, my name is..." I searched for it. A word lingered on the tip of my tongue. A name I'd known only a moment ago had somehow evaporated.

"You've heard of John Manchester, but you'd never want him to be part of your family. Not if you knew what I do about him. He's a real person in the world, but unrelated to you."

"But Dr. Maggie..."

"My name isn't Dr. Maggie, it's Dr. Baum. You see you've got me confused with someone else. Can you tell me about this Dr. Maggie person?"

"Yes, she's... You're..." Again, words wouldn't formulate. Previously sticky ideas cracked and splintered. "I don't know." I put my head in my hands. "What's wrong with me, why can't I remember."

"You will," she touched my hand, "I promise. This process will all be over as soon as you have your surgery. The confusion comes from the tumor growing inside of your belly."

"A tumor?" I couldn't take it. This was too much.

"That's enough for today." The doctor stored the file she

was writing into a cabinet at the same time Rowena appeared in the doorway.

"No." I struggled to my feet and approached the doctor. "I'm confused. I need to have you help me understand." The senator she'd warned me about whispered into my mind and disappeared again. He might not be related to me, but somehow he was the most powerful person I knew. I didn't know what help I needed, but I knew he could do it if only I could get to him.

"Let's go," Rowena clamped my upper arm with her man hand and dragged me from the office.

I peeled at her fingers. "Let me go!"

"Glinda?" Dr. Baum lifted a small purse.

I looked around the room to see who this Glinda person was. No one else appeared. Only the three of us. Dr. Baum swung the small handbag on a thin string. "Take her to get some new shoes."

I stared at the swinging bag.

Shoes.

I blinked, not sure what I had been so upset about. The idea of buying new shoes filled my mind. Something hovered at the edge of my brain. Something I wanted to do or say, but it wouldn't come to me. It felt important. Then again, what could be more important than shoes? I grinned at the women. I waved goodbye to Dr. Baum and followed Glinda down the quaint streets wondering if this town had a designer shoe store.

PART IX

The Present

CHAPTER 42

I stop talking. My past was more than spotty. No matter how hard I try, no events except the ones I already shared exist.

Faith watches me.

Staring at the wall I say, "That's all I know." Studying my belly, I tell her, "Months of my life have disappeared. August, September, October, November, December. Where did they go?"

Faith whispers for the first time. "Are you sure no cameras exist?" She looks suspiciously around the room.

"Yeah, I've looked. Besides, as much as I don't want to trust Rowena, I do."

"She might not have been told." Faith continues to whisper, "Dr. Maggie did find you at her place."

"A neighbor must have seen us." I shift in my seat. "Look, if they are listening, it's way too late to do anything about it. We've been talking freely until now, let's continue to do that."

"Maybe the surveillance is down here." She says staring

at the table. "The Center sounds like a story. A made-up place. What if the 20,000 cameras you remember are here."

"The Center existed." I state firmly.

"Can you be sure?"

"Yes." I glare at her. "I lived there. It was real. I burned it down, remember."

"What if that was a lie? What if cameras are actually here?"

"Stop it. Bunkerville doesn't have the electricity to bug every house or monitor every resident. It would be an electrical nightmare. I think we are safe in here."

"I hope so." Her doubts aren't helping. "One thing your story has confirmed. Dr. Maggie wants to kill your baby, always has."

"I know that." I turn on her. "Trust me. The last thing I need you to do is question everything I say. You got that? This whole situation is bad enough."

She pulls away from me as if I might get violent. And the reaction only causes my fists to clench. Through gritted teeth I say, "Look, let's not talk about this anymore. I don't know anything else. Okay?"

My surrogate mother stands with her back stiff the way my real mother used to when she was mad at me. I walk away from her and head to the bathroom. The entire situation feels hopeless. Completely hopeless.

With the door closed, I balance my butt on the bathtub's edge and fight back tears. I don't have many choices. The woman in the other room is my legal mother if those documents mean anything. Which means I have to trust her and her husband, whom I've never met, to free me from here. To save this baby.

I stare at my toes. I can't trust my shoes. Although they have been kind to me. But, no, Courtney, don't do that. Don't even think of the word.

I have to place myself fully into the power of someone else. I look at the wig stand. "But isn't that what I've been doing since I've been incarcerated? Haven't I placed my trust in others and look where it's gotten me."

Her pursed lips indicate she concurs.

"But this is different, right? Oh my gosh. I never thought I'd miss Uncle John or Nanny Bella, or even father and mother as much as I do right now."

I study the floor. Maybe it's time to make friends. Not the high school, petty friendships of my past, but with people who aren't motivated by my violence or manipulation. Faith scares me because she seems to want to make me believe I'm worth knowing despite my past.

A light tap on the door.

I say, "Come in."

Faith peeks at me, "You okay?"

"Yeah," I say because what else is there to say.

My only hope of escape leans against the frame. "What if we solicit Rowena to help. She seems to think this is all a charade."

"No. She's a rule follower. She might not like what's happening here, but she would never help a convicted felon escape."

"Then, it will be up to my husband and me."

"And what will you do with me above ground?"

"We will contact your parents and the authorities. We'll fight to find you a decent place to finish your sentence. A reliable adoption agency, if that's really what you want. Look, all of us have done horrible things in our lives, but I still believe more good guys exist in the world than bad."

"I hope you're right."

CHAPTER 43

Faith and I return to the dining room table.

"Dr. Maggie is crafty and determined. She's not going to let us just walk out of here, no matter what you signed."

"Then we'll have to make a scene. Statistically, not all these people would support her plan. I think if they knew, they would rally against her rather than for her."

"You want to trust our escape to the masses? No way. That's too big a gamble. We can't trust anyone here. No one."

"What about your former roommate, what's her name? Glinda?"

"Rowena, her name is Rowena." And Faith didn't know the full story between me and the former guard.

"But she's the one who drew your attention to your pregnancy. She's obviously not on board with Dr. Maggie's plan."

"Yes, and Dr. Maggie knows it."

"But Rowena was trusted by the doctor at one time. She

did make her your roommate."

I laugh, "That backfired, didn't it?"

Faith laughs too. "Sure did. I think you have an ally in that guard."

"Maybe, she's definitely the reason I'm no longer hypnotized." I sigh. "What she didn't give me was what happened to me since August."

"I might be able to fill you in."

I threw her a skeptical look.

"Dr. Maggie," she says, "who I knew as Dr. Baum, reached out to us in late September. The interview process took about a month. And then my husband's current project wouldn't end until January. I think she's been looking for parents, prepping all of us for this reinvented life."

"Prepping?"

"Your background, all fake, your medical condition. All stuff she made up. Stuff she's probably been implanting into you. The same history she provided to us would have to become your history for this to work."

"And what about the baby? Why hasn't she taken it by force?"

"I don't think she has as many allies as you do. It would be hard to find enough people to support her taking your child against your will. Two real camps exist when it comes to pregnancy. One is for the rights of the child, so they wouldn't help. The other is for the rights of the mother, and they wouldn't help if you didn't sign off on the choice."

"So, she invented the tumor."

"Yeah, she needs you to sign the papers for the procedure. And from what she told me and my husband, you've been reluctant to do that. It's what got us to come support you. I thought you were a recovering addict who didn't realize an invasive tumor could kill you. I came early to help convince you."

"And you were willing to accept me as your own daughter?"

"Yes. As it was explained to me, you had a horrible past and wanted to reinvent yourself. She was looking for surrogates to aid you through rehabilitation. I assumed for drugs, not crime. Either way, you would still have to choose us when we came. We would have no financial obligation toward you because you're an adult. And she said you'd been trained to not expect your parents to fund your adult life. I never had an idea she was "training" you through hypnosis. She's been lying to both of us about that. But the rest sounded perfect. We would give to each other as we felt called. She was clear about wanting you to be loved sincerely, not via obligation."

"So, you and your husband will not receive any financial compensation?"

"No. None."

"What's in it for you?"

"To help another human being. To become a surrogate family support network for someone in need. That's what made me like the program and Dr. Baum so much. Her heart really believes in this program."

"Don't make her sound altruistic."

"Look, no one is all good and no one is all bad. I believe she's a human with an altruistic plan she's taken too far."

"She's an extremist who's trying to kill my child."

"I'm not disagreeing with you."

"Sounds like it. Sounds like you admire her."

"The enemy you know is better than the enemy you don't. You have to see her for all her layers."

"No, I don't. She's insane, and you can't play with crazy."

"Look, if you can't see all sides of her, you will not be able to escape this place."

"I'm going to be straight with you. I don't think I will escape. You're a sweet person. But there's no way Dr. Maggie will allow me to leave this place." I get up and move away from her. I'm new to trust and I'm new to making friends like this and I don't like it. I don't like feeling unrealistic hope. "This place is like Alcatraz." I say, "No one escapes."

"Sounds like all we need is a fork."

With that crazy statement, the apartment door clicks. The lock disengages. The false feeling of freedom only solidifies how truly trapped I am. And as much as I want to trust Faith, her words sound too good to be true.

CHAPTER 44

Outside the window people happily step into the sunshine, going about their day as if Bunkerville were real and friendly and not a crazy asylum run by a lunatic dressed in altruism.

"Courtney," Faith stands beside me. "Do you know about the only three men known to escape Alcatraz."

I don't answer.

"All they had was a fork. When no one was looking, they dug tunnels from the vents. They made paper mâché heads to represent them when they slept. These heads were there when they were discovered missing."

"Didn't they drown in the Pacific Ocean?"

"Maybe they did, maybe they didn't. But if they did, they drowned free men."

"Are you really telling me you are going to help a convict escape a prison?"

"I'm going to help a pregnant girl save her child. As I said, you will still need to finish whatever is left of your sentence. And I can't speak for my husband, but I will tell you, wherever that is, I won't be far away."

"So, how? How are we going to get past the Wicked Witch and her flying monkeys?"

"Throw a pail of water on her?"

"Very funny." I watch the ocean waves through the window. "Although..." A plan formulates in my brain. "What if we did find a way out. Like Truman did in the Truman show." I point. "Beyond the wave pool is an LCD screen. Beyond the are cords and panels and those places would need to be maintained." I let hope in. "What if we swam to the edge and found a backdoor?"

"Only one problem," she says, frowning. "I can't swim."

"What do you mean you can't swim?"

"I had an aunt who died in a boating accident in Utah before I was born. My father hated the water, from then on. He refused to let me anywhere near a lake, ocean, or swimming pool. He considered water extremely dangerous."

I drop the curtain.

"Courtney, I really think the plan I told you was best. My husband and I have legal custody of you, and we will inform the good doctor we would rather you have your surgery above ground."

"You want me to continue to pretend."

"I want you to trust us to get you out."

"And when she disagrees? Because she will disagree."

"We make a stink. A loud stink. We disrupt Bunkerville with announcements of what she's doing. Trust me, many of these residents aren't inmates. Many of them are patrons who pay big bucks to live hidden away and the last thing Dr. Maggie wants is a scandal."

"But she told me I knew too much to leave. She won't let

us go."

"She will if you sign a non-disclosure agreement. My husband and I already did. This place is private and I'm sure other people have come and decided it wasn't for them. But no one in the world knows why and it all has to do with legal documents enforcing silence."

"That means I have to pretend."

"Yes, only until my husband gets here."

"But I have an appointment with her tomorrow."

"Yes, right before my husband comes. It's only for an hour."

"How do you know?"

"Because the itinerary allows us this day to get to know each other. For you to take me around the town. Then tomorrow is a big picnic celebration for your birthday."

"My birthday?" I search my synapses for the actual day of my birth. "Is it my birthday?"

"Maybe not your real one, but Dr. Baum told me your father would arrive in time for a surprise picnic on the beach. All we have to do is play along."

"Easy for you to say. I have to sit in an office with a woman who can hypnotize me with a pair of shoes. I don't want to be left alone with her."

"It's the only way." She takes my hand. "Look, from our conversations this morning, you have no reason to trust me, but it's very possible I'm your fork. The only way to save your baby and get you both out of this horrible place."

CHAPTER 45

Faith chooses an outfit from my closet. I close my eyes as she ties my shoes.

"I'm feeling peaceful and I don't want to," I tell her as my mind wanders towards calm and happy thoughts.

"Think of the baby." Faith warns.

Baby?

"Think of home, your real home."

Isn't this my real home?

I open my eyes and look at Faith differently. "But mother," I say, "I am home." And for the first time in what feels like days I relax.

"Wow, this trigger is really strong."

I don't know what to say to that. I don't want to say anything. I want to rest for a moment and breathe. To really experience the calm.

My mother's voice softens, "I'm going to try something, and I want you to tell me if it works."

Before I can answer, a sharp pain surges through my

toes.

"Owwww." I push her away and rub my foot as peace ebbs away. "Why would you do that?" All feelings of calm slip away.

"What's your name?"

"Huh?"

"Your name?"

"Why? My foot really hurts."

"That's because I stomped on it, Courtney."

"You what?"

"Yes, I stomped on it. What is your name?"

"You said it, it's Courtney."

"And who is Dorothy?"

While my toes still throb, I remember, and terror surges through me. "No," I say to her. "No. That was too fast. Too fast. What the heck? No. I can't wear shoes. I can't." I reach to take them off when Faith grabs my hands.

"You have to." She takes my face in her palms and directs my attention to her. "Dr. Maggie will know I know if you go out barefoot. She can't know. She can't. We have to pretend until the picnic. The shoes are a strong trigger, but pain is stronger."

"You're going to stomp on my feet when I go under?"

"Sometimes, I think I have to."

I love and hate the idea. I've never been one to take a punch, always been one to give it. I hold my belly and decide, it's time to embrace the pain necessary to save my baby's life.

"Now let's go for the walk."

"And if I go under?"

"I don't know, maybe you could stub your own toe?"

"Kick a rock?"

She shrugs.

In the end, our excursion is uneventful. I have no friends to introduce to her. At the beach we stay on the boardwalk due to her fear of water. We buy fresh fish for dinner and intentionally avoid the shoe store. And whenever a wave of peace comes over me, I kick at rocks and poles and any hard surface I can find. And with sore toes, we return to the apartment where I am still Courtney, the pregnant inmate.

CHAPTER 46

Today's the day.

I'm wearing my Keds because they are soft enough to stub my toe. They also cover the bruises I gave myself yesterday and contain the coffee stains courtesy of Rowena. A memory tied to the baby and a reminder that as much as entering a hypnotic state for me is easy, I still have the power to escape it as well.

At 9:15, a guard shows up ready to take me to my appointment.

"Where's Glinda?" I ask hoping my tone of voice matches Dorothy.

"She's been transferred."

"To where?"

"That's not my business." The guard is obviously not open to further conversation on that topic, so I say goodbye to my mother.

"I'll see you later today."

"Okay." I wave. We practiced being mother and

daughter all morning. No more calling me Courtney. No more calling her Faith. I'm Dorothy and she's Mom.

Navigating Bunkerville, I paste a plastic smile on my face until we reach Dr. Baum's office. Because that's who she is, not Dr. Maggie. In this drama, she's Dr. Baum.

The pretend sun doesn't fool me. I desperately want to be impenetrable. To not get stuck in a state where I'm fooling myself. And while I try to imagine myself strong, I don't believe I've ever been more nervous to face anyone in my entire life. The best way to not get lost again is to convince the psychiatrist, I'm still under her spell

The woman has the power, means, and need to keep me hypnotized. And if she does it, my entire fate and the life of my child sits in Faith and her husband's hands. Until we get free of Bunkerville, I'm at the mercy of another. A stranger who came to help me.

I kick a rock as hard as I can, and it bounces against a wooden fence.

"Hey," the guard says, "Why'd you do that?"

"I don't know." My answer sounds childish. "Is there a rule against kicking rocks?" I allow aggression in my tone.

"No," she squints at the fence. "I was surprised, that's all."

I don't speak.

Any answer might not match the kind of answer I should give. Kicking the rock was a risk, but worth it. My toe hurts and I am fully in my mind Courtney for that moment. I rub my stomach and pray as if I am Nanny Bella.

We enter the foyer and the nurse takes my papers. She points to a seat. "Dr. Baum will be with you in a moment."

"Thank you," I say and sit. The guard leaves and I pick up a magazine. Not to read, but to present myself as casually as possible. The moment reminds me of the anxious wait in a long line at an amusement park before getting on the scariest ride they offer. I feel I am about to be pulled from my feet in a harness five stories into the sky and dropped. The waiting and watching people fly then puke is worse than the two mins of losing your breath and having your stomach rise to your chest.

By the time I am escorted into Dr. Baum's office I am ready to get on the ride for the sole purpose of getting off it.

The scent of grapefruit tickles as I sit in the chair opposite the doctor's desk. I'm suddenly suspicious of smells. They could be another means of controlling me.

So could the chair, or the desk, or the words.

Soft canvas straps and a comfortable insole kept my feet safe. Safe. My brain relaxes. I open my eyes. Dr. Baum stands beside me adjusting her cat-eye glasses. Her warm brown skin stretches into a soft smile. My heartbeat slows.

"How are you this morning?"

"Nervous," I answer honestly.

"About what?"

"Meeting my father."

"That makes sense. What has your mother told you about him?"

"He's an actor."

"What does he look like?"

"I can't picture his face. I can't remember his voice. I wonder if he will like my wig."

Dr Baum pats my leg. "He knows you've been sick. A loving father doesn't care about things like that. He's here to see you. He's worried about you."

"My father named me Dorothy," the words fall from my mouth like a gasp. Involuntary. Yes, my name was Dorothy...

I blink my eyes open. When did I close them?

Dr. Baum smiles at me. A gentle smile. I love her curly hair. She's so sweet. The nice doctor has told me a hundred times—very patiently, I should add—I am getting better. Soon all the confusion in my head will dissipate and my thoughts connect like the pieces of a jigsaw puzzle.

"Ready to go?" She inclines her head toward the door.

"But I just got here." I rub my belly, a strange habit I can't seem to stop.

"You've been her for an hour and it's time to go."

I stand up. Of course, it's been an hour. Why would I think anything else? "Are we going to see my father now?"

"That's right."

I reach toward my neck. A reflexive gesture. "Didn't I used to have a necklace?"

"That's kind of a vague question." Dr. Baum tips her head sideways. "I'm sure over the course of your life you've had many. Can you be more specific?"

My hand moves from my throat to my forehead. Rubbing at the wrinkled worry, I try to remember. But I can't find anything more specific. Nothing.

"Maybe you're thinking of the turquoise beads."

I shrug, that string is new. No, this is something older, more sentimental. The image of a handsome young man forms as a shadow in my thoughts. He stands on a mountain top.

"You did have a gold chain that matched your summer sandals."

I glance at my feet covered in stained white canvas. A blend of confusion and peace battle within me. The shoes are supposed to tell me something. I made eye contact with the doctor.

"You okay?" The sweet lady touches my arm.

"Yeah, I'm good."

I don't tell her about the confusion. I like the smile on her face too much. And although I can't really put my finger on it, I know if I tell her the truth, the smile will evaporate.

CHAPTER 47

Outside the sun is bright. I close my eyes and allow its warmth to stifle my discomfort. Bouncing on my toes, I embrace the soft cushioned sole. The smell of sand mixes with coconut oil. A couple dozen people populate the beach. "Wow, a lot of people are here today."

"They came for you."

"For me?"

"Sure, we have a big surprise." Dr. Baum puts her arm around my shoulder and squeezes.

"Is it my birthday?"

"Yes, how'd you guess?"

"I don't know. The idea popped into my head."

"Did your mother say anything?"

A young girl with pigtails waves at me. I lift my hand and ask, "How do these people know me? I don't have any friends."

"That's because we wanted you to get better first. Today is your birthday. A new beginning brings together people who can help support you through the rest of your life."

A volleyball bounces across a net as a foursome kick up sand to chase after it. Others splash in the water or lay on blankets on the sand. Each person who happens to look at us stops what they are doing and waves at me.

I reflexively lift my hand to acknowledge them. But they are all strangers to me. "Where did they come from?"

"Some live in the neighborhood. Others visit people they know who live here." Dr. Baum's excitement resonates through her tone. "They all want to support your special day."

A warm glow tingles its way from my toes to my heart. Love is such a wonderful feeling. In a sideways hug, I squeeze my kind doctor back. She's been so great. I honestly can't remember the last time I felt so cared about. Of course, that doesn't mean I haven't been. The blank spots in my memory would soon be filled in. We turn away from the beach and up the wooden walkway to a garden I've never been to. Off the boardwalk a cluster of palm trees protect a private picnic area.

"We're here." She extends her hands with the excitement of a small child. Her energy elevates mine. The scene is picture perfect. The small path opens to a perfectly situated scene.

The grass on the side of the path is thick and green.

The sky above our heads is a complimentary blue.

The palm trees aren't as tall as those in town, but still reach high enough above our heads to create shade with their wide leaves.

The path bends before opening to a hidden garden. Neatly placed picnic tables — at least ten — are covered in red and white checkered cloths. On them are wicker baskets and brightly colored presents. A couple coolers rest near trees. The people stop setting up and wave at me.

I want to remember them. I fight to recognize their features. Try hard to think of names. Everything is foggy. Every face unfamiliar.

Until.

I spot a guy leaning against a palm tree all alone.

My heart races.

I know him.

He holds a toothpick to his mouth and chews on it. Once we make eye contact, he throws me a smirk that sends shivers down my spine.

The hum in my ears accompanies a vise-like pressure to my temples. I squint in the direction of my doctor, but she's out of sight. I back away until I can see her at the top of the boardwalk helping a woman drag a red cooler toward the path.

The pressure in my brain releases.

My doctor's name isn't Dr. Baum, it's Dr. Maggie.

The woman with her isn't random, it's my surrogate mother, Faith.

I'm here to meet my new father.

It's obvious I slipped into hypnosis in Dr. Maggie's office, but I'm not sure what caused me to slip out. A guy, next to a tree. Not just a guy.

Fisher.

The rapist from The Center.

His horrible leer yanked me back into reality. Like pain, my brain would only pretend so much. But the idea I might be attacked again has helped me become fully alert. Alert enough to protect myself from a predator.

CHAPTER 48

Fisher and I entered The Center on the same day as Ángel and Dee Dee.

Fisher, the guy leering at me from a nearby tree, is a violent criminal who tried to rape me in The Center's forest.

Fisher, who got sent to The Bunker before the forest fire and has been down here ever since.

Every wisp of fog clouding my brain is gone. His presence verifies Dr. Maggie's lunacy. She must believe she can transform a repeat rapist, or he would not be here. Stalking Bunkerville for his next victim. Possibly living in the same apartment complex as me.

All her pretense of care for those who live here vanishes. It's one thing to try to kill an innocent baby. People do it all the time. Abortion is acceptable in the United States. But rape isn't. And by the look in his eye, Fisher plans to rape again.

Yet he's free to roam Bunkerville. He's probably pretending to be hypnotized like me. Only, he might not be as susceptible to going under.

Fury rises from the tips of my stained shoes.

Sitting at the picnic table furthest from him, I turn away. I can't look at him and stay calm. He probably has figured out I've reclaimed my mind. With him on the prowl, I need to stay alert. Fully alert. I'll let Faith know once it's safe to do so.

My nerves tingle. I want to glance back to make sure he's not approaching me, but the risk is too huge. I keep my eyes and smile focused on Dr. Maggie and Faith as they stroll up the path. The two women laugh. It's not the cackle of witches, but a creepier sound. They crack up like they are old friends at a real picnic.

Fisher's presence has saturated the party with doubt. Is Faith really going to help me escape? She told me she wasn't an actor like her husband. Yet seeing her and Dr. Maggie together, it's as if they've known each other for years.

More than know, they like each other.

As if this is a real beach party, free of violent attackers on the periphery. Their lack of awareness makes the hair on my nape bristle. I rub my belly and tell myself Fisher won't attack me in this crowd. He prefers a more isolated moment.

Dr. Maggie and Faith drop the heavy cooler and sigh.

I fight to drop my paranoia. I'm not a poker player, but I have to find a way. I force happy thoughts into my head and pray they permeate through my eyes.

"Hi, Dorothy, honey." Faith leans over and hugs me.

I hug her, tempted to whisper that I'm alert. But I don't. I don't know if she was only pretending with me back at the apartment, or if she's pretending now.

"What a great setting." Faith says and I follow her eyes across the staged picnic area braving a glance toward the tree.

No Fisher.

Not good. Snakes are better kept in view.

I survey the landscape with more intent.

People begin to come up the path, dusting sand off their swimming suits, drying wet hair with towels. Everyone is smiling and I force my lips to mimic their greeting.

The people I'd like to see aren't in the crowd. Rowena's been transferred. Ángel works in the prison. He's the one who saved me from Fisher in The Center. He would be my best ally in this situation.

"Do you recognize anyone here?" Dr. Maggie asks.

"No," I say in a soft voice. "I don't recognize anyone."

"Don't worry, the puzzle pieces will all be filled in."

The phrase means more since I'm fully awake. When Dr. Maggie speaks of puzzles, she's talking her landscapes, not mine. I exhale.

"Well," Faith claps her hands together. "I think you'll remember that guy over there."

"That's right." Dr. Maggie places a maternal hand on my shoulder. "Here comes your father."

Faith jumps up and hurries to embrace my surrogate father. He picks her up in his arms and swings her around. The thought of swinging equaling love echoes in my brain. The painful memories of my own father's rejections stab at my heart.

And when the swinging is over, I fully expect to see the unknown face of a stranger coming toward me. I'm not supposed to know his face, but I do. And not from being underground.

I pinch my lips together.

This day can't get worse.

My surrogate father is none other than Stan the Man.

Yeah. I know him. He is an actor from San Diego who

does insurance commercials. Anyone might have recognized him for that reason. That's not why I know him. I know the jerk because we met when I was fifteen. To say we met would be an understatement.

I pick at the plastic tablecloth.

My potential father and I have more than met.

The summer of my sophomore year, we had sex.

CHAPTER 49

In high school, I wasn't intentionally promiscuous. The sex I had with a couple dozen different guys—a number hard to admit to myself—happened almost by accident. They whispered loving phrases, and I desperately wanted to be loved. Before moving to Virginia, I naively believed these men loved and wanted to marry me. They all turned out to be users. Stan the Man was no different. He wasn't my first. That was Kurt Foster, when I was twelve. Stan was one more in a long line of losers my adolescent heart believed could love me. And like in movies, this would be the one who would make me his wife.

The actor didn't call or visit after our night in a sleazy hotel. I blamed myself, although I know I was too young to recognize the predators or the players.

The creepy jerk approaches the bench.

I watch my fake mom, no longer trying to hide my awareness.

"He's here," She pulls me into her arms. Her hugs are

genuine with the ability to reach past my skin and embrace my very soul. My arms tighten and I squeeze her back.

Not for one second.

Not for two seconds.

I don't let go for at least thirty.

I hold onto her while real tears stream down my face. The crying isn't an act. I weep because it hurt to remember who I used to be. Gullible. Angry. Stupid. It aches to remember how unwanted I had been. How unwanted I still am.

"It's okay." She pats my back and lets me linger in her embrace. My real mother would never, ever, ever have allowed that. I tried a million times in a million ways when I was small to understand all the distance I felt from my real parents. They are so kind and loving to Kat, which only drove the knife further into my heart.

I can't go there.

I have to focus.

I'm alone and the only way out of here is with skills I've never had, like direct honesty.

I release the kind woman who shared the morning with me, knowing I would need to find a way to exit Bunkerville by myself. "Thank you." I step away and wipe my face.

With my chin up, I face my fake father. I give him a moment to recognize me. But he doesn't.

"Hey, Stan," I say matter of factly, "How you been?"

His chin disappears into his neck as he says, "My name's not Stan." He coughs and looks at Dr. Maggie. He's not talented enough to pretend surprise. He truly doesn't remember me.

My fists clench and I force them open.

Violence isn't going to work in this moment. Even though I feel it rising. This buttwipe took what he wanted from a 15-year-old me and walked away erasing me from his memory. "I was blonde back then." I tug on my wig, ready to pull it off. Faith grabs my hand and holds it. Her grip is soft and firm. "You don't have to do that."

I look into her eyes.

She asks me from a painful place, "Do you recognize him?"

"No and yes."

Dr. Maggie comes closer. "Is everything okay?" She leans in.

"It's fine," Stan clears his throat and speaks in a fake deep baritone, "My little girl is confused. Doesn't quite recognize dear old dad." He smiles and reaches for me.

I jerk away in disgust. If I believed in God, I would have thanked him right then for letting me see Fisher. For pulling me from the fog. One perpetrator helped me recognize another. I face Dr. Maggie. "I know this man."

"Of course, you do," she replies.

"Not because he's supposed to be my father." I stare into the doctor's eyes. She needs to see I'm not under her spell. "I know him from my past. This woman…" the words catch in my throat. I swallow and squeeze the hand still holding mine. "She could be my mom." My hungry soul refuses to deny someone so real. I puff out a deep breath to dispel the steady rise of connection inside of me. "My heart honestly feels that."

Dr. Maggie adjusts her cat-eye glasses.

I maintain eye contact with her. "This man could never be my father."

"Dorothy, I realize you're confused." Dr. Maggie's voice is stern.

"My name's not Dorothy, it's Courtney."

Dr. Maggie moves toward me, but Stan's wife stands between us. "It's okay." She offers me a gift the size of a shoebox. My new mother is more committed to this story than I know how to be. "Your father brought you a present."

"He can't be my father."

"Why?" It's the actor who asks the right question.

"Because, Stan, I wouldn't have had sex with my father." The message drops from my mouth like a bomb.

The fake world goes silent.

Faith drops my hand.

Dr. Maggie audibly exhales.

Stan stutters, "What. No. What? Come on. Who is this girl?" He paces around in a circle. And while he might not know me specifically, he probably "doesn't know" a dozen girls my age.

"Stan?" Faith's question shakes with an anger implying knowledge. Comments she made about her husband during our sequester materialize. This wasn't a happy family.

I shiver. Not because I'm cold, but because she didn't deserve this. Her desire to help someone through recovery was not only genuine, but was lost to me forever. My past couldn't be erased. Dr. Maggie's crazy experiment was impossible. She might have embraced a new family, but that was after meeting them. Connecting with them. Like me and Dee Dee.

But this, bringing in actors who weren't paid to pretend to be related, is beyond reality. Am I supposed to live in Bunkerville for the rest of my life? Would Faith and Stan visit me as if I really lived in a real place? How can someone so delusional get backing and buyers and people like the dozens staring at us now? Do they all sign up to play act in a buried world? The level of crazy grows exponentially in my mind.

"Let's go," Stan reaches for his wife's hand which she forcefully rejects. "What? Are you seriously going to believe this piece of trash over me? She's obviously lying." He kicks a bench and storms around. "I don't know this girl. I've never been to Virginia." He turns to Dr. Maggie. "Come on, help me out here."

The doctor ignores him and directs her attention to me. "Courtney, what kind of game are you playing?" Her glare indicates she would take the word of any random jerkwad over me.

"It's not a game. I met him in San Diego the summer before my sophomore year of high school."

Faith lowers herself onto the picnic table. Dr. Maggie watches her do it without moving her face. Eyes toward the bench, then back on me.

I continue my confession. "We met at Balboa park. He took my number and we a talked a couple times. We planned a date. He took me to a movie and after we wandered through Horton Plaza, we ended up in a cheap motel off Pacific Coast Highway."

I hate myself.

"You bastard." My never-to-be surrogate mother lunges off the bench at her cheating husband. "A teenager?" She pummels him with hits and slaps. "I spent a lifetime believing your lies. Lies about all-night script sessions with single actresses. All the phone numbers and motel visits you said were necessary to your work." She faces Dr. Maggie. "I'm an idiot. I believed he could change. I believed what I wanted to. Ignored the red flags. The warning from my gut." She turns and without hesitation slaps Stan across the cheek. The flat smack echoes, reminding me we're in a cave. "But a high school girl? Teenagers? You filthy creep." She pushes him and turns to a guard who has made her presence know. "That's statutory rape. Arrest him."

Dr. Maggie and I stand stunned.

Stan curses and paces the underground grass. "Get me out of here. I want to leave now!"

Faith crumples into a heap on the bench. "Arrest him," she screeches.

Dr. Maggie grits her teeth and whispers to herself with her jaw clenched. "Reconstruction doesn't work without drugs." She glares at me like I was back in the red room, before signaling the guard to take Stan away from the scene.

My counselor stabs her finger toward me. "Stay put."

I do.

She helps Faith up and leads her away from the garden as other guards quietly escort the crowds away from me.

Gulls squawk from speakers. The ocean crashes in recorded waves. My Reconstruction party is over and so are any additional plans for escape.

CHAPTER 50

I wait in the garden, staring at the empty tables.

In the distance, I hear splashing and indistinct voices. People in Bunkerville have returned to their volleyball playing, sunbathing, ocean swimming lives as mine returns to isolation.

Dr. Maggie is gone long enough for me to recognize the soundtrack loop. For at least the third or fourth time, the ocean birds repeat themselves, just like my life. I'd been to bed with so many men The Bunker couldn't find a random actor without picking someone I slept with. I deserve to be buried this deep. I'm scum and dirt and worthless.

Reconstruction was supposed to make my life better, not reveals truths that would make Ángel blush. Sleeping with more guys than the number of years I've been alive used to make me feel grown up and cool. But facing those numbers in the presence of Dr. Maggie and Faith turns me inside out. All my ugly guts are exposed. Cool becomes stupid. Grown up becomes childish. I can't fool myself in the bright exposure of my guilt. All those one-night stands devalue my worth in ways I hate.

Just imagine Stan as my father.

A shudder runs through me. If I wasn't pregnant, I would have been given drugs. Probably would have been fully susceptible to hypnosis. Faith and Stan would have unknowingly helped abort my baby. Later, Fisher could have attacked me. I rub my belly. This boy has saved me again. Not that I deserve it.

I press my hand against my sternum and fight to breathe as a guard comes to escort me away from my fake birthday party.

"Time to go home." Weariness hangs in her words.

"Where's Dr. Maggie?" I ask standing to follow her. "Where's Faith?"

"I can't say anything." Her averted eyes tell me she's trying to hide something. Something bad. Something dangerous.

I back away from her as my self-pity shifts rightfully to self-protection. With the news about Stan, I'd not only lost an ally, but my baby had also lost a means of escape.

"I want to talk to Faith."

"You can't." The words get lost in her attempt to say them. She clears her throat and says again, "You can't."

"Look, I know she might not want to talk to me. I get that. But I have a right to say goodbye, don't I?" I didn't think I did, but I had to try, for the baby's sake. "Please."

"My job is to escort you home."

"Really? Home?" I say. "To the fake apartment building. To a fake life?" I step off the boardwalk and toward the beach.

"No. You can't go down there." She reaches for my arm and I yank it away.

She runs ahead of me and puts her hands up to block my direction. Over her shoulder I see Dr. Maggie and a group of guards on a distant part of the beach. They are alone. Volleyballs have been abandoned.

"Let's go," the guard moves to block my view.

"What's going on down there."

"Nothing that concerns you," she says, successfully gripping my elbow and pulling me away. Looking over my shoulder, I see two guards lift a stretcher and cart it away from the water.

"Someone's hurt," I state the obvious.

The guard tightens her grip on my arm, and I think to resist her guidance until I spot Dr. Maggie turn toward us. She is too far away for me to see her face, but her determined stance makes it clear that she watches me.

CHAPTER 51

Emptiness drapes the walls and windows and furniture of my apartment. Without Faith or Glinda-Rowena, this apartment might as well be an Isolation cell. I sink into a chair ready to have a great big pity party when someone knocks on the door. Wiping away a single tear, I stand as tall as possible before opening the door.

Nodding at me, Dr. Maggie says, "Hello again."

She doesn't ask, but I step out of the way and let her in. At the couch, she sits in the same location where Faith and I made our escape plans.

Adjusting her cat-eye glasses the doctor says, "Well, this certainly changes things."

I take my former seat. My feet stay flat on the floor. Turning my toes inward, I wait for her to say what she's come to say. While I don't believe the hypnotic trigger has completely left me, my stained canvas shoes bring me no comfort.

"Courtney, I need you to know this isn't your fault."

I pick at my fingernails.

"It's not." She reaches for my hand and I shift to avoid contact. With a sigh, Dr. Maggie continues, "This whole experiment is new. It has been my life's work. But it's all been theory until now.

"The last thing I ever wanted to do was hurt someone. We screened all potential families." She pauses long enough for me to glance her way. Her eyes are not on me, but on the room she's created. "I never wanted you to encounter someone who might remind you of your past." She turns to look at me. "You might not like what you've experienced here so far, but I promise. I built all of this out of love."

Outside a bird tweets from the tree planted near my window.

"You must be very rich to be able to build all this."

"I have money." She shrugs. "But most of the funding comes from donors and federal grants." She crosses her arms. "I don't blame you for Stan. Many young girls have sex in search of love. More than many. It's sad. At fourteen or fifteen a girl should feel cherished and loved by her father enough to never have to seek validation in clubs or bars or the arms of men who are strictly seeking a moment of satisfaction."

"I don't want to talk about Stan." My voice cracks. "I want to talk to Faith."

"That's not possible."

"Why not? She treated me with kindness and deserves to get an apology."

Dr. Maggie stands then moves to the window. "Not all men are like Stan. Or your father. I hope to introduce you to good, kind, loving men. Men who don't see women as objects."

"Like Fisher?" I allow frustration to reign for a moment

over common sense. "Is he on your list?"

She straightens her back. "So, you saw him?"

"Yes, and you have to know you can't keep him down here."

"Oh really?" She faces me.

"Yes."

"That's not really for you to decide, is it." The glare in her eyes adjusts my bravado. Her volatile personality lingers close to the surface. This woman has complete control over my life at this moment, and if I want to maintain the smallest amount of self-awareness, I need to tread lightly.

"He's dangerous," I say with deep respect.

Her expression loosens. "At least he's trying. He really wants to change his life to become better. He's making progress."

"But he's not," I appeal to her, "I saw it in his eyes." I fold my hands into a prayer fist. "He's not hypnotized. I could tell by his expression."

"His expression?"

"Yes, you know, like a hungry predator. I'm sure you are aware he tried to rape me in The Center. He's still a threat. He's not redeemable. He's not. He admitted it to me himself in The Center. He knows he will spend the rest of his life in prison. He wants to get away with as much as possible before he's caught again."

She stares out the window at her creation.

"Look, I realize you don't trust me, but I saw other girls out there, within his grasp. Some in skimpy bathing suits. He'll hurt one of them, if not more."

Dr. Maggie lifts her hand to silence me. And as much as I hate when people do that, I comply. "You've said enough," she says without anger. "I get your point and I will look into it. For now, you and I have matters to discuss." The tone of her voice remains even, which feels more threatening than if she would have exploded in anger. "You might feel it's a good idea for you to return to Truth and Isolation."

I don't answer because either a positive or a negative response could trigger an outburst. She's in control. Not only of me, but of Fisher and every other person in Bunkerville. Including my baby.

"I don't want to send you back to prison."

With all the energy inside of myself, I hold my face completely still. I don't allow my brain to think of how delusional her statement is. I can't risk a slight lift in my eyebrow.

She continues, "You've learned all you need to in the Truth project. More exposure to your past won't help. You might not believe this, but I want you to get better." She taps her finger on the window frame about twenty times before saying, "I'll make a deal with you."

I look directly into her eyes. "I'm listening."

"The doctor will be here tomorrow to conduct the C-section. The procedure is safe, and your baby will be given to the adoptive parents you've already chosen."

I gulp. "When did that happen?"

"I tried to keep as much of this horrible part of your past from you. It's easier to keep a memory away than it is to replace it."

"But why a tumor? Why a lie?"

"I told you, Courtney, I want you to have what I have. I want you to be free from your past indiscretions so you can enter college without a ton of baggage."

"College? I haven't finished high school."

"But you have. You passed the GED two months ago."

"Two months ago?" I stand. This is too much. "I can't. I can't do this." At the door, I turn the knob expecting it to be locked. When it opens, I step into the fake fresh air. Glancing down the mosaic steps, I look for the guard who should be standing on the street. But no one is around to stop me from executing my plan to swim to the edge of the wave pool and find a way out. No one but the woman who runs Bunkerville standing behind me.

"Courtney, please come inside," Dr. Maggie's voice remains calm. She still has control. She could call a battalion if I run. No, any escape plans will have to be done when she's gone, leaving the door wide open. I could keep it open all night without the risk of bugs coming into the space. Paradise. Then again, Fisher and others like him live down here with me so I have to close it. Lock it myself. I face my so-called counselor and say, "I don't want to be hypnotized anymore. I want to know. To choose."

Dr. Maggie exhales a breath. "I figured."

"I want to meet the adoptive parents and have you restore as many memories of the last few months as possible."

She sits up straighter, "Okay." The adjustment in her posture tells me she's lying. She's going to agree with whatever I say, and then tomorrow, she will pull me back under hypnosis and do whatever she wants. Facing me she asks, "Is that all?"

"No," I take a single step toward the couch. "I want to talk to Faith."

Anger flashes on her face. She stands and walks around the opposite side of the couch as if she needs the extra room to regain control of whatever is boiling inside of her. Her voice is forced as she says, "That's not possible."

"Why not?" I inch toward her. "I want to apologize. As

a psychiatrist, you have to admit that's an area of growth for me. It shows you have made a difference in me. Helping me to be better. To own up to my mistakes."

"Faith isn't here anymore."

"What?" I pause my forward motion. I don't know much about Bunkerville, but from what I do know, travel is dependent on schedules and times. Cars or buses aren't waiting to take people to the surface whenever they want.

"Please sit."

"I'd rather stand."

"Fine," Dr. Maggie's eyes lack anger and deceit as she says, "For your own good, I suggest you let this go."

The words carry the weight of a threat, but I don't accept it. "I can't." I say with as much simplicity as I can muster. "She's been very nice to me and I'll take whatever anger she wants to pour on me rather than the regret of not apologizing to her."

"She wasn't angry with you, she was mad at Stan."

"If that's true then why can't we talk?"

"Because, Courtney," Dr. Maggie stands directly before me as if she wants to examine my response. "Faith is dead."

CHAPTER 52

My legs lock. Like a statue, I'm frozen to the floor. All desire in my heart screams run, but my body won't comply. Dr. Maggie talks but I don't believe her. It's all a lie. A lie to keep me from talking to the woman. That one word repeats itself over and over in my brain as Dr. Maggie speaks.

"She drowned."

Lie.

"No one saw it."

Lie.

"A guard found her floating."

Faith is afraid of the water.

"We did all we could."

She wouldn't do that.

"I'm sorry. Don't blame yourself."

My muscles release. Like a puppet, I slump onto the floor. Dr. Maggie comes to my side. I allow the manipulative woman to help me to the couch. I allow her to raise my legs and put a wet cloth on my forehead.

"I can take you to see her body, if you like."

I shake my head. The truth breaks through my shock. If Dr. Maggie is offering to let me see Faith's body, then the woman is actually dead. Not by running into a wave pool and killing herself, but at the hands of Dr. Maggie or one of her henchmen. The murderous woman in front of me would do anything she could to prevent an outspoken person from leaving Bunkerville.

"I'd like to be alone."

"I understand."

But she didn't, did she? This crazy woman whose hands or words killed the first innocent person I met in Bunkerville didn't understand anything but power and control.

"Here, drink this."

I take the glass of water and swallow its metallic contents.

Dr. Maggie carries the glass to the sink and rinses it out. When she returns, she says, "I hate to leave you in this state, but you have requested to undergo no more hypnosis. I don't want to leave you to dwell in the misery of all the immature decisions you've made." She shrugs, "But maybe the consequences of the Truth videos in addition to the day's tragic events will sink in. Maybe in the morning you will reconsider. Do you really want to be who you are?"

In a different time and a different place, Dr. Maggie's words would have catapulted me into a restless night of guilt. And while I recognize The Bunker could tattoo another Roman numeral onto the base of my skull because of my connection to Faith's death. I choose to believe Faith rather than her killer.

Everyone is guilty.

Everyone has a reason to be locked up in a cell for the

ripples our negative decisions cause others. But Faith provided me with a counterbalance as well. She helped me believe in the goodness of mankind. I can't allow Dr. Maggie to kill my child or anyone else. I have to get out of Bunkerville and above ground or die trying.

I drop my feet to the floor.

Time to get ready. Plan my escape.

My arms are tired as I push myself up from the couch. As I stand, a wave of fatigue washes over me. It's been a very long day.

I yawn.

It would be pointless to leave while Dr. Maggie still watches me. No. I'll take a nap. Give Bunkerville's neighbors and guards time to sleep. My eyelids droop. I can leave after the fake sun sets.

CHAPTER 53

Rain.

I hear it before I open my eyes. The uneven rhythm on the windows. The occasional passing of car tires through wet puddles outside my window.

It's nice.

I don't have many memories of rain, growing up in San Diego. But Virginia made up for it. A rainy night in New York lingers in my mind between sleep and waking.

Uncle John laughing over a card game. But, no, I don't have an uncle. The senator in New York is someone I know of.

I rub the heavy sleep from my eyes.

The pattering on the roof slows. The light splash of traffic and the drip of excess water through gutters is joined by the distant bark of a dog.

Only...

My neighborhood doesn't have cars.

My neighbors don't have dogs.

They can't because we are buried deep beneath the earth. My head hurts. I hate when my thoughts become morbid. I roll over the best I can with my growing tumor in the way and push away thoughts of New York.

I've never been to New York. Or had I. To be honest, I remember more about the city than I do this room. My temples throb. The clock shines the time, 1:16 in the morning. The early-morning hour when hallucinations roam.

Across from me, the closet door is closed, and I want to cry. The rain. The confusion. Despite my fatigue, I switch on the lamp beside the bed and try to sit up, but my headache and exhaustion keeps me down.

Memories of cement tunnels and confinement refuse to dissipate. I live deep beneath the earth. The reoccurring nightmare of babies and caves pushes me deeper under the covers. Dr. Baum explained it was because of the cancer drugs.

I rub my tumor.

The growth moves.

More rain. More traffic. One problem. I live in a green space. Bunkerville doesn't have cars. The traffic splashing through puddles on the soundtrack is a mistake. They got it wrong. Pain thumps through my brain. The ache shouts at me, "Get a shoe."

I want to, but a desire deeper than a dream curls me into a ball, the pain in my head escalating.

"Get shoes."

I plug my ears and focus on the curtains covering my fake window, because that's what it is. A fake window. I'm in the Bunker. The angry pain lessens. I remember everything. The rain comes from a sprinkler system. The traffic from a recording. The pretend sky mocks the real one, inaccessible to me. My temples relax. Being buried beneath the earth isn't the nightmare, Dr. Maggie is. Because that's her name. Dr. Baum is an alias.

Standing, I approach the framed wall and I pull open the curtain.

My reflection stares at me from the glass.

My hair is cropped short because a barber shaved me, not because of cancer drugs. I'm not sick. I'm pregnant. I reach over and switch off the light to banish my reflection from the glass. The outside image hesitates a blink. Eventually the view of the horizon registers.

Placing my hand on the glass, which is real, I squint, looking for pixels. The tiny, minute squares will validate my beliefs. But the screen is too far away to touch, therefore, too far away to find a tiny pixel.

My mind is a delicate maze, fighting to find which path is real and which is invented. The street below is made of cement, but this room isn't in an apartment. I live on a decorated set. My baby bump is huge. Months have passed.

Doubt reaches for me from the closet behind me, but I fight it. My brain needs confirmation. Water drips from the limb of a tree.

I shift my eyes.

A building.

From another direction.

A sky.

In the distance, a streetlight.

Yes! If the cityscape is real, my eyes will confirm it. I fix my gaze on the light post. Not one constructed by the stage crew, but a pole at the screen's edge. A real light will burn a reverse pattern into my brain. A recorded image won't, at least not in the same way.

I focus unblinking at the spot.

One. Two. Three. Four. Five. Six. Seven. Eight. Nine. Ten.

I close my eyes. No polka-dot imprint is captured by my retina.

The lamp isn't real.

I'm in a dungeon with a killer. A killer who gave me drugs last night to make me sleep. I came to Bunkerville to save my baby, but Dr. Maggie wants to remove him. My heart hurts. I embrace my stomach. Faith told me I was eight months along, and now she's dead. Killed in the wave pool yesterday. And when the fake sun rises in this place, Dr. Maggie, the murderer, will put me into the hands of doctors and kill my child as well.

CHAPTER 54

I have to get out of here.

Now.

I throw the covers off my fully clothed body.

If I'm still here when the sun rises, Dr. Maggie will definitely regain control of my mind. She can then kill my baby, or worse keep him and experiment on him.

I jump from the bed and avoid the closet. The night's chill has me retrieving a pair of sweats from the hamper. I pull them over my jeans. At the dresser, I grab all the socks I own to avoid any footwear triggers.

Hurrying into the living room, I grab my jacket and a scarf to wear like a vail over my face and head. Without looking at the shoes I discarded yesterday, I put three pairs of socks on my feet and stuff the remaining three or four into my coat pockets. Without looking back, I hurry from my apartment and down the mosaic steps into the dark street. The cement beneath my feet is as cold as the floor of my old cell. Wet but not freezing.

The waves are motionless this early in the morning. No doubt a way to save electricity. I think about the swim Faith and I had planned. It no longer makes sense. The rain from the sprinklers is already soaking through my socks, the last thing I want is to be soaking wet.

Looking from left to right, I quickly cross the street. One of these shops has to have a back door. I head toward the barber. Although, months ago, when I exited the elevator with Rowena, a wall hid the entrance, but that didn't mean I couldn't search the area again.

With the scarf masking my features, I still look for lights in windows, making sure no one watches me. Feeling alone and invisible, I decide to see if I can find an open door.

The handle on a nail salon is locked.

I try the bookstore next door. Locked.

I don't give up.

Dozens of doors.

Blocks of walking.

Walls, water, and other barriers keep me within a ten-block radius. I spend hours under the unmoving moon feeling brick walls for secret passageways. Nothing clicks or opens to free me. Disappointment lingers on the edge of my nerves, but I push it down. Bury it. I have to escape, and not just for my baby. I can't put it past Dr. Maggie to kill me now that I know the depths of her madness.

I stop on a bench to rub my sore feet, peeling off layers of wet socks. One of which has a huge hole worn in it. I replace the worn socks with two new pairs, leaving two pairs in my pocket. The soft fabric elevated my mood. Rubbing my sore back, I think about the baby. I can't keep checking buildings for an exit. There has to be another way out.

The props around me cast phantom-like shadows. They

are all a part of the conspiracy to kill my baby. I bundle my coat tighter around my child as the air blows through vents. I lift my hand to see if I can identify the source. Maybe find an exit like the criminals at Alcatraz. The breeze pushes itself from my left and I press into it. Before my hopes can rise too much, the sprinklers above me click on again.

Thunder booms from speakers.

I rush to find cover under an awning on the main street. The water falls from the pretend clouds, lacking the freshness of rain. The slight smell of chlorine and metal pipes drips from the canopy's edge.

I've run out of options. I can't return to my apartment because giving up isn't an option. The only thing left to do is wait until I see someone open a door. I'll have to slip into a business unseen and search for exits. If I could do that, I might find a back door.

Or I could try to find a uniform or outfit to make me look like I'm part of the staff. See if I can hunker down in place like where Rowena lived. Of course, the odds of finding someone as rebellious are probably not good.

"Son," I say as I place my palm on top of my stomach, "We have to hope we find another kind soul like Faith."

A stab pierces my soul.

No.

I can't put another person's life in danger. The risk for them is too high. My best bet would be to get to the prison. Find Ángel, appeal to the boss. I can't imagine those in charge would support the killing of innocent people. A conspiracy like that would become too large to contain.

No.

The sprayers click off as quickly as they started.

A light in the bakery across the street comes on. I duck from view and slip across the street. The last drops of water fall from the ceiling. The screens on the horizon offer a purple glow. The recorded sunrise has begun. A rooster crows from the speakers like a warning alarm. Morning is near.

The sound of a door opening in the alley beside me draws me toward it. I peek around the corner. A woman in a dirty apron carries plastic bags to one of two dumpsters. I study her and wonder if she would be the kind of person who would help a pregnant woman get free of this place.

With her back to me, I can't see her face. Can't assess her features. She lifts the metal lid. I crouch and tiptoe to the opposite bin.

She hefts the first bag over the rim and drops it.

Swoosh.

I wait for the thunk of the bag landing on the bin's bottom, but it doesn't happen. The swoosh makes me think it's falling into an abyss.

The woman lifts the second bag and I crane my neck to hear better.

The second bag slides with a swoosh into another part of the cave.

Of course! The garbage doesn't land on the bottom of the dumpster, it slides down a chute. The garbage bin provides the magnificent sound of escape. I lean against the brick wall and wait for the woman to reenter the wooden door.

I count to five before I stand and lift the lid and look in.

The smell of food waste greets me.

My hunch is confirmed. No bags. A dark shaft has swallowed the garbage. The Bunker can't put trash into dumpsters because they don't have large waste-removal trucks to pick them up.

No, this bin drops into the prison. A grin stretches wide on my face as I remember Ángel mentioning the job working with the trash.

With the grace of an eight months-pregnant woman, I climb onto the metal rim. I lean forward and take a big whiff, delighted I can only detect the rancid smell of garbage. No smoke.

I place my feet in front of me and straighten my body. I'm not a fan of enclosed water slides, but I get over it. This dark chute is my only hope. I lift a prayer to Nanny Bella's Jesus. "Please let this dark tunnel be safe enough to carry me and my baby to safety."

Closing my eyes, I let go, hoping beyond hope this slide doesn't lead to an incinerator.

CHAPTER 55

The darkness, the stink, and the unknown pull me down the slide until I land with a splat. The bag which preceded me explodes beneath me.

Wet debris splashes into my open mouth. A mixture of flour and salt float over me like powdered snow. It sticks to my wet face. My sweats are caked in gunk, but so what. I lounge like a pig in mud.

I've done it.

I've escaped.

Tunnel walls surround me. I can barely see the artificial light above me. I've landed too deep for anyone in Bunkerville to reach me.

Who would have thought I'd ever be happy buried in garbage? I close my eyes and push away the funk from my nostrils by breathing through my mouth. A vivid memory comes to me as I lay in the filth. Ribbon was the only person I knew who didn't use deodorant or shampoo. We used to call her ring-around the toilet because she peed her pants in the third grade. The teacher had ignored her raised hand for at least fifteen minutes. And when the urine dripped beneath the small desk, Ribbon looked as shocked as the rest of us. Her expression shouted, "How did that happen?" while her voice remained silent.

I wasn't quiet. I was the first to laugh. Not at the pee, but at the bewildered look on my classmate's face. Well, the laugh on that day released the beast in me. I got high-fives from the boys on the playground for days. Being mean became my ticket to attention. My ticket to The Center. My ticket to Bunkerville's waste bin.

The pointed edge of what must be a box poked into my side. I wish Ribbon lived long enough to see me here. Hopefully, she's watching from heaven. I'd like to imagine her pointing her finger and laughing at me, but she wasn't like that. I want her hate for me and not for her.

Typical selfish Courtney.

I have to do better. I have to remember this moment. This place. This trash bin. Ribbon deserved better than I gave her, and I need to make sure I never forget. Time to get out of this mess, and not for me. While I deserve this place, my unborn child doesn't.

I roll over and crawl through trash. Slippery bags and boxes support me before crumpling under my weight landing me face first into another bag.

Hoping to make better progress, I flail my arms as I surf for balance.

Above me the bin door opens.

The light brightens and I realize I'm not as far away from the streets of Bunkerville as I thought. The dimness came from the closed lid.

A white trash bag blocks the light as it descends the chute, missing me by inches.

It thumps onto the pile where I was laying and sends up a new explosion of flour and debris.

A gust of dust coats my throat sending me into a coughing fit.

"Hey," a voice bounces off the walls. "Is someone there?"

I slap my hand over my mouth, but the convulsions from my throat won't stop. I hack half a dozen times as tears roll down my eyes.

"For crying out loud." The voice is annoyed.

I'm caught. No one will confuse me for staff now. Employees don't try to escape, convicts do. I need to find a door before Dr. Maggie finds me.

The surrounding walls are black and smeared with slimy waste. The more I investigate the space, the more I discover there was no way out. The chute is maybe ten feet above me. The trash must empty from below.

As if my thoughts trigger a command, the bags begin to sink. The smell of smoke reaches me first. Rising past the falling trash from the open floor below. I sink into a seated position again as bag after bag shifts under me.

A huge problem reveals itself. Bunkerville, most definitely, burns its trash.

CHAPTER 56

The smell of charred garbage rises as bags inch their way down the smooth walls. Veins of light peek through the dark debris. I position myself at the top of the heap, doing my best to protect my son.

Maybe there's an edge I can stand on until they turn off the blaze. I still have a chance to manage my own descent. One of Uncle John's favorite shows comes to mind. The American Ninja Warriors have a spider move that might work.

Shoving wet socks against the slick wall fails.

I yank the wet fabric from my feet, depositing them next to me in the descending trash.

The chute below is more than half my body length. With my baby facing up, I lean my shoulders against the wall. This time I find a way to press the soles of my feet against the opposite wall and they stick.

The bags fall without me.

This is good.

I'm comfortable for the moment. I have a second to evaluate my next move before my muscles fatigue. What did the ninja warriors do next? Jump?

Light explodes below me.

The scent of smoke grows stronger, but not the actual artifact. The fire causing the smell isn't positioned directly below me.

Leaning sideways, I can see the exit. The bags land in bins. Once a bin is full, it moves and is immediately replaced. Probably by a person, like the manual systems in the laundry. I lean to my left to see better. Big mistake. My shifting body weight pulls me off balance, causing my left foot to slip.

Oh my gosh.

My heart races as I fall into a half-loaded bin of garbage, landing with a hard thump. A burst of pain jars through my left shoulder. Metal wheels squeak beneath the bin as it shifts forward then stops abruptly.

I grab my aching limb. Above me, a girl dressed in green overalls gawks at me. A facemask blocks what has to be her wide-open jaw. A green cap covers her probably bald head to her ears. The only part of her exposed body I can see is the wide-eyed, unmoving shock examining me through her goggles.

CHAPTER 57

Laying in a pile of Bunkerville trash, I shrug and wave with my uninjured arm. Awkwardly I try to climb from the bin. It is hard to roll over with a wounded shoulder and fat belly. Pushing past the pain, I kick a bag out of my way and give myself enough room to adjust my legs beneath me, only to have the bin topple under my weight. Gravity lands me hard on the cement floor.

Pain tingles up my elbow, but I don't care. Garbage bags spill around me, but I smile. I'm free from Bunkerville and free from danger. Cradling my sore arm and shoulder, I pivot, searching for an exit only to realize I have an audience larger than one.

It's not every day a pregnant girl covered in gunk and white flour falls from the heavens. I give them a quick hello-goodbye wave. I want them to stay shocked so I can find a door to escape through before the guards come.

To my left, a humongous incinerator has its mouth wide open. A metal rolling conveyor feeds the beast. Bins rest next to sorting tables near the inmates watching me. I've no time to wonder what is kept or discarded, I need to find an exit and an ally.

I head to the only door I can see, but before I can get there, the smallest sorter grabs my sore arm.

The pain keeps me from yanking away. To avoid it, I lean toward the girl. As soon as she sees my reaction, she releases her grip and removes her cap and goggles.

"Courtney, is that you?"

It's my turn to widen my eyes and stare shocked. "Dee Dee?" I can't believe it. I don't have to look for an ally, I have landed in her arms.

"What are you doing here?" Then she looks at my belly. "And when did you get knocked up?"

"I can't talk," I whisper to her, "I need to hide."

"Where?" The futility in her words sting. She glances around. "All the bags get burned. If you're trying to escape this prison, it won't happen. Nobody gets out of here unless they're a guard. All the doors have locks, all the cells have keys."

"Even that one?" I point to an exit I imagined running through.

"Yes."

I lower myself to the floor in defeat. My body gives into the night's exhaustion. I close my eyes for a moment, too tired to think. Then I remember the person who heard me coughing while in the bin. Opening my eyes, I tell the girl who entered The Center with me, "Dr. Maggie will probably send someone from Bunkerville to get me. I don't want to go back." The statement is futile. Dee Dee has no power to help me.

"You were in Bunkerville?" The girl I startled when I first arrived sounds confused and impressed. "I heard the place is amazing, why would you ever leave it?"

Ignoring her, I face Dee Dee, "Is there anywhere I can hide?"

She studies the room like she's never seen it before. "There's a bathroom in the back, but they'd find you there. Maybe you could climb into the bin again, we could fill it with clothes, but…"

"They will know she's still here." The other girl says.

"I think we should call someone and tell them," a third girl joins in, "we could get in trouble."

I don't respond. I can't. A jarring pain curls me into a fetal position. Clinging to the floor, I moan. I've never been in labor, but nothing else could account for this amount of agony.

Pain folds me in half, turning me inside out.

A severe cramp stretches through my torso. Every ounce of my attention is arrested. I open my mouth in a silent scream, trying to dispel the pain. Pressing my head into the pile of discarded clothing, I grind my teeth.

Tight.

Sharp.

Contractions.

Rolling over, I try to move away from the pain, but it follows me.

"Guys she's in labor," Dee Dee shouts to the other girls.

Footsteps dart past me.

"Hello… Yes, I work in the incinerator room… Please come quickly... We need your help."

I fold into myself rubbing my back trying to chase the agony away. I don't know if the rubbing works, but the contraction eventually loosens, leaving in its wake the awful knowledge it will return.

Tears flow uncontrollably from my eyes.

"It will be okay," Dee Dee sooths.

But she doesn't know it's too soon.

I lean on my knees and weep. My escape from Reconstruction hasn't worked. After all the walking, searching, escaping, my baby is still in danger.

CHAPTER 58

The door I hoped to escape from opens. Careful not to further injure my left arm, Dee Dee helps me to my feet. A guard who once escorted me from Isolation approaches. My friend offers her my right arm.

"Where did she come from?"

"Bunkerville." Dee Dee points up.

"You're kidding."

Dee Dee shakes her head and I say nothing, saving my energy for more important things, like saving this baby's life.

"Let's get you somewhere comfortable." Her voice is calm and reassuring which makes me nervous. It's horrible how kind, soft words have become a trigger of fear in me, but Bunkerville taught me to distrust the quietness in someone's voice.

Dee Dee speaks, "I know she used to be in my cell block."

"Which one is that?"

"Delta."

"Perfect, that's not too far." The guard's voice is firm with Dee Dee, but gentle with me. "How far along are you?"

"Eight months."

"You don't look that big."

"Should you be in labor this early?" Dee Dee asks.

"No," I say as tears choke my throat.

"Don't worry, this could be false labor. That can happen because of stress. How did you get into the garbage in the first place?"

"Oh my gosh…" Tears push past my eyes as the pain tightens and my insides cramp. The guard grasps my hand as I sink onto the floor.

"Stay with her, I'll go get help." The guard rushes away as Dee Dee rubs my muscles.

"Breathe, Courtney, breathe."

I listen and try, but it's hard.

"We'll get through this."

I want to believe her. I want to. This little bit of a girl is the closest thing to friendship I've ever had. As she tells me to focus, I concentrate on believing she won't let anyone hurt my baby.

"I plan to study medicine when I'm free. Do you think they'll let me? Do ex-cons ever get to be doctors?"

The sound of her story and rhythm of her voice doesn't have the power to fully distract me from the pain, but it does make the time pass until it subsides.

"Thank you." I whisper.

From down the hall, the guard approaches and she's not alone. Ángel pushes a wheelchair behind her.

"It will be a few minutes before another contraction comes. We should get you to a bed before then." Dee Dee sounds a decade older than her fifteen or sixteen years. Ángel and the guard help me into the chair as we weave

285

through the halls with Dee Dee following behind.

"We need to call Bunkerville to see if they have a doctor who can help."

"No." I put my foot on the ground trying to stop the wheelchair like Fred Flintstone. "You can't do that."

"They are more equipped…"

"No." I try to get up without success. "No." I appeal to Dee Dee. "Don't let them. They tried to kill my baby. They did. Dr. Maggie and some doctor. They…" The pain returns, but I fight against it. "Dee Dee." I gasp. "Don't let them kill my baby."

"I won't," she says with a conviction she can't back up.

I tighten my arms around my body.

"Courtney?" Ángel says with a calm voice. "We aren't equipped to deliver a baby down here."

"I'm not going back," I say through gritted teeth as the pain releases again.

"But it would be better for the baby…"

"I'm not going back," I repeat as I straighten up in the wheelchair. "Dr. Maggie spent months lying to me and twisting my thoughts to make me believe my baby was a tumor. If you send me to Bunkerville, you will be as guilty as she is of killing my baby. And if that happens, I will find you and tattoo a Roman numeral on the back of your head myself. "

Dee Dee snaps her finger and shakes her hand. "Sorry, Ángel, but she's right. And I'll help her do it."

"Look, ladies, all I want to do is help this baby."

"Then don't send me back there or let any doctor they've got touch me."

"How about if I at least get the nurse that works here to take a look at you."

And as if in agreement, the baby shifts his position. "I'll

do that as long as you let Dee Dee come with me."

"But..." He exhales.

The other guard shrugs her shoulders.

"Fine," he finally says, "but let's get going before your situation gets worse."

CHAPTER 59

The contractions don't ease as I'm wheeled through the cement halls to a small clinic. I'm helped onto a hard, flat cot with a thin blanket. Dee Dee finds a paper towel dispenser. She soaks a folded wad in the sink before returning to place it on my head.

When another contraction comes, she rubs my back and tells me stories. I learn more about this person than I've ever known about anyone in my life because I never cared enough to ask about others. I always made the conversation about me.

Eventually, a nurse enters the room. Something about her features triggers a memory. She lifts a white gadget with a spiral cord attached to it.

"I want to check the baby's heartbeat. I heard you've had some pain and I want to make sure he's alive."

"Wait a minute." I point at her. "Don't you work in Reconstruction."

She pulls away from me.

"Yes, you do." I jab my finger in her direction. "You wanted to drug me. You were helping Dr. Maggie erase memories."

She tenses. "I'm here to help you."

"No, you're on Dr. Maggie's team. You're still dressed in her costume. You wanted to abort him. You wanted to kill this child."

"I didn't know you were pregnant."

I slap at the air between us. "Get out of here. Go away."

She turns to Ángel and the other guard. "Will you please constrain the inmate while I check on the baby?"

Everyone stares at her without moving.

"That's what she does. She injects drugs into people who are tied down."

The nurse opens her mouth wide as if I'm lying. But when no one speaks she stuffs the white contraption into Ángel's hand. "This isn't worth it, I quit." She storms away saying, "I didn't sign up for this. Get me out of here, I'm going back to Kansas."

"No one signed up for this," I shout at her exiting backside and the guard who hurries after her.

Dee Dee rubs my back, "At least she can walk away. Not like the rest of us."

"Yeah," I look at our remaining guard, "I quit too. Okay? I'll move to Kansas if that's what it takes."

Dee Dee chuckles, but Ángel doesn't pay attention to us, he's too busy balancing the baby heart monitor in his hand. "I don't know how this works. In fact, I don't know anyone else who does." He sighs. "Courtney, if you really want to help your baby, we need a professional. Someone with experience to do this."

"But they can't be from Bunkerville. I tell you, Dr. Maggie tried to kill my baby. And if I'm being honest, I think she actually killed my surrogate mother."

"No way. She might be an extremist, but she's not a murderer."

"That's what extremists do. They kill people who try to expose them or stop them. I promise. A woman came to help me. She told me of her fear of water, yet Dr. Maggie wants me to believe she drowned herself."

He scratches his head as if it can help him better understand my situation.

"Ángel, I know it sounds crazy, but she convinced me I had a cancerous lump to remove."

"You never asked for an abortion?"

"Never! The entire time I was there, she kept me hypnotized. When the fog in my brain cleared, I turned all my attention to keeping this kid alive."

"It's hard to believe."

"Why, because she's a doctor and I'm a lowly inmate?"

"No." He pulls off the wall. "I was an inmate too, if you remember."

"Stop it. Both of you." Dee Dee steps between us again. "Seriously. Who cares about this right now? We need to figure out how to bring this baby safely into the world. Can we please focus on that?"

She's right. Ángel doesn't need to believe or even know everything that happened to me in Bunkerville. Time will be better spent on coming up with a way to protect my son once I'm free from this crazy place. My baby has allies, and our time should be spent deciding how to protect my baby now and after he's born.

I'm ready to talk solutions when the door opens.

Turns out we did waste precious time because now it's up. As if summoned from Hades, Dr. Maggie glares at us from the frame.

CHAPTER 60

I yank on my dirty shirt as if it can shield my baby. The guard and Dee Dee step in front of me. The action gives me a smidge of confidence.

"What brings you here?" Ángel asks with authority in his voice.

"I'm checking on my patient." The she-devil responds as if she owns me.

"She's not your patient anymore."

"Courtney chose Reconstruction." Dr. Maggie approaches Ángel.

"And she jumped into the trash to escape it." Dee Dee chimes in, stepping toward the doctor.

"And I'm here to take her back."

"Policy says she gets to choose," Ángel states matter-of-factly.

"Fine, then let her choose." She places a finger gently on Dee Dee's shoulder and nudges her to the side. "Courtney, let's get your shoes. A wonderful warm pair to cover your feet. Cozy and comfortable." She looks around the room, then continues, "Remember, the pair we bought a couple days ago. The soft, smooth leather pumps with the red sole. Let's try those on again. You have them at home, right? In your closet with all the other shoes you own. We can go now." She reaches invitingly toward me. "Ready?"

The room went silent enough for me to hear water in the pipes. Did that come from a sound system? A voice in my head says Bunkerville will give me a calm place with smooth sheets and hot food and a private bathroom and a closet full of clothes and shopping for shoes. Looking at my bare feet, I ask, "Where are my shoes?"

"She didn't have shoes when she came." The young girl in the room comes to stand beside me. For a second, I don't know her. Then again, when I study her face, a name forms in my mind. Dee Dee. Yes, that's her name Dee Dee.

"Let's go home and get your shoes. You'll feel better with soft leather covering your feet." The doctor gives me a sweet smile. I know her face too.

I place my hand on the bed to move when a cramping pain claws its way into my back. The tumor. I curl over. No, no, no. It's not the tumor, it's the baby. The child this woman wants to kill. She's a killer. "Get away from me," I growl through gritted teeth. "I will never go anywhere with you." The pain curls me onto the bed and away from her. "Go away, and never, ever, ask me to join you again." I close my eyes and bang my fist on the cot. "Oh, Dee Dee, make it stop. Please. Make it stop." My friend rubs my back.

From somewhere far away I hear the doctor say, "The boss will hear about this."

"You bet he will," Ángel counters.

"You think he doesn't know about the baby?"

"It doesn't matter now, does it?"

"Look, Courtney, your family connections won't help you. And you'd be stupid to think they will."

I'm in too much pain to reply. This has nothing to do with my family. They don't know I'm pregnant, stupid witch. She's trying to mess with me.

"Time to go," Ángel says.

The doctor's voice is low and threatening. "You think you can tell me what to do? You entered The Center an inmate, you don't want to leave The Bunker one as well."

"Your threats don't bother me. I can see now, Courtney is right. You're trying to perform an illegal abortion."

"What abortion?" The doctor's voice shifts from malice to confusion. Her innocent act doesn't affect me.

"Please," I beg Dee Dee, "Tell them to stop."

The other guard moves as if released from freeze tag. I'd forgotten she was in the room. "Let's take this outside. We can call the boss."

Dr. Maggie's words sound sincere, "I was never going to kill the baby. I have a doctor upstairs ready to perform a C-section."

"It's too early."

"The OB-GYN looked at her film. The baby is fine."

"Then why not let her deliver the child?"

"A C-section better fits the story of a girl whose new life didn't have an unplanned pregnancy in it. The scar and the post-surgery fits with having had a tumor, not a baby." She clicks her tongue. "But none of that matters right now. The best thing for the baby is to be born in Bunkerville."

Ángel is quiet, too quiet. The thinking-of-joining-my-enemy kind of quiet that terrifies me.

Through the pain I say, "She's lying."

Dee Dee squeezes my hand.

Ángel says to Dr. Maggie, "Let's talk outside."

The door closes and Dee Dee and I are left alone, and all I can wonder is if Ángel is about to become the doctor's next victim. He believes me now, but for how long? Tears fill my eyes and I honestly wonder if this nightmare will ever end.

CHAPTER 61

It takes forever for Ángel to reenter the room. The short contraction ended at least five minutes ago if I believe my ability to tell time, which I don't. I keep my eye on the door to see if Dr. Maggie is with him, but no one else comes in.

He raises his hands and speaks, "You're not going to like what I'm about to say, but I need you to listen."

My muscles are too tired to hurry, or I would have gotten up and walked from room. Through gritted teeth I tell him, "I'm not going to Bunkerville."

"I'm not proposing that yet."

"No. No. I don't care what Dr. Maggie told you, but I can't go back."

"I said that's not what's on the table for the present moment."

"No, Ángel, No. You get to choose, you are either on my side or her side, there is no in-between."

"I'm on the baby's side."

"Then we stay here."

"I didn't say you were leaving."

"You didn't say I wasn't."

"If you will stop being paranoid for a moment, I will tell you."

"No. No. You don't get to accuse me of that. I'm not being paranoid. You didn't live up there, did you?"

"I didn't mean it that way."

"Then tell us what you do mean." Dee Dee steps between us. She has enough suspicion in her voice for me to know she's still on my side.

"If this baby is coming now, he might be too small to survive without the incubator available in Bunkerville."

"Bring it down here. Bring it all down here." I say able to sit up enough to swing my legs over the end of the cot.

"We can't. This place doesn't have anywhere for us to set it up and plug it in. The hospital in Bunkerville is wired. We're not."

Dee Dee turns toward me nodding her head. "He's right. Almost everything here is manual."

"What about the laundry room. They have washers and dryers they could unplug. Put us in there."

"If we had hours to move those huge machines around, yes, but honestly, I wouldn't trust them. Dee Dee you know the power in the prison is unreliable. No back-up generators to handle surges or outages."

"More reliable than Dr. Maggie, I can promise you that," I fume.

"But I'm not asking you to go to Bunkerville yet. You might not trust Dr. Maggie, but I have no choice at the moment if we're going to deliver your baby safely."

I'm about to tell him to go to hell with the she-devil when Dee Dee places her hand on my arm. The tender touch is like cool water on my skin. "Let's at least listen to him." Our eyes meet. She raises her eyebrows before giving me a slow nod. She wants me to trust her. We're not enough to form a full mutiny, but I return her nod with a frown.

"What do you propose happens next?" my young ally asks.

"It's my understanding," Ángel omits Dr. Maggie's name, "a midwife lives in Bunkerville. She knows nothing about your pregnancy or your time in Reconstruction. She happens to live there by choice."

"Nope," Dee Dee says, "Nope. I don't believe it. No one would live in a cave by choice. No one sane, anyway."

It's my turn to correct my friend's assumption. "Actually. Most people in Bunkerville are there by choice."

"What?"

"Yeah, it's a thing, I guess. People looking for solace, someplace green..."

"Well, Dr. Maggie says we can talk to a midwife if you like."

"Someone from Bunkerville." I accuse rather than ask.

"Yes," he holds up his hands, "But she will come to see you as an inmate in a prison. I told Dr. Maggie I want to go with her so I can witness the exchange."

"You won't be able to tell if the midwife has been hypnotized. It's not that easy."

"I know that—" frustration fills his voice "—but we have to do something."

"Ask her if she's ever performed an abortion."

"What?"

"Yes, ask her, I have to make sure it's not the abortion doctor."

"Courtney," he steps toward me. "I can't ask her that. We've already chased away one medical professional. But what I can do is hear the conversation. And be here during the examination. I've already got permission for Dee Dee to be present during the more private moments. I understand you are not in the mood to trust anyone, but I'm begging you to trust me. I could be in Bunkerville escorting the midwife here, but I didn't want to go without your permission."

His statement halts my hesitation. I know I can't deliver this baby without possibly endangering him. Neither can Dee Dee or Ángel or anyone else in The Bunker. I absolutely hate the idea of anyone connected to Dr. Maggie helping, but I am a prisoner with limited options.

"You'll be extra observant?" I ask.

"More than that, when I bring her down, if you don't feel like you can trust her, we'll have time to think of something else. I've already got someone working on a plan B as we speak."

"Help from above?"

Ángel chuckles and nods, "I've already spoken to the Almighty."

"I wasn't talking about him."

"God willing, if we need help from the earth's surface, we can get that too. Because of the remoteness of our location, we need at least a week or more for that to happen. This midwife really is our next best option." He pauses long enough for me to see Dee Dee nodding at the idea. "Now, because I want to be completely honest with you. If you are in labor right now, this midwife might suggest you deliver in Bunkerville where there's an incubator. Right now, she knows nothing about the hypnosis or your past. When we talk to her, she will be informed there is a pregnant inmate in the prison. It will all come as a big shock to her."

"Or so Dr. Maggie says."

"Right. We don't have a lot of time. Are you okay with

me going and bringing this woman back?"

"As long as you take Dee Dee with you."

"I don't think I can do that." He frowns, "Besides, I proposed she stay here with you, I thought you wouldn't want to be alone."

"What about the other guard, the lady who found me in the trash place?"

"No problem. She's outside with Dr Maggie right now. I didn't want the doctor to go ahead without us," he says, "but I need to hear you say yes."

As a contraction begins its rapid ascent, I return to the cot and groan, "Yes, go." The pain gives me no other option than to trust the inmate turned guard. As Dee Dee rubs my back, I beg Nanny Bella's baby Jesus to not only ease the pain, but stop anyone from Bunkerville who might be dangerous from hurting my child.

CHAPTER 62

I only have one more contraction while Ángel and the guard are retrieving the midwife from Bunkerville. "I think it's slowing. That's a good thing, right?"

Dee Dee shrugs, "How would I know?"

"I don't know. I'm just so tired," I say as I close my eyes, happy to be free of pain. Dee Dee lets me doze, so I have no idea how much time passes before the clinic door swings open.

"Who's he?" Dee Dee asks as I open my eyes.

"He's the midwife," Ángel says, "And before you get all weird about it. He's heard all the jokes and insults about his chosen profession already."

With a defensive tone, the tall skinny man speaks in a voice deeper than his body shape would infer, "It's why I moved to Bunkerville, to find some peace." He hitches a black bag higher on his shoulder as if waiting for permission to leave.

I ask him a straight question, "Did you find peace in

Bunkerville?"

"Not as much as I'd like. They have some strange ideas I'm not sure work for me."

"Like?" I continue my investigation.

He looks over his shoulder and in a conspiratorial tone says, "They sometimes lock you into your home for a couple hours in the morning. Makes it feel more like a prison than a retreat."

The other three people in the room open their eyes wide, and I nod my head. The man sets down his bag. Obviously, we've both passed the necessary test to begin. The male midwife picks up the white plastic instrument the nurse had given to Ángel from the counter where he left it. From his bag he retrieves a bottle of what looks like gel, and some rubbing alcohol. The abrasive disinfectant smell invades the room as he cleans his tools.

"You good?" Dee Dee asks.

"I think so."

The man washes his hands speaking over his shoulder, "You know, when these guards knocked on my door this morning, I was surprised to find Bunkerville is connected to a prison." Drying his forearms, he turns to me. "Maybe the morning lockdowns are made to protect the city when inmates come through there."

"Maybe," I say feeling better and better about this man. He could be acting, of course, but I don't know many actors who would take on the responsibility of helping deliver a baby. Their wives or husbands, maybe, but not the actors.

Hanging the towel on the rack, he picks up the gadget and approaches me. He drops the conversational tone and says, "So, how far along are you?"

"Eight months, I think."

"Do you know when you conceived?"

"May."

"Your math sounds right," He lifts the instrument. "Do you know what this is?"

"No, I have no idea."

"You mean, during your entire stay in this prison no one's check the baby's heartbeat?"

"Not that I know of."

"You'd know," he says with assurance. Which convinces me my hypnosis is unknown to him. I bet all the hypnosis in Bunkerville is unknown to him.

"Does that mean you've gone all this time without prenatal vitamins?"

"No," I twist my head to show him my patch.

"What is that?"

"My prenatals," I say turning to face him.

"Never heard of such a thing."

"A prison nurse gave it to me. It's supposed to last for three months. This is the second one."

"But if it lasts for three months, you are a month behind for the third. When did you get it?"

"I don't know, I haven't seen the nurse in a while." I can't tell him she might have been a victim of the fire I contributed to above ground. He's here to help my baby and if the morning sequester in Bunkerville raises the hair on his arms, the rest of The Bunker might cause him to pack up and leave before my baby is born.

The man turns to the female guard, "Can you please check with whatever horrible healthcare professionals this prison has and get this girl another patch please?" The female guard looks first to me, and then to Ángel.

"Dee Dee, you stay here while we go check on that."

My friend nods and the midwife watches them go. "I've never been in a prison before, but this has to be the strangest. You're an inmate too? Right? I mean you're wearing that horrible green outfit, that can't be a uniform. And they let one inmate watch another. Strange. But I'm not here to judge, I wanted to make sure this little one is okay." He clucks his tongue as if he would love to talk all day about the goings on in The Bunker. In his deep-smooth professional voice he continues, "So, when was your last contraction?"

"I'm not sure."

The man rolls his eyes with disgust.

"She fell asleep, and I wasn't timing them. It's probably been about an hour."

"Okay. That's good. If they have subsided, they could be Braxton Hicks. How about if you lay down and let me see if I can find a heartbeat."

I let my head fall onto the lumpy pillow and lift my dirty shirt, exposing my pregnant belly.

"This will feel cold," he says as he squirts the goop onto the gadget. He hands me the speaker attached to the device with a twisted cord.

I wince as the clammy gel rubs around my belly. The child responds by shifting away from the device.

"Great." The man's face lightens. "He's moving. That's good." He maneuvers the probe like a pro. I focus every cell in my brain toward the task at hand. A rush, like the sound of wind, comes through the speakers then a slow whoosh, whoosh, whoosh.

"Is that him?"

"No, that's you, I'm afraid. His will be much faster." He reassures me, "Don't worry, we'll find him." He slides the device lower, right above my left hip.

The sound changes.

A quick whooshwhooshwhoosh gallops throughout the

room. Dee Dee's eyes grow wide and I can feel tears form in mine.

It's him. He's okay. He's alive.

My escape from Bunkerville hasn't injured him.

His life, so far, is perfect, and I need to do everything in my power to ensure I don't mess it up.

"Thank you," I say to the midwife.

"You're welcome," he hoots, and I can tell from the thrill on his face he misses his chosen profession.

"This is sooooo cool!!" Dee Dee comes to my side, joy covering her features as well. We all laugh. I hold the speaker to my heart trying my best to cherish this one bright moment in my dark life.

CHAPTER 63

By the time Ángel and the other guard return, the examination is over. The midwife confirms everything is still "locked up tight."

"Definitely false labor," he says as he packs his bag.

"Didn't feel false to me."

"The pain is real," The midwife reassures me as he secures the new prenatal patch behind my ear and says, "your body is getting ready." He dusts his hands as if he's happy with a job well done. "I'll be back to check on you next week. In the meantime, drink plenty of water. Dehydration can lead to false labor." He turns to the guards, "So can stress, so keep her calm. No unnecessary drama."

Ángel agrees.

The midwife lifts his packed bag and departs with the female guard who found me in the trash room. Her name is Lucy.

Dee Dee leans on the counter as Ángel tells us what's next. "The boss wants to respect your privacy, so very few people will know what's going on. He wants you to choose what you want to do with the child."

"Where was he when I was in Bunkerville?"

"I can't answer that," Lucy turns to Dee Dee, "We need to keep this quiet."

"Easy to say, but we're not the only ones who know. Everyone in the incinerator room saw her fall from the ceiling. They know she's pregnant and heard her complain about Bunkerville."

His lips twist sideways, "Oh great, it will be impossible to stop the story from getting out."

"Has the incinerator crew gone to lunch yet?"

Ángel looks at his watch. "Not yet, their break starts in about fifteen minutes."

"Take me to them. I think I can convince them to stay quiet. It might take some doing, but we've all been teased for working with trash. Maybe if I give them enough information, they will feel like they have an upper hand with the snobby inmates in other jobs."

"If you think so," Ángel looks at me. "But I can't leave Courtney alone. This isn't a secure location."

"Then put her in the wheelchair. Having the girls see she's safe will remove some of the mystery. But we should get out of here before another guard takes those inmates to lunch. I promise, they will whisper loud enough to draw the attention of other people. I'll make sure this is an incinerator-girls-only story."

Ángel agrees and helps me into the wheelchair. I ask if I can take the pillow. Fatigue holds every cell in my body hostage. I'm too afraid of bothering the baby to lay it over my stomach, so I tuck it to the side and twist my neck enough to close my eyes.

I'm awake enough to smell the smoke and hear the story

Dee Dee tells when we arrive at the trash room. I wave at the girls and thank them. They wave back as Ángel takes me to get showered. He sets a guard's uniform on the bench next to the towels and turns to leave.

"You're joking," I scoff.

"No, I'm not. The green jumpsuit isn't really designed for pregnancy."

"I could wear an extra-large."

"The boss suggested we use this until we can get you some regular clothes from Bunkerville. The pants and button-up are easier to put on and off if we find ourselves in a delivery emergency."

"And people aren't going to notice me in this." I tap my finger on the uniform.

"Not where you're going," he says before closing the door.

CHAPTER 64

Standing under the flowing water in the communal shower, my brain tries to work out where The Bunker might hide an eight months-pregnant teenager.

Bunkerville is out, if they were taking me there, they would have already done it. My yellow cell has windows, like every cell in my row. As soap and water rinse the remaining trash from the little bit of hair on my head, one location comes to mind.

Isolation.

No windows.

Food is delivered.

A set group of guards maintain the place. It's the perfect hidey hole. I cough out a sarcastic chuckle. Looks like I'll serve the thirty-one days left on my tattoo sentence after all.

I turn off the faucet and dry myself.

The white room might not be as bad knowing I'm not in there alone. Although, I doubt my son will be enough company to keep me sane. With growing anxiety, I put on the uniform, and I'm surprised to find it less comfortable than the jumpsuits. The fabric itches and I feel a jolt of empathy for Ángel and his friends.

Fully dressed, I tap on the door and Lucy opens it up. She and Ángel are the only guards I've seen since falling into the trash room. The wheelchair is gone, and I miss it. I haven't slept for over 36 hours, and the escape and false labor has me exhausted.

We navigate the empty halls to an elevator bank. Memories of getting into one with Rowena trigger panic.

"Are you taking me to Isolation?"

"Yes," she smiles at me. "But you'll get visitors."

"Visitors?" I ask, afraid to hope for too much.

"Yeah." She presses the button and the car descends. "Regular food, rest, reading, writing, visitors. Whatever can keep you comfortable until the baby comes."

"I won't be alone."

"Well, yes, you will be for large sections of the day, but not like it was before."

As the wheels beneath me rattle, I try to think of how to make Isolation less traumatic. "Could I get some items to draw?"

"Sure, there's plenty of paper, pens and pencils."

"What about color, do you have any colored pencils, or chalk, paint or anything like that?"

"I'll check." The elevator stops and Lucy indicates for me to step out. The stark white walls stun me at first. And when I enter the cell, I'm reminded of how silent this place can be. On the table is a lunch tray and I eat for the baby's sake.

"And who will be my visitors?"

"Make a list of those you trust, and we'll run it past the boss."

"Who is this boss?"

"I don't know," she says. "I've never been in a meeting with him. In fact, I believe today was the first time Ángel ever talked to him on the phone. Here in the prison, we get memos. If I'm being honest, I always thought it was Dr. Maggie."

I pick up the peanut butter and jelly sandwich from the tray. "Me too," I admit before taking a bite.

"From what I know, the boss doesn't live anywhere near The Bunker."

"Convenient." I say with peanut-butter sticking to the roof of my mouth.

"All the guards in Truth join a conference call where an admin relays the boss's instructions and reactions to requests."

I swig the apple juice before saying, "So why would this guy care about what happens to me? I'm not anyone important..." I stop, surprised at how quickly I'd forgotten my Manchester lineage. My uncle is a United States senator.

"We have a lot of rich kids here in The Bunker and in Reconstruction. Remember, The Center was full of the children of influential families. If I were to guess, I think the boss is worried about one thing and one thing only. Bad press. I've been to Bunkerville and this place has to be expensive to run. Whoever's backing this experiment doesn't want the world to uncover any dirt."

"That makes sense. But is a pregnant teen enough drama to get the world's attention?"

"One as outspoken as you could."

She has a point. I've never been the quiet type. I finish the sandwich and nibble on the veggie straws.

"Do you mind if I ask you something?" Lucy's tone infers no force.

"Sure."

"I saw your tattoo, and I've heard the Truth Sessions can exaggerate crimes, you know, connect you to deaths connected to your actions. Is that true for you?"

"Yes, you could say that."

"Do you mind if I ask what?"

I wipe the crumbs from my fingers and drink the rest of my juice as I think about whether I should tell her. Based on her earlier comments, this girl worked in The Center, she will know people who died. I shake my head as I push the tray away from me indicating I'm finished. "I'm not ready to talk about that." I add, "Sorry."

"I understand. I was just curious." She takes the tray. "I'll be back with your dinner. You can give me a list of names then. In the meantime, you have a couple bottles of water, the midwife says you need to drink them before dinner."

I nod, wishing I had a story to tell this person who's been so sweet to me. But I don't. I'm locked in this room because of my own actions. And someday, when the memories of people like Jackson have faded, I hope to be the kind of person who can answer any questions without pride or shame.

CHAPTER 65

I sleep through the delivery of my dinner tray as well as lights out. And I would have continued to sleep if my shoulder wasn't being shaken.

Like a patient in a hospital wakened to take her meds, various attendants wake me to eat and drink. The first morning it was Dee Dee, freshly showered and ready to go to work. Then Ángel at lunch and Lucy for dinner.

By the end of the first week, each incinerator girl visited me in succession. Those conversations are more superficial than the ones I have with Dee Dee when it's her turn, but I'm glad to have them.

On day nine, my morning visitor is a complete surprise. When Lucy asked me for a list of those I trust, I couldn't help to put down Sleeves. I still don't know her real name because when I told her how I had to describe her rather than give a name, she told me she prefers the nickname to her own.

"I had no idea you were pregnant."

"Nobody did."

She leans back on two legs of the chair next to my desk and laughs. "The most private thing about an inmate is his medical records. Our crimes are public record, unless there is a court order of suppression."

"Yeah, by the way, how are things in the laundry, that freckled girl still hassling you?"

"Who her?" Sleeves chuckles, "No, she got caught and spent less than a half day in Isolation before begging to go to Bunkerville. She left maybe a month after you did."

"That's crazy. That means she was there when I was. She probably attended my made-up birthday party."

Sleeves shrugs.

Three knocks on the door. The hour is over.

"Time to go back to washing clothes. Some of them I'm sure belong to our freckled friend."

I nod at the irony.

At the door, Sleeves glances at me, "Hey, thanks for thinking of me. I can't tell you how much it means to me. More than you'll ever know."

"Thanks for supporting me before you knew me and keeping my secret now."

Pressing her lips together she doesn't respond. Emotions flow across her face and disappear. My words affected her, but I can't imagine why. I'm eating my breakfast when Ángel returns.

"Sorry," he says, "I forgot to drop these off. I thought about waiting until lunch, but I figured you'd really rather have them now." On the table beside me he deposits a small box of crayons. "Got to get your visitor back to the laundry and make my rounds. Enjoy."

He closes the door and it's my turn to get emotional.

CHAPTER 66

The next four weeks in Isolation are perfect enough to make me anxious for their end. According to the midwife, my baby is officially full-term. He could come any moment and not need an incubator.

Looming in front of me is the pain of delivery.

Looming before me is the question where the baby will go.

Looming on the other side of Isolation is the rest of my prison sentence.

My baby has no choice. He will be born in prison, but he should have a choice about whether he stays or not. But I don't think I can let him go. Not only because it would break my heart, but because I'm not sure he will be taken care of on the outside.

These thoughts have me doodling on a blank page of an amends journal when the door to my Isolation cell opens.

Turning to greet one of my many friends, I'm shocked to see Rowena enter. Up until now, I thought Ángel and Lucy were the only guards who knew I was here.

"Hello, Courtney," she says in her gruff voice.

"Rowena." The name falls from my mouth. "What are you doing here? I thought you transferred out."

"Transferred, yes. Out of here, no."

"But you said you didn't like either program, why stay?"

She leans against the closed door, "Because of you."

"What?" I set my crayon down. "Don't blame me for whatever you've done."

"I don't blame you. And when I said you, I should clarify. I'm here because you are pregnant. I suspected it for a long time, but when you finally agreed to premature surgery, I felt it wasn't fair to the little person growing inside of you."

"You know I didn't choose premature surgery. I was tricked into it."

"Yes, which is why I stayed." She crosses her arms, "Satisfied?"

I'm not, but I don't tell her that. "So, what are you doing here now? Come to deliver my baby?"

"Not quite." She pushes off the door and approaches the table, her posture maintaining military attention. "The boss has sent me to bring you to your last Truth session."

"What? Are you telling me I haven't seen everyone who died because of stupid choices I made?"

"I don't know, I only work here."

"Same old line." I return the crayon to its cardboard container.

"You are such a pain. I hate this place."

"Then why not tell me straight about the baby when you had the chance?"

"Do you honestly think if I'd have told you about the baby while you were still Dorothy that you'd have listened?" She rolls her eyes. "You don't have to answer, because I know you wouldn't."

"But I'm not hypnotized now."

"Maybe not hypnotized, but you are still under the influence of lies and deceit. Most of us are. But your baby is in a safe position. The boss has assigned the task to me to bring you into the second part of your Truth. Specifically, your family story."

"My family?"

"Yes."

"Why do I need to see footage from my family?"

"Because," she pauses to ponder my question before relaxing her posture and saying, "You want it straight?"

"Yes."

"Fine, I've not been given permission to give it to you straight, but I believe you have a right to know. The person running this place, the one everyone calls the boss, he's related to you."

"Related?" I scoot my chair around to face her. "In my immediate family?"

"Yes, very immediate."

Pressing my hand to my heart in an attempt to slow the pain growing there, I watch her lips as she forms the words.

"Senator John Manchester."

CHAPTER 67

"Uncle John," the words barely escape my lips. It can't be possible. He couldn't, wouldn't do this to me.

Rowena tells me to breathe and I realize I hadn't really inhaled since hearing my uncle's name. I intentionally take air in and out of my lungs a half dozen times.

I say my thoughts aloud, "He couldn't. He wouldn't."

The guard leans forward, speaking in slow, even tones. "I've never lied to you. Never. Not even in Bunkerville. And I'm not lying now. Senator Manchester became The Center's largest donor once you arrived. After The Center burned down, your Uncle became the controlling partner in this failing experiment. He's the boss. The one in charge of what happens both here and in Bunkerville."

"I don't believe you."

"I heard it from his own mouth."

"You're saying he knew about everything."

"Everything."

"The hypnosis?"

"Everything."

"Killing the baby?"

"Yes, everything. Courtney, until Dr. Maggie signed off on my transfer to this section, I was in every intel meeting there was. He picked what you would see in Truth. He approved of your Isolation. He said you wouldn't be able to handle solitary for so long and knew you would choose Bunkerville."

"But why?"

"Personally, I believe his motive was to have your memory erased."

"Even of him?"

"Especially of him."

"But my memory of him is positive."

"That's because it's not real. He's a game player. You'll never understand people like that. Don't try. Honestly, I didn't see his mania until your pregnancy came up. That totally freaked him out. He said babies ruin everything. Dr. Maggie agreed, although I've come to learn, she never planned to actually abort the baby, only tell him she had. She loves experiments too much. She planned to document the abortion while keeping the baby in Bunkerville to monitor and manipulate."

"She's sick."

"They're both sick."

"No. No. Not him. There has to be a good reason for what he's doing. It has to be honest and kind. Has to be." I rub the top of my belly. "Dr. Maggie, yes. She's a killer. She'll do anything to keep her experiment running, including murdering my surrogate mother."

"Faith?" Rowena takes a step back. "Faith is dead?"

"Yeah, she drowned in Bunkerville."

"I didn't know. Oh my gosh. This can't be happening.

They've gone too far. No one is safe." Rowena's strength melts. Her vulnerability terrifies me. This all has to be some crazy nightmare. Panic laces her voice as she says, "I need to take you to Ángel. Let you see whatever video your uncle has prepared. I'm going to look into what happened to Faith."

The idea of leaving the safety of Isolation frightens me. "Can't you tell me?"

"I don't know what's on the tapes. I only know he did all he could to keep them from you. But now you've fully embraced truth. He's become the doting uncle again." She waves her arms around the room. "All of this has been orchestrated by him. The visitors. The midwife."

"The crayons?"

"Yes. But that's all I know." She frowns at me, "And more than I should have told you."

"Could you get in trouble for telling me he's the boss?"

"Yes. Very big trouble. I believe he's capable of drugging me and erasing my memories. Or, if you're right about Faith, worse than that."

"Then why tell me?"

"Because, I believe you have a right to know. Now, come on, we're wasting time." She opens the door to the sound-proof room and I follow her from it.

CHAPTER 68

In the video room, Ángel nervously rolls the remote control around in his hands.

"Let's do this thing." My tone sounds brave, but anxiety courses through my veins. I have no reason to believe Rowena is lying about Uncle John's role in this place. The elaborate story rings of politics and truth. What doesn't make sense is why the senator would want to reinvent me. We've always been close. But if Rowena's right, our closeness was either one-sided, or a mirage. The thought generates a physical pain in the core of my heart.

Ángel sinks into his corner seat.

I climb into the chair.

The lights dim.

The screen comes alive with images. The ache in my heart expands as Uncle John's happy face stretches wide across the wall. I recognize the location. Reagan National Airport. He personally escorted me away from DC and my normal life. The film is muted like the other times I'd been in this room. A chill cascades down my arms from the occasional blast of air through ducts.

Because I was a seventeen-year-old minor, he was able to take me to the gate where he handed me off to a police officer. Back then I believed he accompanied me out of love. I desperately needed to believe he found me important enough to fly from his Manhattan apartment to see me off. I figured it was extravagant. Since the senate wasn't in session, he must have come to D.C. to be close to me. Now, I can't piece together a motive.

A close-up of his smile hurts like the rejection of my father. I look away and the video stops. A couple bulbs above me bring light into the room.

"Are you okay?" Ángel comes to my side.

It hurts too much to talk. I curl onto my side and allow the emotions to flow. I miss him. I know I ignored him while in The Center. In our last phone call, I'd been demanding and petty.

"Why?" I ask the room. "Why would he abandon me to Bunkerville?"

"Who? Your uncle?"

I press my lips together. Ángel doesn't know the man on the screen is the boss. For Rowena's sake I don't say more. As far as the guard standing next to me is concerned, I'm watching home videos. Unless he's not being honest with me either. I wipe my eyes and ask the guard directly. "Do you know my uncle?"

"I recognize him."

"From where?"

"From TV. My father's obsessed with politics. Watches CSPAN like it's a sport."

"But that's all you know?"

"Yeah."

"And you don't know what I'm about to see?"

"No." He looks down. "I hope he's not dead. That would be too cruel."

"No, I don't think he is."

"Then why the tears?"

"Honestly, it's hard to connect who I was to who I am today." I sit up again. "I'm not the person I used to be. And it's very possible he's not the person I thought he was."

"We all change. But love doesn't."

I wipe my eyes. "I hope you're right."

"Of course, I am."

"Do you think my Uncle has the power to get me out of this place? Do you think he could have?"

Ángel shrugs, "Yes, I think someone in his position could have moved you to another detention center after the fire. Other influential parents did." Then he turns to me, "But he doesn't know what goes on down here. He couldn't. Don't start thinking about another person's motives when he's not here to talk to you. To tell you."

I let the words sink in. They don't conflict with what Rowena said, but they don't support her story either. Maybe Uncle John is more complex than Rowena's two-dimensional villain. Uncle John would have to be a heck of an actor to pretend for the last seventeen years. Something in this video has the answers and I'm ready to see them. Whatever pulled the man on the screen away from me, he's back and I want to see why.

I face the wall.

The lights dim again.

The video starts.

The next scene takes me back further, to the Halloween night in New York when I concocted the stupid idea to buy oxy over the internet and drug Nicole into being my best friend. I fight each inhale. I wish they would get beyond my stupid and dangerous decisions. I've learned how my revenge was beyond over-the-top.

More images including birthday vacations, surprise picnics in Balboa Park. Each scene slowly taking me backward through the parts of my life I shared with Uncle John, all of them good. When Uncle John isn't present, the events deal with the lack of affection from my own parents.

A lonely day in the park with my friends.

The day my mother and father took my sister, Kat, to Catalina to celebrate her second grade report card. Then Nanny Bella holding me close when I discovered I wasn't invited. I rub my belly, allowing sadness to flood the little girl I used to be.

A new scene blinks onto the screen. This one dimmer. The other images had come from security cameras, this one from a traffic cam. Even without sound, I remember the conversation with Ashley. Dust casting a gray tint over the formerly green summer scene.

All the kids in the neighborhood had been playing "ditch", the adolescent version of hide-and-go-seek-plus-tag game. The darker it got the better the game. Problem was, once the sun set, the stupid streetlights would come on and person after person would disappear into their houses along Point Loma. That night, Ashley and I were the last to remain.

I didn't remember the look on Ashley's face because back then I was too busy staring at my feet. And I never would have seen the blended look of anger and loneliness on my own if not for this moment. Ashley's lips move and my memory fills in the words.

"Don't you have to go inside?"

"Nope." I picked up a rock and tossed it into the street.

"No curfew? Lucky you."

"I guess."

"What?" She pulled away from me in shock. But there I was, the younger version of me on the screen, still chucking random rocks into the street as I told her what I'd known my whole life. A curfew meant someone cared when you came and went. A curfew meant someone worried about you getting nabbed by the boogie man. I didn't have that. And at twelve or thirteen, I realized how pathetic my childhood had been. And so did Ashley.

Pity. That's what she wore on her face as she left me sitting in the ever-darkening evening tossing stones into the street.

"What's the point of all this?" Ángel complains. Embarrassment clouds his face. His shoulders slump as younger versions of me flicker to life.

"Hey! Don't you dare feel sorry for me." I shift in my seat seeking a more comfortable position.

"I'm human, okay? I'm not a robot. These videos don't make sense. They aren't like anything I've seen before. This is borderline bullying."

I stare at the frozen image of a mini-me with red braids making a sandcastle. "But why? There has to be a reason."

"I don't know, but we can stop if you want." He stands and approaches my chair.

"Why do you care?" I pour my frustration on him. "You didn't seem to mind the others. You didn't offer to stop when the images were of Jackson and Ribbon. This is just a job to you."

His eyes glisten as he says, "This was never just a job for me. I've come to believe in this place. I've seen people benefit."

"From prison tats and guilt trips? I never thought you'd be good with any of that."

"I'm not. The tattoos are excessive and crazy. But Truth can be about more than a guilt trip. Like I said, I've seen people I knew from The Center gain honest perspectives on their lives. Become people who cared more about others than they did prior to sitting in this chair."

"Like me?"

"Yes, to be honest, like you. You have to admit you were a nicer person after you saw what effect your actions had on the lives of others."

He's right. The earlier videos, while not completely fair, did force me to see myself as others saw me.

"But this," he points at the screen. "This doesn't seem to be about giving you an honest perspective on your contributions to the world, but to humiliate you."

"I think the boss wants to send me a message," I insist. "Apparently everything boils down to my childhood. Maybe even my birth."

"Sounds more like Dr. Maggie than the boss."

"Maybe they aren't so different." I sit back triggering the show to continue. A happy little me skips toward the camera, and Ángel stays next to me. The comradery lights a candle of courage inside of me.

Uncle John can show me whatever he wants. Nothing he shows me will alter the past. Except I might learn why he decided I should experience these horrible experiments. What part of him did he want to erase from my life via hypnosis? Or what part of my life did he want me to accept in Truth?

The scrolling videos stop on a picture I know well. The one of my uncle holding me as a newborn. My mother smiled in the background, happier than I ever remember her being. The still pictures came from the photo album my uncle sent me. Each shot taking turns occupying the screen.

325

This video isn't new.

This video existed before the fire.

It had to because, these snapshots had been left on the bed in my dorm room on the day of the fire. My uncle sent the beloved book to me in the mail. Whatever message he wanted me to learn, began in The Center. And what I thought had been forever destroyed now shines on the white wall.

The photo slideshow is replaced with a video made from an old handheld recorder. My very pregnant mother sits on a lawn chair next to a resort swimming pool.

An urge to pee comes over me. I push it away. Not that I want to see my mother and father on vacation before I was born, I'm just ready to get this over. We must be near the end and the answer. I bounce my leg as I watch.

The radiant joy on my mother's face is disarming. Her stern features are relaxed in ways I never knew they could be. The young, vibrant, pregnant woman in her two-piece bathing suit, unashamed of the growing child within her. Like an old TV ad for sunscreen, she gets up and sits next to the sapphire blue water before slipping into it.

I tighten my legs, hoping the need to urinate will subside.

With the palm of her hand, mother splashes water toward the lens. The scene jiggles around as whoever holds the camera places it on a table so they can join the fun. A wall-to-wall mustache comes in view as the camera shifts.

I don't remember my father ever having a mustache.

The thought is jarring. Of course, this was filmed before I was born, and he could have had one then. I lean closer to see, but the man moves out of view and the image blurs then zooms before being returned to the table.

My mother's face is closer. She encourages the man with the mustache to join her. I struggle to picture my father with facial hair. Not his style, but it could have been.

Unless.

The baby shifts.

I adjust my position.

The need to pee hits me so hard, I can't contain it any longer. "Stop." I turn my face away from the images and the flickering swimming party pauses.

"I need the bathroom."

Ángel helps me and I waddle-run down the corridor. The whole time I pray I won't pee my pants. The bathroom isn't far, although the journey feels like it's a hundred miles away. Ángel pushes open the door and lets me enter alone. I don't need to add more humiliation to my list of experiences. I make it to the toilet right in time.

Relief empties from me. My mind is able to think. To connect dots. The mustache man is not my father. Uncle John wants me to know my mother had an affair. This is his big reveal. The news he wanted to erase or for me to accept. I'm not a Manchester, which honestly doesn't bother me the way it should. My father isn't my father. Which means Uncle John isn't my uncle since they are brothers. That thought would have made me incredibly sad a day ago. Now, I'm not so sure what to think of the New York senator.

I wash up in the white porcelain sink.

Why didn't Uncle John tell me this years ago? Why the elaborate video? He knows the news would have given me great joy, explaining my father's distance toward me and greater love for my sister.

I dry my hands, moving the paper towel between each finger as I think. Maybe Uncle John isn't the sociopath Rowena thinks he is. He might want me to embrace my real father and let him go. The love in the thought warms the cold sting of rejection I have been worried about.

Ángel pushes off the wall as I exit the bathroom. As we return to the room, I tell him, "I've figured it out. All these videos about me and my life come down to information I never would have believed about myself. I'm not a Manchester."

"What do you mean?"

"That man on the screen, he's not my father. My dad never had a mustache. My mother had an affair."

"I was thinking the same thing."

"Really?"

"Yes." Based on the way he says the word, he's concerned. "Are you okay?"

"I am. I honestly don't care I'm not a Manchester. I'm glad Benjamin Edward Manchester is not my real father. I'm over the moon glad. You were right earlier. These videos have helped me. I no longer care about the money or position. And to be honest, I'm excited to discover I have a father I've never met. Maybe if I find him, I'll find me." For the first time in months, excitement bubbles inside of me. "I want this. I really do. Having a different father explains a lot."

"Courtney, I think you are partially right."

"Partially?" I enter the room.

"Yes."

"How could my mother have a partial affair?"

"I think you're right about the affair part. But maybe wrong about who it was with."

"I don't know who it was with, so how can I be wrong about someone unknown to me?"

Ángel quietly closes the door but doesn't take his position in the corner. "I think you do know him."

The idea stops me cold.

The guard approaches and says, "I think I recognized the man with the mustache."

"What? How could you? His image only flashed on the screen a couple times."

"Long enough for me to know. Long enough for me to be worried about how the news will impact you."

"What? Why? No." I insist. "This is good news."

"You know him too."

The pain of doubt returns full force. "No, I don't. I don't. How could I?"

His words are barely a whisper, but are loud enough to burst the hope building inside of me. "Because you've known him all your life."

His tone scares the snot out of me. He points to the screen and says, "Look closely."

In the frozen image on the screen, the guy leans close to my mother.

My heart hurts.

My palms are wet.

I bite my lower lip.

Dr. Maggie's proverbial puzzle pieces fall into place.

The man with the mustache is none other than the young, up-and-coming senator from New York.

My Dad's brother.

My Uncle John.

CHAPTER 69

Time slows.

The shock hits me the way an unexpected car slams into another. Broken glass floats as the harsh impact crumples unsuspecting passengers into crunching metal.

Prior to Truth, I was the neglected niece of a US senator. I'm the byproduct of an awful affair. My father didn't swing me as a child because he must have hated the very sight of me. My memories have been fitted together all wrong. My life began as a lie. A betrayal.

And to make matters worse, I'm still a Manchester. Still connected to the warped dysfunction of money and politics. As much as I want the man I grew up thinking was my father to love me, I never deserved it.

I can't move.

Not fingers.

Not face.

Nothing.

How can I ever be loved by Benjamin Edward

Manchester? I represent the worst moment of his life. Not only did his wife cheat on him, she used his own brother to do it. I am the family's dirty little secret.

The adults responsible for me probably thought a horrible announcement in the press would have ruined their image. Uncle John would have had to resign. And in the end, all his love was fake. Built on guilt, probably. He didn't love me enough to impact his career. He chose to preserve his name over acknowledging my true connection to him.

Uncle John…I swallow.

No, not my uncle. My sperm donor.

The only man who ever showed me affection is a fake. As the jacked up, jigsaw puzzle pieces fall into the right places, he approves of my being here and signed off for me to be a rat in a social experiment. All his acts of affection on the outside must have been fueled by shame.

A pain wells in my back, shattering the ache in my heart.

The stabbing cramps crawl their claws across my belly as my abdomen turns inside out. A splash of water erupts between my legs and I scream at the top of my lungs.

CHAPTER 70

Pain replaces every thought of my own messed up birth. One hundred percent of my attention is drawn into the insane cramping and the short reprieve between contractions.

Ángel gets me blankets and calls for the midwife.

My labor isn't long, but it is excruciating. The twisting convulsions of my uterus aren't the worst part of delivering a baby. The movies got it all wrong. The worst part of delivery is the burning tear of muscle as my son pushes his way into the world. His head forcing its way through a hole too small for him.

But as unbearable as the pain is, the moment I hear the child's first cry, thoughts of pain fall away.

"It's a boy!" the midwife's deep bass voice proclaims.

He's here. Safe. Whole.

"I'd hand him to you, but we want to get you into a clean gown and deliver the placenta before we can do that." With the small child squirming in his hands, he asks Ángel if he'd rather hold the child or cut the umbilical cord. He chooses to hold the baby.

"Go wash your hands, all the way to the elbow. Don't just wet them, lather, and scrub to the count of twenty. Then dry off with the towel and grab the baby blanket."

While the guard is busy, the gloved midwife points the child in my direction.

"He's strong. You did good."

"Thank you," I say looking at the squashed face and sticky limbs.

"Grab some gloves from the box and put them on."

"Why wash my hands if–"

"Because you're going to touch the gloves. Now, come on and hold this boy close against your gown while I snip this cord."

The baby's eyes are wide when Ángel turns for me to see him. "He's so beautiful."

"Yes, he really is."

"I can't believe he's here. I've imagined him for so long."

"What are you going to call him?"

"Oh my gosh, I never thought of a name. I'm going to make a horrible mother."

"No, you won't. You risked your life to save this child. To me it's the best sign of what mother's do than any. His name will come to you. In some societies, a baby doesn't get his name until he's over a week old. Take your time."

I nod. I have time. We all have time.

"Courtney." The midwife draws my attention away from the baby by patting my leg. "We have one more step before we get you cleaned up to hold your son. When you feel another contraction come, I need you to push some more."

"Is there more than one?"

He chuckles, "No. We need to deliver the placenta, or

you could bleed to death."

I push, and with the midwife's help, deliver the afterbirth.

"Good job," he says, "We're almost done. Ángel, will you please get Courtney a clean gown while I wash the baby. "Courtney," he turns to me. "Take this rubbing alcohol and towel to clean off your upper body as best as you can. Normally I wouldn't be so excessive, but this is still a prison and not a hospital or your home."

I'm okay with the request. Anything to hold the boy in my arms. Which is exactly what happens within the next five minutes.

The baby is bundled.

I'm clean and in a gown open in the front for nursing.

A warm blanket is laid across my legs and peace floods my soul.

The midwife stays with me while Ángel goes to prepare a room for the baby and I to use. "You look really tired. This chair isn't a safe place for you to hold the child, so if you get sleepy, let me know."

"I will," I say, although I'm not tired at all.

He sits and tells me he's been doing some research. "I don't know when your sentence is over, but above ground, some prisons allow inmates to keep their baby for eighteen months."

"Really?"

"Unless you were thinking of adoption. If that's the case, the less you bond with him, the better."

I draw the child closer to me as if his words could pull my son away. "I thought about it."

"Most teen mothers do."

"Do you think it's selfish for me to keep him?"

"As an adopted child myself, I don't think so. I met my

birth mother and she's an amazing lady. But she was thirteen when she had me. She told me her parents had split up and her mother threatened to kick her out of the house. In the end, she wasn't financially or emotionally equipped to raise me. My adoptive parents were loving and supportive. They couldn't have children, so they saw me as a gift. But every situation is different. This child is a gift. The question is, to whom?"

The baby's slate gray eyes stare blankly at me.

"If you'd like, I'll make a call to a counselor I talked to. She really helped me understand all the dynamics connected to being adopted and giving a child up. You might not have planned his conception, but that doesn't mean you can't be very intentional about his future."

I pull the child even closer. "Is she in Bunkerville?"

"Oh, God, no," he scoffs. "I wouldn't trust someone to give me a manicure in that place. No. This is someone who lives above ground."

"Sounds like you're not a fan of Bunkerville."

"Hmmm." The bass sound comes from deep inside of him. "I wouldn't say that. I think it's no longer the place for me. If I were to compare it to someplace. It reminds me of an old fun house with its tricks and whistles and twisted mirrors. Entertaining while testing your nerves."

I agree with him completely.

"I do plan to leave once I know you and the baby are in the safe health zone. And I do mean both of you."

"Thank you."

"No, thank you. If I hadn't met you, I wouldn't be planning on returning to the profession I loved so much. I'm going back above ground to work as a midwife. I no longer care as much for the rejection I receive as I do experiencing the greatest miracle ever created by God."

I rock the small child entrusted to me and think about how hard it would be to give him up. He's a part of me. He has saved me from drug injections and reprogramming. I'm not in the same situation as the midwife's birth mother. I'm not poor. In fact, I'm related to some immensely powerful people.

Powerful, manipulative, possibly even sociopathic. If I keep him, I'm not sure I can shield him from the rejection he will probably receive from my father—the one who fed and clothed me, not the one who played the part of doting uncle. And I wouldn't want to spend a lifetime lying to him about the uncle who tried to trick me into aborting him. I'm not sure I want this precious baby exposed to the dysfunctional mess I call home. The decision in front of me isn't as clear or distinct as the movies make it out to be.

CHAPTER 71

The midwife stays in the video room long enough for me to nurse the baby, bundle him, and use the bathroom on my own. He provides me with a squirt bottle to rinse with rather than the pain of toilet paper. I'm given a maxi pad the size of a diaper and some ice packs before getting me into the wheelchair.

Lucy hands me a small bottle of Tylenol which I put in the pocket of my gown and a ring to sit on. The baby is wrapped tightly in a blanket and sound asleep. I wave goodbye to the midwife who promises to return in the morning. I don't mind the bumpy ride to Isolation because I'm still too enamored with the small bundle in my arms.

I would love to show him off to the entire prison, but the halls we travel are empty. It's probably best. I need to be careful about how I feel about this sweet child. Bunkerville robbed me of thinking time. Four months passed where I could have considered what would be best for him. Adoption has always been an option. Something I honestly considered, but keeping him has also never left me. But now he's here, I truly need to consider what's in his best interest, not mine.

The door to the white room opens, and it already smells fresher than I remember. Not the fake baby-powder scent from Bunkerville, but actual smells of lotions and linens. Inside, the room feels brighter and more welcoming with the added baby fixtures. Next to my cot, a bright pink basinet with a musical mobile of butterflies and flowers. In the empty corner near the exposed toilet is a blue changing table decorated with gray and green elephants, hippos, and rhinoceroses. Diapers and baby clothes lay folded on the writing table.

I'd love to cling to the doll-like infant in my mind, but I focus on what he needs. The midwife said he's exhausted and could sleep up to eight hours. He has worked as hard to come into the world as I have.

Lucy gently lays the bundle into the basinet before coming to help me from the wheelchair and onto the bed.

It takes both her hands and mine to move from chair to bed. I accept the offer of water and two pain tablets before curling onto my side with the icepack resting between my legs.

"We're bringing you a small dresser for his clothes and maybe a rocking chair."

"I'm going to stay here?"

"The boss thinks it's the safest place."

"So, I'm still a secret."

"You could say that, but I don't know his intention."

"That's because you don't know him."

"And you do?"

"I think I've figured him out." I say and close my eyes. Sleep overtakes me and consumes the time in ways only sleep can. I'm awakened by the grunting newborn cry.

I rise too quickly and have to wince through the pain. "It's okay," I whisper as I lean over the basinet to pick him up. Sitting on the side of the bed, I bring him to my breast the way the midwife showed me, and I'm surprised at how easily he latches on. I've never cooed in my life until that moment, but the sound escapes my lips involuntarily.

The door opens and I'm surprised to hear Dee Dee ask, "Is everything alright?"

"Yes, he's hungry." I shift my eyes to her and ask, "What are you doing here?"

"I've been outside working on homework for about three hours when I heard him cry through the monitor." She points to a white speaker I never noticed sitting on the writing table.

Looking into my baby's eyes, I speak to my friend, "Have they made you a guard or something?"

She chuckles and moves to get a better look at the boy. "Not hardly," she says, "All the visitors you had before have signed up to take shifts to be here to help you and this little guy as much as possible." Her voice becomes singsong when she refers to the baby. "Isn't that right little man?"

"So, I have an entire crew of people to help me?"

"Yup," she reaches towards the baby's finger and then pulls back. "Wait, let me wash my hands."

An entire crew of inmates has been assigned to help me. That could only be the work of one person. The man who refused to acknowledge his parentage. He chose his political position over raising me. And his choices started when he chose to have an affair with my mother. Even recording the event for others to see. Not the world of course, but maybe his brother. While I'd love to consider his actions as kindness, the new information helps me see the desire to control imbedded inside of them. A control I used to mistake for love in my own life.

"My uncle is excessive, that's for sure."

From the sink Dee Dee turns toward me, "What's your uncle have to do with this?"

I don't respond to her question directly but voice my thoughts aloud. "One minute he's trying to kill the child, now it's as if the boy's a crowned prince."

"Whoa, hold on." She holds up a soapy hand. "Let me do this right, and then I want to know everything."

I nod my head and study the baby monitor. After Dee Dee dries her hands I tell her to turn it off. "What I'm about to tell you has to stay within these walls."

Her big brown eyes widen with interest and remain animated throughout the entire saga about my uncle being the boss as well as my biological father.

"That's messed up," she whispers.

"You're telling me." I jut my chin toward the monitor, and say, "probably should turn that back on before someone gets suspicious."

She does it while I unwrap the small boy and change his teeny-tiny diaper and try to bundle him back up. The blanket is looser than when the midwife did it.

"Can I try?" Dee Dee asks.

I nod, pushing back the feeling of failure rising inside me. Her small brown hands work slowly and perfectly, which doesn't help. "I've been practicing."

"On what?"

"The midwife gave us all a baby doll and a blanket. All the incinerator girls know how to bathe him, change him, comfort him. The midwife's been teaching us for weeks."

"Why didn't he teach me?"

"He said he would, but he was worried. Until you gave

birth to a healthy child, he didn't want to get your hopes up too high."

"He thought my baby was going to die?"

"No, not that. He said he experienced a mother who'd given birth to a stillborn child in circumstances less risky than this."

The word kindness bounces around in my heart like a beachball. And it doesn't stop when Dee Dee leaves. For the next few days, I push away thoughts of my uncle and his motives and accept the kindness of the gentle and competent midwife, the visits and gifts of inmates, and the growth of a little boy whose life I have the power to change.

For the first time ever, I spend every waking moment considering the needs of someone else rather than myself. And by the evening of day seven, I'm ready to tell the midwife I think I'm ready to be a parent. Ready to spend the rest of my life doing the easy and hard things necessary to care for another human being.

I watch my newborn's eyes drift closed and the slight rise and fall of his chest as he breathes. I close my eyes to sleep not knowing in the morning every ounce of peace and comfort will be stolen from me.

CHAPTER 72

I sleep through the night. The entire night. I'm beyond rested. Sitting up and stretching stiff limbs, it feels like I've had eight to ten hours of dreamless sleep. I smile through all the seconds it takes for me to toss off covers. For milk to leak from my breasts. For me to bend over and reach into the void where my newborn son should have been.

Frozen, I stare for a moment before calling to the monitor, "I'm up and ready to nurse, you can bring the baby back."

But the door remains closed.

I waddle to the device. It's turned off. I flip the switch on, but the red light doesn't glow. The idea of my baby being kidnapped first enters my brain at this moment. My hands are shaking as I turn over the monitor and see the batteries have been removed.

"No. No. No." The device crashes to the floor where I drop it as I hurry to the door and pound. "Open up. Hurry, please, the baby, he's gone."

My fist crashes against metal as the door swings inward.

"Whoa," Ángel steps back to avoid crashing into me.

"Where's the baby?" I grab the lapel of his uniform.

"In the..." he points to the basinet then stops midsentence.

"He's gone." I push past him. "Someone's taken him. Oh my God, help me." I rush down the hall ready to fight my way to Bunkerville and find my child. "She took him. She had to."

"Courtney, stop," Ángel reaches for my arm, but I slap him away.

"No. He's gone. He's been taken."

One white hallway leads to another.

"And we'll get him back," Ángel races in front of me, blocking yet another dead end. "Let me help, please. You're not alone. You're not."

"But I am. Without my son, I'm nothing." The reality of my circumstances breaks through my search. I'm lost. In this place. In this life.

"You don't know this maze like I do," the guard says. "Please, Courtney, we're wasting time. I can't let you run through the halls, I can't. And the more time I spent trying to stop you is time I could be looking for the baby."

I crumple to the floor. "He's gone. She took him, I know she did."

"Who?" Ángel gets me to look into his eyes. "Did you see her? Who was it?"

"I didn't see anything. I was sleeping." The tears gush from my face. "I was sleeping." The words cave in around me. No decent mother sleeps through the abduction of her child. Real mothers wake at the slightest sound. The slightest movement.

"Let's go back, please. I'll send Lucy to get Dee Dee for

you, and I promise we will turn this institution upside down. Whoever took him can't be far."

I return to my cell to perform the hardest act a parent ever has to do for a child.

Wait.

CHAPTER 73

Sitting on my bed, I fight to exhale. The dreams of a better life for my son evaporate like mist. The unselfish action of saving him has failed.

The idea carves a hole in my soul.

I search the cot, and tables, and bassinet hoping to find a clue. Praying to a God I don't know for a miracle I don't deserve. "Please," I say through unstoppable tears, "Please don't let her hurt him. Please," I fall to my knees, "Please keep him safe. Bring him back to me."

Nanny Bella comes to mind. Her prayers and her words of reproach when I behaved badly and her just because hugs. She taught me how to love. She's the one constant in my life. "Jesus," I say to the ceiling. "She'll help me. I'll do whatever it takes to live with her and raise my son right."

Dee Dee enters the room, her face as terror-stricken as mine. She doesn't whisper false hope but holds me as we weep and wait.

Hours pass like weeks.

Minutes feel like days.

Each second brings on new terrors of what might be happening to my son.

The lunch tray arrives with Sleeves and Lucy. They join the worrying and waiting. By the time Ángel returns, I've become numbed by shock.

His words seep over me like I'm made of plastic. "Your baby is nowhere to be found."

I don't move from the place where I sit. I can't move. My body no longer belongs to me. I gave it to the baby. And without him here, I'm frozen.

"But he's not the only one missing."

"What do you mean?" Dee Dee offers the question I'm too frozen to ask.

"Three adults are also missing. One or more of them must have taken the boy."

"Who else is gone?" Sleeves asks.

"The midwife, Rowena, and Dr. Maggie."

Advocates and enemies. The words formulate in my mind as my eyes remain fixed on the white wall. Any one of the three might take the baby for very different reasons.

The midwife because he senses the child is in danger. Maybe sick and needing medical attention.

Rowena because she doesn't trust me. She was always more interested in making sure the baby was safe, not me. I can see her protecting the child over my feelings.

And Dr. Maggie, she would steal the baby for her experiments. But I'm not sure the mad psychiatrist would give up her precious Bunkerville for the sake of one child. On the other hand, I did a pretty good job at casting doubt on her crazy plan to erase the history of an adult. With a fresh canvas...

"It's her," I say aloud. Turning to those seated around

the room. "It must be her."

"Who? Rowena or Dr. Maggie?" Ángel asks.

"Dr. Maggie. Think about it. She wouldn't abandon her life's work for any other reason. Bunkerville is her child."

Sleeves pokes out her bottom lip and nods in agreement.

Dee Dee asks, "What can we do about it?"

"Find her." I'm adamant.

"But how?" Lucy asks.

"By asking the boss," Ángel offers. "He has the power to find her."

"No," I tell him. "Ángel, he can't be trusted. He was part of the plan to kill the child."

"You don't know that."

"I do," I say. With Rowena gone, I no longer feel the need to keep her secret. I tell the group what I told Dee Dee.

"That's messed up," Lucy says.

"Very," Sleeves agrees.

"The only people who I trust to help me are sitting in this room."

"But two of us are inmates," Dee Dee reminds me. "We can't help."

"If we escape, you can."

"Are you nuts?" Sleeves asks.

"No, I'm not. We don't have time, and my baby's life could be in danger. Dr. Maggie is unstable. If the boy has a hope of a happy live, we have the power to deliver that. Which means escaping this hell hole."

Dee Dee and the female guard are on board. Sleeves sides with Ángel as he lists all the risks. He concludes his stupid sermon with, "We'll all be fugitives with limited power if we get out of here."

"Seriously?" I lean forward, feeling stronger than I have in years. "I'm my uncle's dirty little secret. The bastard daughter he's kept hidden from the world. As long as I'm underground, the secret holds no leverage. But once I'm above ground, I'll have access to all the money and power I need to find my son."

"Blackmail plus a prison break." Ángel throws his hands into the air, "There goes my future FBI career."

"Then you'll do it?" I ask.

"Yeah."

I face the inmate who I met months ago in a laundry room. We spent only a couple hours together back then, and since I've returned to the prison we've become closer, but she owes me nothing. "Sleeves, you don't have to come if you don't want. It's up to you."

Her voice lacks enthusiasm, but she shrugs and says, "What, and miss all the fun?"

Dee Dee grins.

For the next hour, the five of us plan our escape, which will happen first thing in the morning.

CHAPTER 74

Without talking to the boss, Ángel moves me to my old yellow cell. It's closer to Dee Dee and Sleeves, and time will be crucial once the escape begins. I don't look too long at the baby's things, it hurts too much. I do think of grabbing a memento, but Lucy reminds us to carry as little as possible. No extra clothes or souvenirs.

"Just walk through the halls with the same silent obedience as every other day."

She's right.

Raise no flags.

I stay alert as I march through the weaving corridors to where life in The Bunker began for me.

When the door clicks closed, I sink onto the cot surrounded by yellow walls and monitored by my mural friends, it seems fitting the place where I started should be the last place I sleep. Not that I can sleep. The idea I might miss the lights coming on keeps jolting me awake. Hopefully Ángel, Dee Dee, and Sleeves aren't as restless.

I need them rested. Alert. Lucy too. She's not leaving The Bunker but will divert attention away from us.

The plan is rock solid.

Ángel will begin before lights up. Once the corridors come awake, he'll pick up Sleeves, then me, then Dee Dee. We have thirty minutes to get above ground from the time the lights come on. Sleeves recommended we carry some kind of "shank" just in case. Ángel didn't like the idea, but Lucy agreed.

Our exit will be from the prison. Bunkerville is out of the question. To escape, we won't use the elevators. Guards don't trudge up the dozen or so flights to the command center. From there, we'll have a three-story ladder to climb before reaching the pyramid entrance of The Bunker. The forest fire has been out long enough to navigate the paths made by fire fighters and guards. Ángel's car is parked with others on the gravel driveway where The Center used to keep buses and snowcats.

We'll drive to Ángel's apartment, where I'll call my uncle and make my demands. The first and most important is to locate my son. We recorded a video of my statement in case something happens to me. Everyone on the team has all my uncle's phone numbers. With four of us, the odds of at least two of us making it out are extremely high.

This is going to work.

Not only because it's a great plan, but because it has to for all of our sakes. We've been through hell together and we deserve to climb from hell and see the sun again. And my son deserves to know I'll do anything for him. Unlike my DNA donor.

The single bulb in the ceiling of my cell clicks on.

The thin blanket tumbles to the floor.

The clock officially starts. Thirty sets of sixty seconds to get to Ángel's car. Not much time.

I reach into the fitted sheet's tucked corner for the pencil I'd sharpened into a point. I march to the locked cell door. With my face pressed against the thick window, I look for Ángel. The dirty walls bleed into harsh cement floors and ceilings. Wire-encased bulbs cast light and shadows along the empty corridor. The recycled air smells of dust.

I tap on the glass as if it's an elevator button. No sign of Ángel. Across the aisle in the small window, a frozen face glares at me. I gulp down a gasp. She shouldn't be there. Ángel told us no one lives in that cell. I stare at the potential witness.

Narrow pupils.

Hollowed sockets.

Dark circles.

The hair on my forearms lifts. Her eyes don't blink. Her mouth, a straight line, frozen in her face like a dead person. My heart thumps hard in my chest. No people roam through the hallway. The girl across from me looks left and right when I do. I squint at her. She squints. That face, that ugly face could ruin everything. If Ángel comes now, this crazy phantom can mess up our plan. I shake my head and she shakes hers.

I step back. She steps back.

I click my tongue. How stupid can I be? The scary phantom in the other cell is me.

"This is no time to be going crazy," I scold myself. "Calm down. Everything's okay. Sleeves and Ángel are less than one minute away. Stay cool."

I pace under the single bulb in my cell. My shadow stretches and shrinks. A minute can take a long time. I examine the tip of the pencil I took from Isolation. I'd love to use it to improve my mural. Horace's whiskers. Natasha's eyelashes. Jasper's knuckle hair.

Not much of a shank.

But a million years ago in junior high, I saw a girl jab someone in the leg with a pen. It did some damage. Drew blood. As the thick instrument thumps against my skin, I hate the idea of having to stab someone. As much as I want to put my violent tendencies behind me, I won't hesitate to attack anyone who comes between me and the exit.

At the wall, I place my head on the yellow cement, pushing my forehead against it, trying to replace the emotional ache with a more tolerable physical pain.

Harder.

Bone against concrete.

Harder.

Bruising of skin.

Harder.

Three knocks on the door startle me. Rubbing my forehead, I swallow unsurfaced tears.

"Finally," I whisper as I hurry to the door. My heart fights to escape my ribs. My head hurts. The grate of a metal key in a steel lock means our plan is still in motion. We are going. We are really going. Today I'll see the sun again. Breathe non-recirculated oxygen. Find my son and feel his small frame enclosed against me.

"Let's go," Ángel whispers.

I exhale and follow him and Sleeves to Dee Dee's cell just down the hall. Once we have the full group, we sprint as fast as possible to a hallway I've never been down before. Our feet pound the cement floor until we stop at a door. Ángel pulls it open and we enter a stairwell.

Ángel leads. Dee Dee, Sleeves, and I climb.

At the end of three flights, Ángel opens the door and we navigate an unpainted gray hall. Sleeves and I hustle behind him with the faster, younger Dee Dee taking the rear. If we get divided, we won't escape. As inmates we've never been through this section of the maze. Ángel makes his third left turn, going full out when he slides to a stop.

He turns and waves us back around the corner.

He doesn't speak, but mouths the words, "Go back. Go back. Go back."

Our momentum stops with the clock still ticking off precious seconds.

CHAPTER 75

Dee Dee grabs the sleeve of my green jumpsuit. We stumble awkwardly back around the corner. With our bodies flat against the cement wall, I take slow, deep breaths through my nose to quiet my panting.

Sleeves braves a peek, before tucking herself against the wall.

The surprised voice of a female guard sneaks around the corner toward us. "What's up, Ángel?"

I cover my mouth with my hands to ensure nothing from my brain falls out. She isn't here to help. Her job would send us to our cells or worse. Lucy told us no one has ever tried to escape The Bunker. I can't let my mind wonder to the horrific consequences of being the first.

"Hey," Ángel shouts. "How you doing? I didn't expect to see you this early."

"Yeah, I wanted to get my rounds in so I can go home before the game starts. That's why I switched schedules with you today."

My freakin' heart smacks loudly against my chest. Dee Dee's eyes widen as the rest of her body stands frozen beside me. Sleeves rolls her eyes at Ángel's mistake.

"No, that's not until tomorrow," Ángel drops an f-bomb.

My heart hurts. Physically hurts.

Papers rustle before the female voice says. "Look, I have it printed out. I'm not about to miss the game."

"But I've already done Alpha through Delta."

"Awesome." A loud clap of hands startles me. "You've already finished half my shift."

"Don't do that," Ángel begs, "Switch with me."

"No way," she laughs. "You already asked me to switch and I made a date with a ballgame this afternoon."

"Please…" He sounds desperate. Too desperate. He doesn't need to do his rounds. We need to get out of here and time is ticking.

Ángel's loud sigh reaches me and Dee Dee around the corner and the female guard responds, "Later dude." Her voice drifts away.

"Fine. But you owe me." Ángel shouts.

"Right." Her chuckle fades as the echo of footsteps disappears.

As hard as I can, I shake my head, trying to Etch-a-Sketch the concerns away. Ángel handled it. The guard left. We're getting out. When Ángel comes around the corner, Sleeves asks him through clenched teeth, "What the hell was that?"

"I screwed up."

"You screwed up? That's all you have to say?"

"Stop it." Dee Dee rubs her temples. "We don't have time to do this."

"Are you sure?" Sleeves asks as she unfurls a long rope from around her waist. "Maybe he's not the friend he claims to be, maybe this is all a trick."

"I can walk out of this cave at any time," Ángel points at her. "With or without you, I'm leaving today, for good. Join me or not, I'm done arguing." He storms away.

"Sleeves," I say, "Put your weapon away. I know this place is crazy, but we need to trust Ángel."

"It could be a trick."

"Look, if this escape is fake, it's too late to change our minds." Dee Dee pushes me toward the path Ángel takes.

I grab Sleeves' hand and drag her after us. "You don't have to believe him, but we need to go. Besides, if you think about it. He's an ex-con with a short career as a prison guard. He has as much to lose as we do."

The skeptic lifts a single shoulder shrug before we catch up with Ángel who holds a door open for us.

Another stairwell.

We climb, Ángel staying one flight above us, ready to shout down a coded warning. Sleeves follows closely behind him. The cement enclosure looks like the kind killers chase their victims through in movies. I never liked slasher flicks when I lived above ground and now, I'm suddenly afraid I'm in one. But no one watching this scene would tell me not to climb those steps.

Dee Dee matches my pace and whispers to me, "You know Ángel already tried to get your boy."

"Really?"

"He goes above ground once a week. Do you know what people say when he tells them about this place?"

I keep climbing but lean my ear closer to her.

"They say, 'Stop watching so many movies.' Or 'Get a life.' Or 'Write a novel.' He needs someone with your connections and your story if we are ever going to stop this madness." My connections. The dysfunction of a family build on money, lies, and very little love.

"How do you know all this?"

"We talk. Ángel and I," she lifts one shoulder in a shy shrug, "we talk."

Of course, they do. He and I talk too, but he never told me he tried. Our rare free moments were always about me. Never really about him. One day, if we survive all of this, I will ask him about his life.

Fighting negative thoughts, I focus on climbing. Seven steps up, circle the cement stair wall, take another seven steps, a door on the left.

"How many floors?" My breathing gets heavy after only three flights.

Ángel's too far to hear me.

Dee Dee's hardly winded.

Whatever. Ten flights or twenty, knowing how many steps doesn't matter, taking them does. I count the floors by the number of doors we pass.

Number five.

I open my mouth wide to get more air into my burning lungs.

Dee Dee puts her hand on my back and pushes me up as we ascend step after step. Our pace becomes slow and steady. Door six, door seven, door eight with no clear end in sight. We must be close. Somewhere above us the sun shines. Real grass smells wet and sweet. On the ninth floor, I get my second wind and smile.

I round the corner and bump into Ángel.

"Hey," I exclaim as Dee Dee crashes into me.

"Go." I push him, but he doesn't move.

I peek around and discover what stops him.

Sleeves has her rope wrapped firmly around his neck.

CHAPTER 76

"Sleeves," I ask. "What are you doing?"

My fist tightens around the pen in my pocket. Sweat causes it to slide around in my palm. This isn't who or how I thought I might use my weapon.

"I've got orders from the boss."

"Orders?" Dee Dee asks, "What orders?"

She ignores the younger inmate and says to me, "He doesn't care if they get out. He's even willing to help them find the baby. But you're a different story."

"Me?" I point to myself shocked.

"He's not interested in being blackmailed." She pulls a taser from the back of her pants and places it on Ángel's neck. "Courtney, the choice is yours. I can zap the mess out of him, and no one gets out. Or you shut up and let them go without you. Remember, time is ticking."

I don't answer her, but my fist relaxes. I don't want to be brave, but too many sets of sixty have passed. If Dee Dee and Ángel get out, they can find my son and make sure he's safe. I have to trust them to send help. I'm not a heroic person, my past proves that, but I have no choice. Someone has to get out.

"Okay." The word tastes bitter on my tongue as I lean against the wall. "Let him go. I'll stay."

"No," Ángel says as Sleeves loosens the rope. "She's not right. Your uncle will never speak to me alone. I've been above ground. I've tried."

Sleeves places the taser against my neck. "Things are different now. He wants the baby found."

"Please, Ángel go. Take Dee Dee. Find my son."

"Listen to her," Sleeves says. The taser presses hard against my skin. I force myself to stand. I make eye contact with Dee Dee and she nods.

"Come on, Ángel." The youngest of the group guides the guard by the sleeve like she's been doing with me. He shakes his head and turns to follow. I sink against the wall. The earlier climb stole all the fight from my muscles. I'm so stinking tired, but Sleeves stops me from sitting.

"We can't stay here. Time to return to our cells." She wraps the rope tightly around my neck.

"Why are you doing this?" I ask as she steps behind me and ushers me down the steps I'd fought so hard to climb.

"Your uncle pays me." She says, pushing me against the wall at the end of the flight so she can open the door.

"You're a plant?" I ask as she drags me into a dark corridor.

"Yup," she says. "I wasn't born into the one percent."

My feet shuffle under me. My life is and never was what I believed it to be.

"Think happier thoughts." She responds to my slip. "At least Ángel and Dee Dee are on their way out of here."

The idea of them making it into the sunlight keeps me

moving. The longer she restrains me, the further they can get. Someone has to escape today if my son is to have any hope.

"We could still join them," I say as we reach an elevator.

"No way. I'm not about to abandon this contract until I'm paid. I'm not a criminal, yet I've had to live the same crummy life you've lived for the last ten months."

"Your job isn't legit. You aren't innocent."

"Maybe not, but at least I'm not stupid."

"I'd rather be stupid than motivated by money."

"Oh, ouch." She mocks while pointing the taser at me while we wait for the elevator. "Your uncle is a very powerful man and I'm not about to get on his bad side."

"I wish I could be disgusted with you. But all I feel is complete and utter disappointment."

She coughs out a laugh. "You sound like your uncle. He really wanted you to come to him. He doesn't like losing control. He fully expected you to honor the relationship you've had. You were his one bright hope."

"One big secret, you mean."

"Oh, poor Courtney had to suffer as a niece of the senator rather than as his bastard daughter."

"Don't make it sound like my life doesn't suck."

She clicks her tongue. "Everybody's life sucks. But you had choices that would have made it suck a lot less. Money, connections. You could have remained set for life. Instead, you decided to become a teenage delinquent. The senator had no choice but to hedge his bets. No one invests in a risky liability. Politicians will do anything to avoid the scandals you continued to bring his way."

"Did he take my baby?"

"I don't know. From what I've seen, he doesn't care about the child one way or another. Ultimately, he thought you'd see his parentage as a blessing. In fact, he fully expects to have a productive conversation with you in a week or two when you calm down."

"A little too late for that, don't you think?"

Again, the condescending half shrug.

The sound of the elevator's approach stirs the fight in me. I can't stay here. I can't. Dee Dee and Ángel have had enough time to distance themselves from this traitor. They should be far enough away I can at least try to get out as well.

The rope at my throat tightens, making me believe I'd spoken my last thought.

"Just so you know," Sleeves leans against my shoulder and whispers into my ear, "This taser doesn't have to be against your skin to work. I can be as far as 20 feet away to shoot you with it."

"Did I say anything?" I put anger into the question to cover the fear of a slip.

"No, just making conversation."

Pinching my lips tightly together, I think. If I stomped on her foot or kick my foot backwards, she might fall without releasing the rope. An elbow in the gut wouldn't be enough for her to let go. Only one thing might work.

I need to stab her.

With her positioned to my left, I slip my hand into my pocket and pull out the pencil. The elevator opens without a ding. Sleeves pulls me off the wall and I make my move, shoving the shank as hard and deep into her thigh as I possibly can.

The rope loosens from around my neck as Sleeves drops her end. She's off balance, so I shove her to the ground and rush into the elevator. She examines her wound for only a second while I push the button for the command center.

With gritted teeth, Sleeves lays on her good side to reach for the taser gun. I repeatedly press the close door button. Leaning on her elbow, she aims the weapon at me.

I turn away.

As the doors come together, I feel a dart enter my right butt cheek. Electric current hums through the wire and I brace for the shock but feel nothing. The doors close and the elevator rises. The wire goes taught, yanking the dart from my skin. I wince at the sting, but the pain brings relief as both darts are dragged to the door and I hear the wire snap. Looking toward earth and heaven I whisper a soft "thank you" as I rise toward freedom.

CHAPTER 77

Like all the other elevators in this horrible cave, there aren't floor indicators. Only buttons with destinations. This one doesn't have Bunkerville, only the Command Center, and three others marked Prison Level A, B, and C.

My butt cheek hurts like I'd scraped it against a thorn bush. I cautiously press my hand against the hole in my pants, happy not to feel blood. Maybe the shock didn't work because one dart missed and the other never fully made contact. I don't know. I'm relieved the shock didn't work. Sleeves' revelations were shock enough.

As I ascend, I have to wonder if the guards are on duty yet. Sleeves didn't restrain me long, but Ángel did want to avoid the elevator. For all I know, when the doors open, I could come face to face with someone ready to start their shift.

The only weapon I have is surprise, but when the doors open, I'm not in the command center but staring at a cave wall. I turn right only because there's a sign pointing that way with the words, Command Center. The smell is different too. Damp and musty, but fresher than what I've been breathing for months. No more cement. No more paint. The lights guide me to an open cavern.

The lighting here is brighter, although still artificial. Computer monitors swirl with screen savers. Chairs unoccupied. Water drips from stalagmites on the edges of the vast open space, both beautiful and creepy. In the cavern's middle, metal escape ladders reach down like dinosaur legs to the cave floor.

Across the room, I spot Ángel halfway to the ceiling. No sign of Dee Dee.

"Ángel," my voice echoes in the empty chamber.

He stops and peeks through the lattice surrounding the ladder. "Courtney," surprise fills his voice. "Hurry."

I run as joy circulates through every cell in my body. I've made it. I'll be free. I'll see my son. The steel rungs are gloriously cold. Above me, the zigzag treads of Ángel's shoes block my view of the upper chamber and natural light, but I'll be there soon.

"Courtney! Thank you, Jesus," Dee Dee shouts from beyond him. "I wanted to go back for you, but..."

"It's okay, Ángel was right to keep going," I shout victoriously.

I pull myself up rung by rung until I hear a door behind me open.

"Hey, you, what are you doing up there?"

I ignore the voice and climb faster. I shouldn't have been so loud. I could have kept my mouth shut and climbed. The encased ladder offers me some protection. But what about after that? He's sure to call for more help. He's sure to get others to stop not only me, but Ángel and Dee Dee as well.

I look up and see Ángel pressing his index finger against

364

his lips. He's thinking what I'm thinking. The guard below me doesn't know I'm not alone. At this moment I have two choices. One, keep climbing and let this guy get to a phone to call for an army to stop anyone attempting to drive out of The Center's parking lot. Two, stay buried for the sake of my son.

The choice is obvious. Not easy. Not painless. But obvious.

"Okay, okay." I say as I intentionally lose the progress I've made. "I'm coming down."

My surrender does what I hoped it would do. It keeps the guard away from the phone.

I want more than anything to keep climbing, but I don't. Looking up, Ángel's shoes have been replaced with the two faces of my friends. I can't wave goodbye. I can't watch them worry about me for a second longer. My eyes sting with the desire to escape, as I glance at the young man who's nervously pulled a gun from a holster and points it at me.

My brain runs through ideas of disarming him as I descend. But all plans of escape evaporate when another guard enters the command center.

"What the…"

"She was climbing the ladder."

"How'd you…"

"Are you alone?"

"No," I say pointing toward the path I took and away from the exit. "The girl with the tattoo sleeves and I got into a fight and I left her at the elevator."

"Call for backup." The guard says keeping the gun on me. As I step off the ladder, he looks up and I follow his gaze. The pyramid above us is dark. The faces of my friends are gone.

The other guard says into the phone, "I'll go and check."

The guard with the gun at my back asks again, "Did anyone go up before you?"

"No, I got here first." I hang my head and he tells me to sit as the other guard climbs the ladder.

On the chilly stone floor, the sting in my butt cheek returns. Dropping my head into my hands, I cover my mouth to make sure none of my prayers for Ángel and Dee Dee slip out.

The guard returns and says, "The only one up there is Ángel. He's shoveling snow from outside of the pyramid."

"Why's he doing that?"

"Says when he's done, the boss wants him to run the snowcat to the maintenance shed. I told him to watch for prisoners. But, honestly, the snow is too deep for anyone to escape at this time of year."

The guard nudges me, "You hear that? No one could survive on the mountain in the middle of winter."

With my head still bowed in prayer, I don't answer.

"Is it winter?" The question was sincere.

"Yeah, a bad time of year to be trying to escape."

While some part of me knew it was February, I'd forgotten about the snow. When Ángel spoke about the parking lot, I forgot about the ride I took in the snowcat last May. They would have to bundle up in boots and parkas. Snowshoes would have to be worn to cross slopes deep enough for skiing. The guard had plans on top of plans and they were good. He and Dee Dee will succeed. I know it. Their victory is bittersweet, but I believe my uncle will help them to save face.

"Call and have the hallways searched. Tell them we've got an inmate in custody and one more on the loose." He tells the other guard and pulls me to my feet. "Also call for a headcount. We want to be fully informed before the staff meeting in an hour."

The young man no longer sounds nervous. His gun hand no longer shakes. His confidence is contagious. I willingly follow him to the lighted pathway. A strange sense of satisfaction covers me. While my body remains trapped, for the first time in a long time, I had a choice in the matter, and I made the right one.

I haven't been a mother long. But since his birth, I've been a caring one. I kept him close when that was the right thing to do. His needs superseding my own. And as I descend into the deep, I realize when the time came to trust his life into the hands of others, I did that too.

PART X

The Future

EPILOGUE

I remained in the underground prison for the next fourteen months as a model prisoner. My time was filled with a mixture of the peace and pain connected to "no news is good news." I never saw another inmate, guard, or doctor previously connected to me again until after I served my full sentence and made it above ground in May 2021.

In June of 2023, my cousin Bailey introduced me to the author who helped tell my story. The investigative reporter wanted to expand beyond serial killer true crime stories and called me to do a tell-all book about The Center and The Bunker. I met her at a raw fruit bar in Owings Mills, Maryland. She introduced herself as Sheridan Alexander. Early into the interview, we discovered we had a common history. She attended the same high school where I bullied Ribbon. Sheridan was part of the reason my old friend Ashley went on a talk show leading to my family's relocation to Virginia. She was a link in the chain leading to my metamorphosis.

A change significant enough to allow high school enemies to bond over smoothies. The high school counselors were right. Adolescent hatred really does become trivial for mature adults. I gave her other names to interview besides me. The last thing I wanted was to make this story about me.

"So, you didn't see Lucy and the girl you called Sleeves after the failed escape?" Sheridan asked.

"No. I continued to work in the laundry without Sleeves. I think my uncle covered up everything."

"Do you know where he is now?"

"No. As far as my family knows, he left the country after the massive defeat of the Republicans in the 2020 election. You already know about his illegal activity. He disappeared before I left The Bunker."

"From the research I've conducted," Sheridan said as she set her plastic cup on the metal table, "The Bunker and The Center were sold in the fall of 2020, during the COVID-19 Pandemic. Your cousin had evidence of your uncle's connection to other illegal endeavors. He had plenty of reasons to flee the United States."

"My uncle is a very powerful man."

She tipped her head to look at me. "There's always someone more powerful."

The futility in her statement stirred up frustration I refused to get into. Besides, I wasn't here to talk about my family. She could ask me all she wanted about The Center and The Bunker, but I refused to invite her into my current life, and asked, "What was the pandemic like?"

She sipped her blended fruit drink. Dabbing a napkin to her mouth she said, "I forgot. You totally missed the height of the spread, didn't you?" Without answering my question, she volleyed one back to me. "What news did you receive down there?"

Since the conversation returned to the prison, I responded, "After Dr. Maggie left, Bunkerville stopped its experiments. Violent criminals, like Fisher got locked up in the prison. Cooperative prisoners could participate in work-release programs within Bunkerville. I did that a few times."

Sheridan offered information I didn't know. "The Pandemic became unnecessarily political in the United States. Misinformation confused a lot of people in rural locations. But as the number of dead in New York rocketed, the investors in Bunkerville turned the city into a quarantine safe hub. The pyramid entrance was closed. One mile from the mine entrance used by Bunkerville, anyone entering had to be tested and wait in private rooms until the test results were analyzed. If they were virus-free, they were escorted to the train and into the underground city. Those testing positive were escorted to either hospitals, hotels, or their homes to recover."

"What about the guards and prison staff?"

"You were always safe. Bunkerville citizens demanded it. They recognized the risk. The pyramid entrance was locked up and everyone had to come through Bunkerville."

"It's funny, when people ask me about if I have any COVID stories, I tell them I had no idea because I lived in a cave."

Sheridan politely giggled, making sure to cover her mouth when she did, a COVID habit I still struggle to remember. When she regained her composure, she continued with interview questions. "What was it like for you to return to Bunkerville on work-release? Did it frighten you?"

"Not so much. Guards were with us as we cleaned the

park or swept sidewalks. The people who lived and worked there were supportive, but cautious when we came down. They no longer were required to sequester when we arrived. They could stay in their apartments if they wanted, being fully aware of the prisoner's presence."

"Sounds like the second half of your sentence was better than the first."

"Don't be fooled. Prison is prison. The yellow cells were still cells. When someone wept, we wept together, never touching, but touched. I spent exhausted nights lulling myself to sleep trying to move limbs I couldn't see."

Sheridan's recorder captured my words, but she also took notes. "Would you recommend The Bunker as a prison option?"

"Yes and no. I don't think people are meant to be buried, the darkness was overwhelming. At lights-out when you can't see your fingers and become forced to trace cheeks and ears and hair, reminding your brain they exist. That's not humane. Do you know how hard it is to believe in things you cannot see? When the lights came on, the hours became days. So as far as I'm concerned, I was down there for decades. On the other hand, I'm a better person because of it. Not all people rise above that kind of trauma, but I'd lived a very selfish life before then."

"But not now."

"I do my best to volunteer and contribute to society rather than just consume."

"And what about your son? Did you ever find him?"

I finished the rest of my drink before telling her. "I'm open to sharing my experiences in The Center and The Bunker for your book."

"I'm sure my readers would like to know what happened after you got outside."

I stood and slung my brandless purse over my shoulder. "I believe they would. However, my life on the outside is a whole other story, best told at another time."

She nodded her head and clicked off her recorder, thanking me for my time. The interview was far less painful than I expected. As I walked away, I considered what she'd said. The time will come when my son is safe enough to tell the rest of the story.

THE FIRST BOOK IN THE SERIES

Courtney's story beings in *The Center*.

Hidden high in the Rocky Mountains, The Center houses inmates ages 12 to 22. The experiment in reform isn't without controversy. Blogs report students being tasered or tortured in a dungeon. 18-year-old Courtney doesn't buy the hype; concentration-camp tactics wouldn't fly in America, especially not for the niece of a US senator.

EXPECTED IN 2024

The Trilogy concludes with Courtney's release and the epic search for her son in *The Outside*.

If you are reading this book prior to 2024, the author appreciates your patience.

To try other books she has written go to www.kodzobooks.com

If you subscribe you will be given up-to-date release information as well as special offers.

You can also follow her on Instagram at KodzoBooks or on Facebook under L.T. Kodzo.

WHERE IT ALL STARTED

LT Kodzo's first award-winning novel, *Locker 572*. Is not a prequel to *The Center*, but Courtney does appear as a side character.

All that is necessary for the triumph of evil is for good men to do nothing.
– Edmund Burke

Welcome to North Harbor High
…where a girl can get bullied to death.

Sheridan Alexander moves to her fifth foster home since kindergarten. Her two goals are to graduate and exit the system without any more trouble. That is until she is assigned locker 572 and finds the abandoned journal of Ribbon Barber.

The journal pages reveal the endless insults and abuse flung at an innocent girl. "Sticks and stones may break your bones, but words will never hurt you."
Yeah, right.

Words of hate scar forever. Sheridan needs to find Ribbon and protect her before it's too late even if it means giving up her most stable home in years. Ribbon has a right to be left alone.

OTHER BOOKS BY THIS AUTHOR

Sixteen-year-old Jimmy Hunter loves dead things. Decaying fossils and buried men no longer have the power to bite or abuse. Jimmy's problems exist with the living. The half-Ute-Indian boy must survive the angry white men his mother insists on dating without killing them. Because like it or not, he has killed. The list he keeps has over 500 names on it. He doesn't want to add any more. Can Jimmy escape to the reservation for the life he's dreamed of? Or will he die trying?

COMING SOON

A new Thriller series.

ACKNOWLEDGMENTS

I'd like to thank God for speaking to me through stories and blessing me with the desire to tell them. I'd like to thank my children who have grown weary of first drafts while being my greatest support and encouragement.

Thanks to The Cover Collection, I love our partnership. Thanks to Rebekah Ruth, for your honest critique of what I thought was a final draft; the entire rewrite saved this book. Thanks to Heather Thompson for the amazing editorial proofreading; if the book suffers from any flaws it's from my stubbornness, not her skills. Thanks to Leah Voysey for adding your beautiful voice and editorial thoughts to Courtney's continued story.

And finally, THANK YOU to those of you who continue to read the stories; you are the reason I my dreams live.

ABOUT THE AUTHOR

LT Kodzo has been writing stories since she could put letters on a piece of paper. Her first published novel, *Locker 572*, quickly became a favorite for young and old alike which encouraged her to continue to polish and deliver this trilogy. She loves to visit schools, libraries, and book clubs as both an author and as a reader.